MICHELLE RENE

THE WITCHES OF TANGLEWOOD : BOOK THREE

GODDESS STORIES

Black Rose Writing | Texas

The author grants the final approval for this literary material.

First printing

This is a work of fiction. Names, characters, businesses, places, events, and incidents are either the products of the author's imagination or used in a fictitious manner. Any resemblance to actual persons, living or dead, or actual events is purely coincidental.

ISBN: 978-1-68433-902-0
PUBLISHED BY BLACK ROSE WRITING
www.blackrosewriting.com

Printed in the United States of America
Suggested Retail Price (SRP) $19.95

Goddess Stories is printed in Garamond

*As a planet-friendly publisher, Black Rose Writing does its best to eliminate unnecessary waste to reduce paper usage and energy costs, while never compromising the reading experience. As a result, the final word count vs. page count may not meet common expectations.

Dedicated to my fans.

Thank you for going on this journey with me.

GODDESS STORIES

CHAPTER ONE

In a place of sadness, rain must fall.

A gentle tether linked the occupants of the old farmhouse to the very elements around them. All mourned in their ways, but the sorrow was too much for the world around them. It saturated the soil and plants and leeched into the very air they breathed. Finally, the world gave up fighting and wept with them.

In the realm of Tanglewood, rain cascaded downward in a steady curtain. It had done so, soaking everything for over a month.

Natalie peered through her kitchen window as the water streaked her view. It was her only window; and, therefore, her only portal to the outside world. She was more or less immovable. Being the anchor child of a living goddess made you that way. Natalie's feet were rooted to the ground, just like any shrub would be. A living piece of scenery easily passed without notice.

"You ready?"

Natalie peered up to see Vivian, the lovely, tattooed woman. Blond and lean in her black dress with a pink satin belt. She had various angels inked on her shoulders. Vivian enchanted the ink used to make them emote her innermost feelings. Right now, they were looking down at Natalie somberly. A few held back barely veiled tattoo tears.

A sniffle and cry came from the nearby sitting room. Many thought of it as the winter room because it was so cold. Natalie gave Vivian a questioning glance.

"It's okay. Percy and Jack Jr. are in there with her right now. Buck swears he's gonna sing her a melody to keep her calm. Not that a taxidermied deer has much of a voice for lullabies, but she seems to like it."

Vivian gave her a heart-hearted smile, but Natalie could not seem to return the favor. She reached across the table and took the framed photograph positioned to the right of her chessboard. She held the gilded frame and traced her hand over the faces in the image.

Nat and Polly stood in their wedding clothes, smiling at the camera. Polly wore a simple white dress with lace panels across the bust and toward the end of her skirt. Vivian had sewn it for her. Nat was in a grey suit that Vivian had helped him choose from a fancy store in Amarillo.

They both looked so painstakingly happy. Nat's grin almost appeared too wide to fit his face. It was hard for the young goddess to seem awkward anymore, but he did so in the picture. He was just so damn proud he could barely stand it.

Polly, always the serene one, grinned easily at the camera as if this all were normal, as if everything was as it should be. And in that photograph, it was. She was standing next to her new husband and holding their new baby in her arms. Faith had only been a few weeks old when the photo was taken.

Polly cradled her newborn bundle in front of her waist to conceal the remaining bump from her delivery. Natalie did not know the ins and outs of childbirth until little Faith was born, including that the baby bump did not automatically disappear after the birth. Nat had not known either and was made to suffer several nights in the barn when he asked about it.

Still, she married him. When they spoke their vows at the wedding, her words to him comprised long lifetimes together and true, undying love. Apparently, even when he was an idiot.

New tears welled up when Natalie thought about that day. Holding their picture now, she remembered how they positioned the ceremony in front of her window so she could be there without discomfort. She thought about how beautiful it all was. How happy. They even let her hold Faith during the ceremony. The picture had been taken shortly after.

Another fussy whine came from the winter room. That half-cough, half-cry sound babies did when they were revving up for a proper wail. Natalie flashed another worried glance at Vivian.

"I promise she's safe in there with them. If things get too dangerous, we will all take cover together. It's up to you to make sure that ain't gonna happen."

They both startled as the screen door shut and a blond man stood before them. It was David Frost, the witch who had created Buck in the first place. He was tall and broad-shouldered, taking up much of the doorway. He did not seem to notice he scared them until he saw how wide Vivian's eyes were.

"Sorry. Didn't mean to spook you. It doesn't look like the rain is getting any better. If we are going to get this done, it should be now." David turned his eyes back down to Natalie. "You sure you want to do this?"

Natalie nodded sharply. She set her mouth in a hard line.

"Alright then, let's see about gettin' you up," Vivian said.

David and Vivian grabbed both of Natalie's arms and hoisted her to her feet. It was not the easiest thing to do. She may have the body of a young girl, but she never moved. One was bound to get stiff.

"Okay, now pick up your left foot. Good. Now, you're right," Vivian said.

Each one was agony to move. David pulled his Bowie knife and cut the tiny white roots that connected her feet to the floorboards of the kitchen. Natalie felt every snap and break vibrate up her legs.

"Okay, let's get to walkin'. We don't want you re-rootin' yourself before we get you outside," Vivian said.

Natalie nodded and moved as fast as she could. It was not terribly quick. Each step felt like she was wearing shoes filled with cement. She was an anchor child. They stayed put. That was their job, to anchor the goddess. But she had to move. She had to get to the grave.

With David and Vivian's help, Natalie made her way out of the house and through the yard. The rain fell steadily over them, soaking her overalls and braided hair from the top down. Camille Lavendou turned around to greet them as they approached.

"There you go. Almost there. Good job, Natalie. Here, you get under the umbrella," Camille said as she pulled her closer.

Camille held no physical umbrella. She was the teacher of *Camille's Home for Wayward Children* and the head of the household. Camille had dominion over just about everything relating to the weather. Her umbrella was more of an invisible dome she made over everyone that kept the rain off their shoulders.

Before Natalie could take another step, she was enveloped in the arms of a blond young woman with a silver hand. Delphia, David's twin sister, hugged her a little too hard. Natalie was unable to speak to anyone except Nat, but she let out a gust of air.

"Easy there, sis," David said.

"Sorry. I'm sorry. I just… this is all so… I'm so sorry!"

Delphia released Natalie and flung herself into Camille's arms, nearly knocking her over.

"It's alright. Now, come on then. There are enough tears all around us," Camille said gently into her hair. "We can be brave, can't we, Delphia?"

She did not stop crying, but she lessened it to a whimper. After being kidnapped by a horrible monster years earlier, the poor girl never had quite recovered emotionally. The ordeal had cost her a hand and a good bit of her self-esteem.

Delphia pulled her tear-streaked face away from Camille's bosom when the commotion attracted their attention. Everyone turned when they heard cussing coming from the barn.

"David, won't you see if Crow needs some help?" Camille asked.

"Be right back."

David jogged to the barn, leaving the women to gaze down at the ground. They stood before two graves. One was a mound of flowers, all different colors and sizes. They were gorgeous, never dying or wilting, no matter what the Texas weather threw at them. It was a tiny garden of perpetual life.

The grave next to it was the opposite. Having been dug merely six weeks before, the ground was still raw. The soil stacked higher than the green grass around it, black and dead-looking from the constant rain.

The two men came back before Delphia could wind up and start crying again. Each took a side of the large tombstone. With much grumbling and difficulty, they placed it at the head of the blackened grave.

There was no need for a grave marker where the flowers grew. That was where the previous goddess died. The one who came before Nat and Natalie. The one who came after so many others. The goddess Nan passed her magic onto Nat in that spot, and she died there a happy woman.

Now, the dark grave had a marker. One that everyone could read. Somehow that made the whole thing more real. It felt worse. They had buried the poor soul weeks ago, but Natalie found the loss to be more permanent as she stared at the words carved in stone.

It seemed so dark. So solid. So undeniably forever.

Polly Jones
1920-1940
She was loved as she loved others.
Completely.

Delphia began to wail again, and David held her close, soaking her mourning dress with the water and mud on his shirt from hauling the tombstone. Natalie heard Camille sniffle, and Vivian's angels cried silently on her shoulders.

Crow's sharp chin stiffened as he stared at Polly's name. Natalie did not know his tribe. Navajo, she thought she heard Nat say once. They must have been a people with few words because he used them sparingly. Perhaps that or the fact that he spent much of his life as a bird.

"Crow, you don't have to leave again," Camille said, breaking the silence of the moment. "You are welcomed to stay as long as you like."

"You asked that I send for the nun. I did so. I came back to honor her grave with a headstone. It was the least I could do for her. But I will take my leave now," he said with a nod at Camille.

"But really, we would love you to…"

She did not get to finish her sentence. Crow leaped into the air with a flutter of feathers and squawks, turning into a large, black bird. His clothes fell in a heap on the ground, and he flew away. Camille watched him until he was merely a speck disappearing into the cloud cover.

"You didn't really think he'd stay, did you?" Vivian said as she stood next to Camille, interlacing her fingers with hers. "He ain't been the same since Polly left him for Nat. He didn't even come to the weddin'."

"I can't blame him. I know what it means to see the love of your life go off with someone else," Camille said darkly.

Vivian pulled Camille closer.

"I came back though," she said. "Crow doesn't have that option. There's nothin' here for him except memories. Painful ones. You can't persuade him."

"No, but I had to try. I wager he'll be gone for another year or two again. Maybe more."

"Nothin' you can do," Vivian said.

"It just feels like there must have been somethin' I could've done. Somethin' to save Polly. If I did, maybe Nat…"

Camille did not finish that sentence either. Lightning lit up the horizon, and thunder roared around them. The very ground trembled as the sound broke the fabric of the world. Everyone jumped in the air, except Natalie, who was already rooted in place.

"Camille, is that your doing?" David asked.

"Not me," she hollered over the building wind.

"Maybe it's just another burst like the others," David said.

The wind abated, and the lightning eased as though the storm had been listening to them. They could still hear the rolling thunder, but it was moving away. The rain did not stop. It never seemed to these days.

"There it goes," Camille said.

"We gotta make a move. If'n we don't find Nat, this storm might tear us apart. The weather's only gotten worse since he left," Vivian said.

Suddenly, they were all aware of the sound of hooves hitting the mud. That slopping sound horses make when clomping through wet soil. Now that the thunder had gone, the sound felt louder than it had any right to be. Each strike of the hooves felt like a building earthquake.

Everyone turned to see the most enormous horse they had ever seen making its way down the road toward them. It was chestnut brown with a dark mane. A Clydesdale, Natalie thought. She had read books about them, but to see the creature in real life was a whole other experience.

There was not much to do sitting in front of a window. Reading the books Nat brought her filled the lonely hours. If she could not experience the world firsthand, at least she could adventure through books.

On top of the beast road, a small figure. A woman, it appeared. She wore a wet cloak with the hood over her head and clutched an oversized book to her chest. The sunflowers at the front of the house blossomed brightly as she approached.

"Who is that?" Vivian asked.

"Out best chance at finding Nat and getting him to come home."

A shiver rippled down Natalie's spine as another jolt of thunder cracked the air. Everyone jumped, and the colossal horse reared. When the beast settled, the woman gazed down at them with a melancholy face. She locked eyes with Natalie with an unnervingly focused stare.

"But Cammy," Vivian whispered. "What if she can't?"

"Then we are all in grave danger," Calliope said.

CHAPTER TWO

Camille expanded her invisible bubble to cover their new guest and her horse. She offered a smile, but the young woman did not return the favor. Calliope handed the book down to Camille before she dismounted the enormous horse.

Natalie strained to get a look, but her feet were already rooted to the ground, making it hard to move. Natalie had never read this book, but in a way, she knew of it because Nat did. Everything he knew, she knew. However, seeing it in person was a whole other experience—a more permanent one.

Camille stepped back as Calliope approached the lot of them. She was Mexican, beautiful, with the most prominent almond eyes Natalie had ever seen. She wore the dress of a nun, a modest uniform of grey and white. Her unkempt hair flowed behind her like a cape.

"I am sorry I did not come sooner," she said with a slight bow.

Her eyes flickered to Natalie, and they widened with recognition. Natalie felt suddenly hot all over with embarrassment. Everyone was gawking at her now.

"You are his anchor child," Calliope said.

The nun moved toward her as if gliding over the earth. Her gaze was intense. If Natalie had not been rooted to the ground, she would have jumped back. No one paid this much attention to her. She was just the anchor. Unimportant.

"You should've come sooner. As soon as Nat jumped in the book," David said with a sneer. "It's a good thing I enchanted the Clydesdales to run faster before I left, or you would still be in the hill country."

The words snapped in the air. It was almost as startling as the thunder, which immediately followed it. The humid air around them grew cold for a few seconds. Calliope did not flinch. She merely broke her stare at Natalie to focus on David.

"David!" Delphia exclaimed.

"What? It's true. We had to send Crow to get her," he said, glaring in the nun's direction. "Otherwise, she might not have come."

"I will not defend myself. You are correct. I should have come sooner. My only reason was that I thought Nat would come back. When he came to me in the cathedral's library and requested the book, I gave it without thought. It is, after all, his book."

Camille turned around so that Natalie could get a closer look at the book in question. It was red with gold filigree. When Natalie took it in her hands, she breathed in the smell of leather, paper, and candle wax. Written in gold on the cover was the title, *The Goddess Stories.*

"Did he say anythin' before he went inside the book? Anythin' at all?" Camille asked the nun.

"Not much. He mumbled something about needing to find *her*. He was going to in to find someone," she said.

"He meant Polly," David said sharply. "He went inside the book to get Polly. And he's been in there for weeks. How could you not tell us sooner? I mean, look at this place."

The rain poured heavier, and another crack of thunder shattered the sky. Everyone flinched except Camille, who gave David a level look. Delphia walked over to her twin and took his hand.

"Come now, brother. Calliope wouldn't have done it on purpose. It's not her fault Nat hasn't come back."

David relaxed his jaw, but only by a degree.

"No, Delphia, he is not wrong. I should have come sooner, but this is not the time for arguing such things. The longer Nat is in the book, the longer the world lives without a goddess. We see the signs at the cathedral as well. I have read some of the stories in this book, and it seems like the world suffers when the goddess is not inside it."

"What do you mean?" Vivian asked.

"Look there," Calliope answered, pointing into the distance.

In Texas, one could see miles and miles in almost every direction. Along the horizon, they spotted the anvil-like clouds building high and dark. The very air grew heavy and harder to breathe. The bottom of the clouds flashed rolling colors of greens and purples—all signs of an impending tornado.

"Camille can fend it off," Vivian said.

When she shot Camille a hopeful look, she did not respond. Camille merely stared at the system, rolling miles away. The witch clutched her hands. Her face was tense all over, and her brows knit together.

"You can, can't you?" Vivian asked her.

"I… I can try, but I don't know. If it's Nat's doin' then it might be too much for my powers."

Delphia moved closer to David and whimpered. Vivian took Camille's hand in hers, squeezing it with shared tension. That left only Natalie and Calliope, and the nun focused her gaze right back on top of the anchor child.

"That book holds all of the histories of every goddess who ever existed. I believe Nat went inside the book to go inside his history. He could not stop yellow fever from killing Polly. He cannot bring her back to life. I think he jumped in here to find her in his story and bring her back that way," Calliope said.

"But he hasn't come back. If that was his goal, surely it wouldn't 'ave taken so long," Vivian said.

"There must be somethin' wrong. Some reason he hasn't returned," Camille said.

"Can't you read his part of the book and tell us, Calliope?" Delphia asked.

The nun looked down at her feet and shook her head. She seemed smaller somehow at that moment as her eyes watered around the edges. Calliope held up her hands as though she had nothing to offer them.

"The Goddess book works unlike any I have known. I can read whole chapters only to find them vanish hours later. One day, half of the book will be visible, and the next, it will be completely blank. I even tried to step inside it the way Nat did, but it refused me."

"What does all that mean?" Vivian asked.

"I think it means only another goddess can go inside it. That, or a piece of a goddess," Calliope said.

Everyone turned simultaneously to stare at Natalie. She was, in fact, a piece of a goddess. The anchor that kept that all-powerful goddess from flying into the heavens. Her ears turned red, and she felt a burning on the back of her neck.

Natalie knew this was coming. After all, it was her idea to send for Calliope and the book. One of the few perks of being an anchor child was that you could see into the immediate future. She used her chess set to interpret what she saw and wrote the instructions down for Camille.

In her vision, Natalie had seen Nat step inside the book. She felt his desperation as he did so. Her deep intuition told her someone would have to go in after him, and the squirmiest part of her gut told her that someone would need to be her. Now she knew she was correct.

Natalie looked down at the volume in her grip. It hummed to her as she ran one small hand over the cover. Camille moved to her side and placed a gentle hand on her shoulder. It felt warm and reassuring, but her nerves still refused to calm.

"I would love to say you don't hafta do this, child," Camille said in her deep, tender voice. "I would take the burden if I could. But it has to be you. No one else can go inside the book and look for him."

Natalie raised her head and locked eyes with the wise witch. She felt like crying. This whole thing was so terrifying. Her vision had not gone beyond this part. She had no idea what would happen when she got inside. The future beyond this point was a mystery to her.

She had to be brave. Nat would be brave. Nat was Galahad. She had to be like Nat.

"Are you okay to do this, Natalie?" Camille asked.

"We are here for you, child," Vivian said, squeezing her other shoulder.

The anchor child clenched her teeth and nodded to them both. She fixed her eyes on Calliope as the nun approached with a minuscule brass key. Everyone held their collective breaths as she inserted the key into the lock on the front of the book and turned it.

Nothing happened. Natalie was not sure what she thought was going to happen. Maybe the winds would pull her inside. Maybe Nat would leap out of the fluttering pages. She expected anything and nothing at all. Natalie looked up at Calliope with a question in her eyes.

"I think I know what the problem is. You will need to cut her roots," Calliope said, pointing at David.

Without question, David pulled his knife from his belt and made his way to Natalie. Camille and Vivian helped her lift her heels as he snipped away at her tiny, white roots. Once she was free, Natalie gazed back down at the open pages of *The Goddess Stories*.

Oddly enough, the dread she felt before was gone. There was a lightness about her being. Usually, if someone cut her roots and made her move, the experience was nauseating. Anchor children were meant to do just that, anchor. Set solidly in the Earth. Ground the goddess in reality. Yet, at that moment, she felt lighter.

"I think you have to put your hand on the cover page," Calliope said as she flipped to the right spot. There was a burned handprint that made Natalie cringe. "That is where Nat touched the book when he created it. I watched him touch this mark before he stepped inside. Perhaps you must do that too."

Natalie's mouth went dry as she hovered her hand over the book. Her handprint was so much smaller than Nat's. A shiver began in her toes and worked itself into her liver. It was not until she heard the gentle humming that she felt better.

An old song. Something sweet, earthy, and familiar.

It was not coming from the surrounding people. No. The song came from inside the book. It vibrated up from her fingertips, telling her that this was the way. Here there may be monsters, but none she could not face.

Natalie took one last gulp of humid air and stepped inside the pages of *The Goddess Stories*, leaving the world of Tanglewood behind.

CHAPTER THREE

Natalie tumbled through the air. The solid ground of Texas was gone. For once, her roots had no place to grow. She dropped into a world filled with brutal winds and the scent of fire, gunpowder, and tar. With a jarring splash, Natalie plunged into a vast body of water.

She did not dare to open her eyes. The salt around her burned her nostrils and pulled at her lips. The water was freezing against her skin. Natalie flapped helplessly, trying to make it to the surface. After all, no one had ever taught her how to swim.

There did not seem to be a bottom, and she could not find her way to the surface. Natalie flailed helplessly in the dark void of suffocating salt water with no light or direction. Just when she thought her lungs might burst, she felt the top of her head breech the top.

Breaking free from the harshness of the ocean, Natalie gasped in a lung full of air. She snapped her head around wildly, trying to take in where she was. Of all the places she expected to land, the middle of a wild ocean was not one of them.

She shielded her eyes with one hand as the slowly setting sun blazed down on her head. Being half-blinded made her panic all the more. A wave pushed her aside as a large ship passed dangerously close to her body.

Natalie had never treaded water before, and her attempt was clumsy. She kept splashing herself when she tried to paddle. The wake the ship produced knocked her underwater again, and she popped back up, spitting.

"You there!" cried a gruff voice from above. "Grab the rope!"

A thick rope splashed about six feet from her head. Natalie flailed wildly to get to it. A deep rush of relief flooded her when she wrapped her arms around it. The cord felt rough under her hands.

"Hold on tight!" the voice yelled.

Natalie wrapped it like a boa constrictor around her arm and braced herself. With one good tug from the people above, she was free from the water. The cold air stung her body as she clung to the rope. Pull after pull after pull hauled her upwards. Once she finally reached the top of the impossibly tall ship, two sets of arms pulled her on board.

"Are you alright?" said the man to the right of her.

"Where did you come from?" said the man to the left.

Natalie focused on her saviors and was shocked to see that one was Chinese. At least, she thought he was. You did not get many Chinese people in Texas, but she did remember Nat seeing a few working along the railroads. This man's face appeared worn from the sun, and his dark hair was pulled up in a scarf.

The other one was black, darker than Camille or Nan. He had dark brown and grey knots of hair falling around his shoulders. Intricate cords and beads wove in and out of his braids. When he smiled, she noticed he had a dimple on his chin and a smattering of light freckles underneath his eyes.

Natalie had never seen such a thing before. Freckles were usually darker than a person's skin. She had seen red-headed people with red freckles, but never someone with light-colored ones. It was like a painter took a small brush and flecked beige spots underneath his golden eyes. She found herself fixated on them.

The men looked her up and down. Natalie suddenly realized that her thin shirt and overalls were clinging to her body. She felt like a drowned rat, and the fact that her eight-year-old body was on display made it so much worse. She wrapped her arms around herself, cheeks flushing with embarrassment.

"Don't worry," said the Chinese man. "We won't hurt you."

"Thank you," she said through chattering teeth.

"I am Bambang, and this is Claude," he said, gesturing to the other sailor.

"We are pirates, but do not worry, child. We are not the type to take children," Claude said with a French-like accent.

The men both smiled at her, and she felt both apprehensive and relieved. Pirates definitely sounded like trouble, but these men had pulled her from the water. That meant they were safe. Maybe. Possibly. Hopefully.

Natalie suddenly wondered how she could understand the men. The ship looked old. Not ratty old. It was aged in the way pictures in history books were. This was a sailing ship made of wood and tar. There was a mast with ribbed sails and red flags. She could smell gunpowder. No one in her time sailed ships like this. At least, she did not think so.

Likewise, the men in front of her dressed like pirates from a history book. They had long tunics bound around their waist with sashes and pants underneath. One wore a scarf around his head, and the other had a wide-brimmed hat. Both carried curved swords at their hips.

If she was in some goddess story with Chinese pirates, how were they speaking English? How could she understand them? When was this?

"We should take her to the captain," Bambang said.

"First, here's a blanket," Claude said.

They threw a ratty blanket around her shoulders and led her through the ship's deck. She stumbled on ropes and nearly fell this way and that as the vessel pitched with the waves. Luckily, her saviors were patient with her. They made it to the main mast and encountered a group of people crowded in a circle.

"Make way for the accused!" yelled a voice behind them.

Natalie and her saviors jumped aside as two sailors dragged a man across the deck, kicking and screaming. His eyes were wild with fear, and when he spotted Natalie, he tried to reach for her. Claude pulled his blade and pointed it at the man, and the captive recoiled. She moved closer to him, thankful he came to her rescue.

"It's not true! Don't listen to her! My brothers, are we not friends? You must let me go!"

When they heard his cries, the crowd parted. All scowled at the prisoner as he passed. Natalie wanted desperately to follow and see what was happening.

"If you want to see the show, you better hurry," Claude said, as if reading her mind.

"It is a good one," Bambang added.

Natalie clutched the blanket tighter around herself and made her way through the crowd. There was one advantage to being so small. She could wiggle herself into almost any place. Weaving in and out of legs, Natalie squeezed in between two thinner men who shifted aside, unaware of her presence.

The burly men dropped the terrified captive on the deck in front of a small man. He wore a long-sleeved shirt underneath a high-collared vest adorned with embroidered patterns and jeweled beads. The vest flared out around his hips, falling just above the knees. Beneath that were loose pants and black boots. He had a scarf around his head and a tricorne hat on top of that.

This had to be the captain. He was better dressed than anyone, and he held himself straight and confident. It was not until he turned to face her that Natalie got a good look at his face. He was not a *he*. The captain was a *she*. Her delicate features and the feminine point to her chin made her no less formidable. The captive shuddered under her gaze.

"You are accused of the attempted molestation of a prisoner," she said in a booming voice. "What say you, Cai Qian?"

"I am innocent!"

The captain moved close to him as the two men forced the Cai Qian on his knees. She scowled down at him, and he averted his eyes. Natalie had never seen a man so afraid of another person.

"Bring out the witness!" she said.

The crowd parted again as a tall man escorted a disheveled and terrified woman to the captain. Her hair was a mess of knots on her head, and she wore the loose clothes of a man. She pulled a blanket around her body as her eyes darted around her. She looked to be Chinese, like most of the people on the ship.

Ching Shih approached the woman carefully. She seemed to be afraid of spooking her more than she was already. Even though the witness was taller than the captain, she demurred as she drew near.

"You accuse this man of attempting to molest you," the captain said in a gentle voice.

She moved toward the woman slowly and placed a small, gloved hand on her shoulder. She relaxed a touch. Her knuckles, which had been nearly white from her grip on the blanket, loosened enough to turn pink once again.

"He… yes. He came to my cell and tried to force himself. I screamed. The guard stopped him before he could do anything," the woman said.

"Lies! She is a liar!" Cai Qian screamed.

"Silence!"

The captain turned on him with a force that seemed to silence the world. With one hard stomp of her boot, everything froze in place. The waves and the wind stopped. The ship ceased its pitching back and forth. The world held its breath, leaving only a vacuum on the deck of the boat.

Everyone held their breaths. Natalie did as well, afraid that there may be no oxygen to breathe anymore. Nothing would be scarier than trying to take in air and find out you could not. The captain stole the world's breath, if only for a moment.

Luckily, the moment passed, and the ocean crashed against the ship once more. The wind howled around them. The boat righted itself and continued its incessant rocking. Everyone around her gulped oxygen as if they were drowning men.

"I believe her," the captain said. "I do not believe you."

She pointed at the man, and he shivered on his knees. Suddenly, Natalie smelled a familiar tang in the air. It was unmistakably urine. When she focused on the accused, she spotted a growing stain on his pants.

"What say you all? Are you with me?" the captain yelled above the wind.

The mob hollered in resounding applause. Everyone agreed, except the prisoner. Not one person was listening to him.

"We have but a few rules here. Female captives are freed at the nearest port. They are to be treated respectfully. That means no molestation. No rape."

"But… I didn't," he said in a tiny voice.

"Because someone stopped you," she growled. "A thief who is caught with his hand in someone else's pocket is no less guilty. Whether he made off with the coin or not."

Cai Qian shook his head back and forth as if trying to will this to be over. His mouth hung open without words.

"You have disobeyed my decree. Everyone knows the rules, and your punishment will be swift. Lift him to his feet!"

The mob found their collective voice and cheered. All were terrified of their captain, yet they respected her. They respected the rules. They applauded the sentence and pumped their fists into the air. Everyone shouted as one, except Natalie.

They lifted him to his feet as the captain approached him. She pulled a long sword from her hip. He sobbed and shut his eyes as she grew closer. Natalie clapped her hands over her mouth and tried to swallow back the bile rising in her mouth.

The captain slashed his thigh with one quick motion of her arm, cutting clean down to the bone. Blood poured from the wound, staining her blade. He yowled in pain. The female pirate remained stoic, unmoved by his blubbering. She wiped the blood from her sword onto the leg of her pants.

"Now, throw him overboard!" she yelled.

The crew cheered once more as the burly men dragged the bleeding man across the deck. A slick of blood followed behind them like a gory snail trail. He wailed, but the raucous din of the crowd muffled it.

"May the sharks find you swiftly," the captain said.

"No, please!" he cried.

Those were his last audible words. They hurled him overboard. If he said anything else, Natalie did not hear it. The crew cheered so loudly they blocked out the wind. The captain made her way back to the frightened woman and spoke gently to her. Natalie strained to hear.

"It is done. We will drop you at the next port."

"Thank you. Thank you so much Captain Ching Shih."

The captain snapped her attention away from the woman. Much to Natalie's horror, Ching Shih found her among the crew and met Natalie's eyes. She looked both confused and curious, staring at the anchor child.

With a snap of her fingers, she froze the world yet again. This time, everyone froze as well. The crew stopped in the middle of their party; some stopped in mid-jump in the air. Bullets whizzed from mid-air above their heads. Smoke hung static from smoldering pistols.

At first, Natalie feared she could not breathe or move. When she tried to wiggle her fingers, they did as she commanded, so she felt confident taking in a lung full of air. Natalie was grateful until she saw the terrifying Ching Shih walking straight for her. She waved a bullet and a plume of smoke away from her face as she did so.

"You, child. You are not supposed to be here."

"I... I know."

When the words came from her mouth, Natalie realized something altogether strange. She spoke. In fact, she had spoken to the pirates who saved her. She never talked. That was part of being an anchor child. There was no talking. Not to anyone but your goddess.

Suddenly, she realized something else as well. There were no roots. Nothing forced her feet downward. She was just another person.

"Why are you in my history?"

"I need your help. I have to find my goddess. He's here. Somewhere in this book."

"You are an anchor child?"

"Yes, and the world is in trouble. I need your help."

"Well then, that is a predicament," Ching Shih said, offering a hand to Natalie. "Truly something new. Fascinating. Let's get you up and moving. There's someone I think you should meet."

CHAPTER FOUR

The captain did not unfreeze her crew until she escorted Natalie into her quarters. Ching Shih snapped her fingers as soon as the door slammed behind them, and the party began anew outside the heavy door. Natalie nearly jumped out of her skin at the sound.

"This is a safe place," Ching Shih said, as she rested a hand on her shoulder. "You will meet my child, and all will be well."

Darkness haunted most of the room, and it smelled of wood stain and incense. A few red lanterns hung here and there. Away from the constant wind of the elements, the air felt heavier and wet.

Her soaked clothes clung to her body, and she felt sorry she was dripping seawater over the ornate rugs as Ching Shih guided her through the room. The captain grabbed an oversized blanket and tossed it to her as they rounded a corner.

It took a long time to make their way in the captain's quarter. There were several twists and turns. Judging by the outside of the ship, this room should not be so large. Of course, Natalie remembered who this was and what a goddess could do. When Nan was still alive, she enchanted their farmhouse to look dilapidated and small on the outside while expanding as far as they needed on the inside.

They passed another series of doors and walked into a spacious bedroom. In the center stood perhaps the largest bed Natalie had ever seen. It had four posts intricately carved with elephants, tigers, and dragons and stained a deep maroon. The blankets were perfectly taut over the mattress and made of silks and embroidery. She had more fine pillows than a French aristocrat.

Yellow and maroon curtains draped about the room, hanging over carpets with milky fringe on the edges. Every lantern glowed with blood-red light filtered around strange shapes Natalie had never seen before. All of it was such a difference from the deck of the ship. This was lavish. All silk and comfort compared to the wood, rope, and the elements.

Ching Shih moved past her to a curtain in the room's corner. When she pulled it aside, there sat a little girl on a grand blue pillow. The girl was about Natalie's age, dressed in blue robes with her pitch black hair held back in sharp pins. She knew the girl at once the way siblings might know one another after years apart. Like recognizes like. This was Ching Shih's anchor child.

In front of the child sat a short table, almost like a lap desk. There were several long sheets of paper in front of her. She painted in vertical lines with a long brush and black ink. The girl had to hold back her sleeve with one hand to not mess up her work. When Natalie peered at what she was drawing, she saw the same symbols as the ones on the lanterns.

"Child, we have a visitor."

The little girl snapped her head up and put down her brush. Her eyes focused on Natalie as her brows pinched. The gaze matched Ching Shih's so closely, Natalie almost laughed. Such sharp features for a young girl, but what did she expect? This was, after all, Ching Shih as a child.

"Why can I speak in front of her?" the child asked.

"She is like you, and her goddess is missing," Ching Shih said plainly.

"That is not right. This never happened in our history."

"No, it did not," Ching Shih said as she sat on the bed. "But here she is."

The great captain appeared smaller. Younger, even. Outside among the pirates, she was the fierce warrior queen. In here, her guard dropped, and she looked like a young woman. Too young really to be such a force of nature. Maybe even a teenager. Natalie knew all too well that the goddess could make herself into anything she wanted, so determining her age by appearance alone was pointless.

"My goddess, Nat, made this book back in my time. He created the history of the goddesses with all of your histories in it."

"This we know," the anchor child said.

"What we do not know is how he is lost to you," Ching Shih added.

Natalie took a deep breath and readied herself to explain. This was the most conversing she had ever done as an anchor child. It was definitely an adjustment.

"We had somethin' happen in our time. A person died. Nat's wife. He left us and jumped into this book. I wager he's lookin' for her in his history, but he's been in here for weeks. I need to find him. Things are bad at home."

The two stared at her for a long minute. Matching brown eyes piercing her very soul. She wondered if they were trying to reconcile the idea that Nat, the goddess, was a boy, but his anchor child was a girl.

The goddess could be anything they wanted. Nat never wanted to be a girl, but that did not change what Natalie was. The magic of the goddess was all about self-perception. When Nat was her age, he had no concept of different genders. He had been born a girl, and everyone told him as much. That was how he saw himself at the time. Therefore, Natalie was a girl. The perfect representation of how Nat saw himself at age eight.

It was not until he got older that he questioned what he should and should not be. When the teenage years came, so did the uneasy feelings. The ones that pointed his focus somewhere else. Only when he was granted the goddess's power could he change his appearance permanently to that of a man.

Ching Shih did not ask. Perhaps it was just an understood fact among the goddesses. After all, Nan had been the same way. Her anchor child was a young boy named Jacob, but she looked like an old woman named Nan. Natalie wondered if there was a way all goddesses could speak to one another. Then another thought leaped into her brain.

"Why can I understand you? I don't reckon you're speakin' English, and I know I can't speak Chinese."

"Why is it you can move freely?" the anchor child asked.

She unfolded her legs and leaned to one side to display the tiny, white roots running from her rump to the pillow beneath her.

"I don't know," Natalie said, lifting her feet to show that they were free.

"I am not sure either," Ching Shih. "This has never happened before. The rules must be different for you here."

"What do I do? How do I find him?"

"I do not have an answer for you as of yet, child," she said with a questioning uptick in her voice when she said the word *child*.

"Natalie," she offered.

"Natalie," Ching Shih repeated. "We will help you in any way we can. The world needs the goddess, and he must be returned."

"It will have to be after," said the anchor child.

"After what?" Natalie asked.

"The battle, of course," Ching Shih said.

"What battle?"

As if the world took its cue, a tremendous blast shook the ship three times. *Boom! Boom! Boom!*

Natalie fell to her knees and clutched her hands over her head in a pitiful attempt to shield herself. The entire ship shivered beneath her, and she was afraid it would crumble beneath their feet.

"That battle," Ching Shih said.

CHAPTER FIVE

The goddess marched through her quarters with Natalie hot on her tail. Nothing phased the great captain. Perhaps it was because she had already lived this. Maybe that did not matter, and she was always this unshakeable. Either way, Ching Shih threw back to the doors and strode onto the deck with the commanding power of a giant.

Natalie followed her like a shivering dog, hoping not to be noticed by anyone. Never before had she missed the calm farmhouse this much. The din alone of the ship was enough to make a person deaf.

Boom! Boom! Boom!

Another round of cannon blasts shook the world as Ching Shih unsheathed her sword and screamed orders over the battle growing around them. Men hustled here and there, loaded balls into cannons, pulling ropes, and arming with pistols.

The ship pitched hard to one side, throwing Natalie across the deck. She barely caught herself on the edge and held on for dear life. When the boat righted itself, she peered out at the horizon beyond with wide eyes. She could barely believe the sight.

Dozens—no hundreds—of ships sailed together. Even in the hazy, purple light of the early evening twilight, Natalie could see for miles around. Great ships like the captain's, bulky ships filled with cannons, and smaller boats barely more significant than a train boxcar. The ones flying the red flags of Captain Ching Shih faced off against an unknown Navy. Bursts of orange color bloomed around the ships as their cannons fired against one another.

Rough hands grabbed Natalie's arms and hoisted her away from the edge of the ship. When she turned around, she found one of the nice men who pulled her from the water. The dark one with the long knots for hair. The white freckles. A wave of renewed gratitude filled her body as he helped her find her footing.

"Are you alright, little one?" Claude asked in that French accent of his.

"I think so," she said with a quiver in her voice. "What is happening?"

"The Mandarin Navy has decided to fight back against our captain. The Emperor is not a fan of losing all his riches to a woman."

"The Emperor?"

"Do not fret, petite. We have hundreds of ships and tens of thousands of pirates. There is no way they will win. Not with the goddess on our side."

Natalie froze and stared at the strange man. He regarded her with an amiable smile. One that said he knew worlds more than he should. Great depths of secrets swirled inside those dark eyes of his—obsidian stones flickering with the cannon fire all around them.

"You know about the goddess?" Natalie asked.

"Of course, I do. I am her right hand. And you are not supposed to be here," Claude he said with a slight crook to his head.

"Yes, I know. I've been gettin' that a lot lately," she said.

Boom! Boom! Boom!

Another round of cannons exploded near to their ship. The din of constant battle resounded in the distance, but those were merely echoes of bloodshed. This one was close. So close it rang in Natalie's ears and kicked in her chest like a mule. She wanted to scream in terror but found no voice to do so.

Claude grabbed her shoulders again and squeezed. It was as if he were trying to keep her from flying off into the ether. To protect her from what was to come. It did not work. Another round of cannons blasted even closer than the last one.

Boom! Boom! Boom!

"Get to the captain's quarters!" Claude yelled over the explosion. "No cannon ever hit it. You will be safe inside!"

She had no voice. It almost felt like being back in Tanglewood, where she could not speak at all, but this was suppressive. A reverberation in her chest that restricted what could come out of her mouth. All she could manage was a nod.

"Take this," he said, handing her a dagger.

Natalie took it and immediately regretted it. The thing was heavy in her hand. She could sense the weight of the dagger was not just the metal. It was also from the blood saturated in its blade.

A ship rammed the side of their vessel, and a barrage of sailors leaped over, screaming horrid battle cries. Claude turned and pulled his curved blade with a determined spin. He ran forward, slicing and cutting down men effortlessly.

Natalie winced and ran in the other direction. She clutched the dagger in one hand and raced toward the captain's quarters. Pirates fought all around her. Blades clanged together. Pistols fired randomly. The cannons blasted at a steady pace, shaking the world again and again.

Ching Shih screamed her own battle cry, cutting two men down with one sweeping arc of her sword. Three more rushed her from behind. Natalie was about to call out and warn her, but the Pirate Queen wheeled on them. She kicked one overboard, shot one with her pistol, and sliced the third from neck to gizzard. The smell of blood permeating the air.

Natalie had to jump over the fallen men. The door was in sight, and she focused on getting there in one piece. She stumbled over a coil of rope and crawled the rest of the way. Just as Natalie reached for the doorknob, someone grabbed the back of her shirt. They hauled her to her feet.

An angry face sneered mere inches from her nose. The only thing she could see was a man with a dry, reddened face. Pockmarks ran down his nose and into his cheeks. His breath stank of smoke and foul fish. This was not one of Ching Shih's men. It had to be the other ones, she thought.

"This must be the child. You come with me, brat. Ching Shih will pay any price to get you back. Cut the dragon by the throat."

"No! Let me go!"

He dropped her to the ground and grabbed her wrist. She whimpered as he wrenched her arm behind her back. The pain shot white-hot up her arm. At that moment, Natalie did not think about anything but the pain. She knew more was to come if this man made off with her. Horrible things would happen if she could not get away.

Much to her surprise, the door leading to the captain's quarters faded in and out of focus. Natalie blinked hard, but she was sure of it. A violet haze passed over the door as though someone had blown purple smoke in that one spot. The man must have noticed it as well because he relaxed his grip on her wrist.

A thin, white hand jutted out from the haze. How could a hand just appear like that through a solid door, she wondered. It seemed impossible, but here it was. The hand reached out, a golden bracelet dangling on the wrist. Even in the darkness, the image of a jeweled snake glinted like a star.

"What trickery is this?" he asked as he released her hand to reach for the magical one.

He grabbed the stranger's wrist and pulled. They pulled back, struggling against his attack. At one point, he tugged hard enough to bring a person's head through the mysterious portal.

It was dark, and a billow of cannon smoke wafted past them, but Natalie could have sworn the person turned their face and looked right at her. They met eyes, but she could not recognize who they were.

By the time the air cleared, the struggle was over. The mystery person got away. They retreated inside their hazy portal, and the captain's door returned to normal. The man fell onto the floor when the hand disappeared into the haze. The only proof any of it had happened was the bracelet. It slipped from the mysterious wrist and clanged to the deck.

Instinctually, Natalie crawled over and picked it up. Something about the snake made her forget where she was. It was beautiful the way precious things were, but it was more than that. It seemed somehow familiar, like she had seen it before. Natalie slipped it on her wrist without a second thought.

"Give that here!" the man yelled, grabbing her shoulder.

In a flash, the battle resumed around her. She wondered if Ching Shih had frozen time again or if she had been under some spell. Either way, she was suddenly all too aware of where she was and her predicament. The man squeezed her arm until her breath caught.

Without thinking, she squeezed the dagger's handle in her other hand. She turned in his direction and stabbed the blade into his shin as hard as she could. It only sank about an inch. To be fair, she had never stabbed anyone before. But it was enough to make him scream in pain.

"You little demon!"

Natalie scrambled away from him. He pulled the dagger from his leg and tried to reach for her. Just then, Ching Shih came into view. She kicked him in the shin directly where Natalie had stabbed him. He wailed again and crumpled to the ground.

"Run!" the Pirate Queen yelled.

There was no need to repeat herself. Natalie pushed to her feet and ran away from the writhing man. Unfortunately, it meant she was also running from the sanctuary of the captain's quarters.

Boom! Boom! Boom!

Natalie ducked as her legs pumped faster. She did not realize she was nearing the end of the ship until the edge caught her in the waist. It nearly knocked the wind out of her lungs.

The scent of sulfur burned the inside of her nose as smoke filled her view. It was so dense she could barely see feet in front of her. All she could do was hear the sounds of the battle and see the occasional explosion of pistol fire.

Boom! Boom! Boom!

One cannonball came whizzing so close it nearly took her out. It flew, shattering rigging and splintering wood. At that moment, Natalie knew nothing but deafness and fear. The very air whined around her as she shut her eyes and readied herself for the inevitable impact—her death.

Back home, they would never know what happened to her. Just that she failed. She failed, and she was lost. This was the end.

Strong arms wrapped around her and squeezed her close. She could smell salt and oil as Claude pulled her against his body. Everything happened so fast. Claude jumped from the ship and into the ocean with Natalie in his arms with a quick leap. A second later, one cannonball smashed into the part of the deck where they had been standing. It missed them by mere inches.

CHAPTER SIX

When one expects imminent death, surviving can be quite shocking. It was a kick to the nervous system from a metaphorical donkey. In that moment of terror, there was no breath and no clear thought. Just falling.

Natalie splashed into the ocean with a pirate wrapped around her and waited for what was to come next. Her mind went blank. She was about to die one second, and the next, cold water enveloped her whole body. The sudden need for oxygen snapped her back to life, and she flailed out of Claude's arms.

He released her, and the two swam to the surface. This time, she was more prepared for swimming. Natalie was still terrible at it, but she figured out how to let the air in her lungs push her upward. In a dark ocean, it was easy to lose all sense of direction.

They broke free, taking huge gulps of air as they did so. Natalie spun around wildly, waiting for the next danger to run from, but the world was calm. No more cannons. No more raging and fighting.

The orange and purples of a sunrise stained the sky, but that made little sense. It had been the early evening mere seconds ago. How could time have passed that quickly? She and Claude had not been underwater long.

Something drifted along the surface of the water nearby. It floated closer and closer to where she swam. At first, she thought it was a barrel or a buoy with fabric on top. Her arms were exhausted, so she reached for it, hoping for something to keep her afloat. When she grabbed it, the material relented under her hand with a sickening squish. She splashed it away as the thing rolled over.

A man faced her. Well, it was not a man anymore. It was a body. A bloated corpse bobbed in the calming waves, looking at her as if begging for help. Natalie realized it was the accused man, Cai Qian. The one the captain deemed guilty and sentenced to death. His legs were missing and part of one arm. The sharks found him swiftly, just like the captain said.

Natalie did not realize she was screaming until Claude turned her around to face him. He had one arm wrapped around a rope, and he pulled her close with the other.

"It is alright. Petite, come on. Stop screaming. It will be alright," he cooed.

His words worked. Natalie went silent. She hung limply as the pirates on the deck above pulled the two of them out of the water. It had all been a step too much. The book, the battles, the alien world with Chinese pirates. All of it. By the time they hoisted her back on deck, she felt like a mute, drowned rat.

Claude wrapped a blanket around her and steered her toward the mainmast of the ship. The place where the drowned man had been sentenced to death. His bloated face flashed in her mind, and she flinched. Claude pulled her closer. Natalie realized she was extremely tired of wearing soaked clothes and pulled the blanket tighter around her.

Ching Shih stood proudly with her men behind her. Several were injured, and all had smears of blood and gunpowder on their clothes. A red, almost rusty stain adorned Ching Shih's right hip. A part of her sleeve was missing, torn at the elbow.

The Pirate Queen faced off with a much larger man in a uniform Natalie didn't recognize. Even though he probably stood five inches taller than the captain, he shrank when she approached, sword unsheathed.

"What say you, Captain? You may surrender and join my fleet, or you can die at the hands of a woman. It is your choice," Ching Shih said loud enough for everyone to hear clearly.

The man dared to look her in the eye and seemed to regret it instantly. He cast his eyes this way and that, trying to find a purchase on someone else. For a sickening minute, he locked his gaze on Natalie. There was a mixture of confusion and resentment on his face. Perhaps even a little malice.

Natalie felt Claude hold her tighter and move a hand to the blade on his hip. She was not sure why he protected her so, but she appreciated it. This world frightened her, and any savior was worth cherishing.

She wondered why Ching Shih did not watch after her more, but this was her story. Natalie was just a tourist. Just because Ching Shih did not coddle her did not mean she did not care. She saved her from the kidnapper, after all.

The Pirate Queen drew her blade quickly and pointed it at the captive. She nudged the tip underneath his chin, forcing him to stand up taller and face her. He gasped as he stood on his tiptoes, jutting his chin up as high as it would go.

"You do not look at her. You look at me."

"My apologies, Captain," he said.

Ching Shih lowered her blade, but only enough for the man to stand comfortably. If he did so much as gazed down, he would have a rather large hole in his chin.

"Do you yield?"

"I yield! I surrender all of my ships to your will. My men and fleet are yours now," he said quickly, eyes bulging with fear.

Ching Shih lowered her sword, and the Naval captain slunk to the floor. A sly grin crossed her face as the defeated man lowered his head in defeat. She turned to her men and held her sword in the air. She did not need words. They all knew what it meant. Everyone cheered so loudly, the men on the other boats heard. They followed suit and applauded.

The cacophony of voices was so deafening Natalie did not hear the Naval captain creeping toward her. Everything was so loud here. Claude was cheering by her side, oblivious to the new visitor. She nearly jumped out of her skin when the captain whispered into her ear.

"You are the child. The one who gives her the power."

"What!" Natalie cried, turning on him. Her heart nearly pounded out of her chest. "Why do you say that?"

"Children do not normally sail with pirates. I hear tales Captain Ching Shih has a child on board. A magical one. It gives her unlimited power. It is why she is so formidable. Are you that child?"

A part of her wanted to blurt out the truth. She was not the child he meant. When she opened her mouth to speak, something stopped her. This man pleaded with his eyes, but he was also hiding a weapon. He had a hidden knife under his belt, and he was so close now she could see the handle.

There was no telling what a desperate man would do. What if she said she was the child, and he tried to kill her? Perhaps he was too afraid of her, and telling him this lie would be a good thing. Recounting the actual story would take far too long and make no sense to him.

Who would believe the actual truth that the old gods were vicious and cruel to their humans in ancient times? One day they found a human so wonderful, they fell in love with her and painted her all the colors of the divine. She had immense powers and ruled the land until new gods came along and flung the old ones into the ether to die. The goddess would have been pulled to heaven with her gods, but they could not stand the idea of her death. To save their treasure, they created an anchor to keep her tethered to the earth. A child who would root themselves to keep the goddesses from spinning away. An anchor who was the representation of the goddess in a younger form.

Of course, he would not believe that. Even if Natalie could say it all, and even if he understood, there was no explanation for her presence. An anchor child without a goddess. It was unheard of. So, Natalie lied and hope the captain would be too frightened to do her harm.

"Yes, I am that child," she said confidently, even though her teeth were chattering from the wet clothes beneath her blanket.

"Good. That is good," he said with a relieved sigh.

"Why?"

"I need you to get a message to her. The Emperor wants a meeting. Tell her he wants to parley,"

"Why don't you just tell her?"

"Because she is about to kill me."

CHAPTER SEVEN

When Ching Shih rounded on the captain, Natalie knew she only had seconds to act. She did not understand why she felt beholden to the man, but she did. By all rights, she should just let history play itself out. In the end, the bloated face of the guilty man in the water motivated her. She just could not stand bearing witness to another murder.

She broke away from Claude's grasp and leaped between Ching Shih and the captain, throwing her arms wide. He seemed just fine, cowering behind a little girl. Ching Shih had begun the horrible swipe in the air with her sword. It was a move that could fell any man. However, when she saw Natalie, she stopped her blade inches from her face.

"What are you doing? This is not how the story went," Ching Shih said.

"Can you do that snappin' thing? The one that freezes everything?"

Ching Shih stared at Natalie with a puzzled look. She thought the Pirate Queen would have been angry, but she seemed more confused than anything else. The crew murmured around them, as if noticing that this was not the way things ought to go. Thankfully, Ching Shih raised her right hand and snapped. Everyone and everything froze and fell silent.

"I killed this man," she said, pointing to the captain behind Natalie. "He dies in the real history. How can you save him now?"

"I don't know. I'm not supposed to be here. Maybe that's why. I mean, Claude's not supposed to save me neither."

Ching Shih turned her gaze to Claude, who was frozen in a perpetual state of concern, pointed toward Natalie. The Pirate Queen's face softened while looking at her soldier, and Natalie could not help wondering if they had a romance between them.

"None of this is correct. Why did you stop me?"

"The captain told me the Emperor wants a parley with you. I don't rightly know what that means, but it sounded important," Natalie said.

"He does, and in the real story, we did have a parley. We met and discussed the surrender, but it was not this man who gave me the information. It was one of his subordinates. Perhaps I acted too swiftly. Perhaps I did not need to kill this man."

Natalie stood stock still, trying not to make a sound that agreed or disagreed with the powerful woman. Ching Shih stared at the captain, cringing on the deck with a questioning glint in her eyes. Her brows knit together, and Natalie thought she resembled her anchor child so much at that moment.

"I... don't know what you should or shouldn't have done. I just couldn't watch it again. We don't do much killin' in my time. At least, none that I hafta watch."

"I see," she said as she slowly turned her attention back to Natalie. "I should stop playing out my story, I think. You do not belong in it, and your presence is changing things. We must find your goddess."

"Thank you," Natalie said.

The words came out in a great gust of air like she had been holding it in for too long—a burst of relieved intentions.

"I have an idea."

"Really? What?" Natalie asked.

"We will go to the parley with the Emperor. I will skip ahead in time."

"How will that help me?" Natalie asked.

"You will want to hear what he has to say, and he has something in his possession that will help you get to someone else who might be better suited to helping you. A wise man. A king among men. Another goddess."

CHAPTER EIGHT

Ching Shih skipped ahead a few days. The Pirate Queen stashed Natalie in her quarters to lessen Natalie's disorientation. The damp shirt and overalls were dubbed unfit, so they dressed her in a fine blue dress made from silk and embroidered with flowers. Her anchor child fashioned her hair in a bun on the top of her head, sticking several long, sharp pins to keep it all together.

Natalie stared at her reflection in the gilded mirror and barely recognized herself. Partly because the mirrors on the ship were not the type she knew. Back home, mirrors were perfectly straight and clear. These mirrors were warped and cloudy in places. Her body appeared too long, and her face swelled when it passed over a divot in the glass.

At first, the anchor child handed her shoes that reminded Natalie of ornate ballet slippers. She respectfully declined, preferring her old boots. Ching Shih reached a compromise by giving her black leather boots in the same style the pirates chose. Something far more practical and appropriate for the time.

While she would never pass for one of Ching Shih's Chinese crew, she appeared far less out of place. No longer the sore thumb. That, at least, gave her a modicum of comfort.

Before they left her quarters, Ching Shih brought out a small doll. It was faceless and made of white silk stuffed with straw. The thing wore a smaller version of the Pirate Queen's outfit and a mess of dark hair made of string. She pricked her finger with a pin and rubbed the pearl of blood onto the doll's forehead. When she handed it to her anchor child, the young girl nodded.

Natalie knew this trick. It was one they used often.

Usually, the goddess could not move far away from their anchor child. That invisible tether did not allow for much maneuverability. Any time Nat would try to walk away from her, he rarely got further away than past the sunflowers at the end of the road.

The doll trick allowed for more flexibility. When Nat needed to go to the *Canyon Cathedral*, they made a comparable doll to Ching Shih's. Something similar enough to the goddess. All you needed was a drop of their blood. The doll acted as a goddess stand-in. Natalie would be linked to the Nat doll so that the real Nat could go on adventures unhindered.

The Pirate Queen's anchor child took the doll with a solemn face. Natalie knew that look, and she knew the reason for it. It did not matter that anchor children hated moving. Snapping roots and walking were ingredients for a bought of nausea. It was the fact that they had no choice. They were perpetually left behind while the goddesses set out for grand adventures.

Natalie flashed her a compassionate look when their eyes met. The girl did not return it. She merely held the doll to her chest as she stared down at her papers. Natalie could not stay and console her. The captain was already hurrying out of the room, unaware of her anchor child's sadness. She had to rush to catch up.

Ching Shih, Natalie, Claude, and few more armed pirates took a smaller boat to the mainland. The port was far too shallow to dock her massive ship. The Pirate Queen stood straight and proud at the front of the boat as the others rowed toward the land. She wore a regal uniform of her own design, which looked expensive.

Red silks with a new, elaborately decorated vest flapped in the breeze. Golden chains and earrings glinted in the sun. The Pirate Queen painted dark makeup around her eyes, making her look even fiercer. Her tricorne hat was now edged with golden filigree. A bespelled addition Ching Shih added at the last minute.

Natalie had never been so happy to step onto dry land. The constant pitching of the boats made her chronically queasy. Even when the solid ground was beneath her toes, she still felt like the world was swaying a touch. She made a valiant effort to stand still and swallow down the bile rising in her throat.

When her balance returned, she suddenly had a sickening thought. What if she never rooted to anything in the book because they were at sea? What if everything was back to normal once she touched land?

If that were true, it would make finding Nat far more difficult. There was no telling how far she would have to go to find him, but Natalie doubted she could sail the entire time. She lifted one heel and peered down at her feet.

No roots. No heaviness.

Natalie was too busy inspecting her feet to hear the captain coming. Ching Shih sidled up next to her as if reading her mind about her anchor child situation.

"Do you know why anchor children have roots?" she asked Natalie.

"Not really."

"Because we are the kites. Always flying out and creating history. We destroy and conquer. Flying dragons. But there is nothing if we do not have you. If you do not keep us tethered to the Earth, we would spin away and never realize our dreams. We would float into the ether and die. We need you to have roots for us."

Natalie stood silently for a moment and let that sink in. She had a thousand different questions whirling around in her brain, but chose the most urgent one to ask. Ching Shih was not much of a talker, and Natalie wanted to get out what she could.

"If I have no roots, then will Nat spin out and die?"

"This is a question for which I have no answer. It is why you should talk to the Wise King. He will know."

"The Emperor is the Wise King?" Natalie asked.

Ching Shih barked with laughter. It was so sudden, Natalie jumped back an inch.

"No. The Emperor is a moron. A man who has never worked for anything a day in his life. He is like an angry boy who wants to hurt me for taking his toys."

"Then what are we doing here?"

"Hush, child. You will see. They await us."

Ching Shih pointed to the line of people positioned in front of them. They were well-dressed and stood with the straight backs of people in charge. There had to be at least two dozen staring at them. The party stepped away from their partners as if on cue, creating a narrow opening between them. A space Natalie and Ching Shih would need to venture through.

Ching Shih stood tall and guided Natalie in front of her. Claude and the other pirates filed in behind. As they walked the gauntlet, Natalie noticed the disdain in their eyes as she passed. Most bowed to the Pirate Queen, but none were her friends by any measure. Ching Shih marched along, seemingly carefree.

"Why are they all so mad at you?" Natalie whispered to the Pirate Queen.

"Probably because I robbed them all blind."

Natalie gulped audibly as she slowed her pace. Ching Shih placed a firm hand on her shoulder and pushed her onward. There was nothing she could do but move among the angry nobles and toward the massive building in front of them.

Most of the people in line paid her no mind. They spared the anchor child only a fleeting glance as they scowled at the infamous Pirate Queen. One man caught her eye because he was glaring at her. Not at Ching Shih. At Natalie.

When she spotted the military uniform and the bandages around his face and leg, she recognized him. It was the soldier who tried to kidnap her. The pockmarked one she had stabbed in the shin with her dagger. He ground his teeth and fixed a murderous scowl in her direction.

Natalie stiffened all over. Her limbs were so frozen with fear she could barely move forward. Only the surge of the pirates behind her kept her going.

They moved closer and closer. Natalie spotted the hilt of a sword beneath his belt. He moved his left hand over it, waiting for an opportunity. She saw every tendon when he clenched his jaw and gnashed his teeth.

Natalie was a mere five feet away when he lunged for her. In one quick motion, the man unsheathed his sword and brought the weapon high above her head. He released something between a growl and a battle cry as he swiped downward. She shut her eyes and braced for the impact.

Nothing happened—just the clang of metal on metal.

When her eyes flew back open, there was Claude in between her and her attacker. He held the man at bay with all of his strength. Swords clashed together. One hand locked over the man's fist, and the other clenched around the hilt of his own sword. The steel scraped as the two men struggled to dominate. Claude's long hair jittered this way and that with the strain, beads clacking together.

Everyone fell silent and watched the two men combat for dominance. The attacker threw Claude off of him. He grabbed the hilt of his sword with both hands and attempted to strike the pirate. Claude dodged easily and kicked the spot on his shin where Natalie had stabbed him in the battle. He yowled and crumpled to the ground.

Claude grabbed the man's sword and squatted behind him. He wrapped his arms around the man's neck with one and braced it with the other. His face began turning purple as he tore ferociously at Claude's arm, trying to get free.

"Let go!" shouted the man. "She deserves this!"

"I do not think so, mate. Yield or things will get worse for you!"

Some of his fellow soldiers moved to the front of the crowd and tried to wrestle Claude away. He did not waver. Natalie judged him to be powerful, but there was only so much one could do when the numbers were against you. They were winning.

Suddenly, a pistol exploded. Everyone turned to see Ching Shih with a gun raised in the air. The smallest line of smoke wafted upwards.

"Get away from my man," she said simply.

"He is attacking a soldier," said one man.

He looked more official than the rest, wearing a uniform similar to the attacker. The others bent to his word when he spoke. Natalie reckoned him to be an officer.

"He is defending a little girl. If your man wants to continue to fight him, that is their business. Claude is surely a better match than her," she said, pointing to Natalie. "And while my man may be capable, twelve against one is not an honorable fight."

"A pirate speaks of honor? That is ridiculous," the officer said.

Ching Shih moved faster than anyone expected. Even Natalie flinched as the small captain strode forward and pulled her sword in one fluid movement. She rested the tip of her blade underneath the officer's chin before he could reach for his weapon. Everyone gasped, and the crowd fell silent, waiting for the impending bloodshed.

"We have honor. We have rules. We do not bully little children. Tell your man to yield and walk away. If you do not, I will alert my extensive Navy to burn this place to the ground."

"How will you even tell them in time?" he said carefully. It was hard to appear intimidating when your primary focus was not getting impaled. "My men will kill you before you get word to them."

Ching Shih smiled in a way that made her look part sensual woman and part demon. The officer's eyes grew wide.

"Have you not heard of me? Have you not seen my power with your own eyes? Do you really think I lose?"

He swallowed gently and stepped backward. The officer waved his men away from Claude, who stood up with a jolly grin on his face. It took three men to lift the would-be kidnapper to his feet.

"Let us depart. She is not worth it," the officer said.

The group grumbled as they backed away. Natalie's attacker rubbed his neck as the blood began rushing back into his face.

"And the yield?" Ching Shih said.

He scowled at the Pirate Queen and then at Natalie. She did not think she had ever seen a person who hated her this much. His nostrils flared as he regarded her, and it made him look like a wild beast. At that moment, it would not surprise Natalie to see smoke come from his nose.

Instead of yielding to Claude, the man spat at Natalie. The wad of spittle landed in the dirt inches from her foot. She frowned down at the gob and braced for what was next.

Maybe it was the time spent with the great goddess Pirate Queen. Perhaps it was some divine knowledge she was privy to inside the book of histories. Either way, Natalie sensed the blow before it happened.

Ching Shih spun around with her sword. The steel sang in the air as it thrust into the attacker's body. The blade entered from behind and stuck out through his gut. It all happened so fast. Even he was surprised when he sputtered blood from his mouth.

No one moved for a long second.

The Pirate Queen pulled her sword back, and he slumped forward. He gave one last gurgled breath before leaving the world forever. Ching Shih used his pant leg to wipe his blood off her sword.

Natalie tensed. The crowd tensed. Everyone froze, except Ching Shih and Claude. They smiled at one another with the effortless affection of lovers. She patted him on the back and turned to make her way to the palace as though nothing unusual had happened.

She hurried after Ching Shih, eager to get moving after the murder. Natalie was sure the crowd of the Emperor's supporters would rush them at any moment for killing one of their own. The masses gasped and grumbled as the story made its way through the people.

Natalie clutched her stomach as she walked faster. It cramped again and again, sending her wincing fits. The air grew thick with the collective rage. A bubbling cauldron just ready to spill steaming violence onto the Earth.

Suddenly, Claude was by her side. He smiled and took her tiny hand in his. A warm sense of security filled her body, and she relaxed into his presence. Well, she eased up enough to stop the cramping in her stomach.

"Do not worry, petite. The path is clear," he said.

"How do you know?" she asked with a squeak in her voice.

"We have done this before, and we always win."

CHAPTER NINE

The palace appeared to be constructed without economy in mind. Nothing but ornate, elaborate architecture. No simple block structures or flat paths. Everything was decorated with patterns or filigreed with paint.

Natalie had never seen curving roofs or ornaments fashioned on a building before. She imagined sliding down the slopes of the rooftops and leaping into the air as if catapulted into a world where she could fly. The dream of the palace shimmered in the daylight like it was fashioned with gold.

When they approached the stairs that led up to the mighty doors, Natalie faltered. She did not want to enter this palace, but she knew she had no choice. Claude grabbed her hand and held her close.

Emperor Jaiqing was not at all what she expected. He wore a golden robe with blue and red silk ribbons along his collar and sleeves. His hat was red with pearl and golden spikes jutting up from the center. He sat cross-legged on a lavish, gold throne. Carved dragons and waves made up the back, legs, and arms.

What Natalie found terribly unexpected was how short he was. Even though he had the face of a man, he looked like a child sitting in his father's chair. She suddenly had a hard time holding in a laugh. This was the great, frightening Emperor? A tiny man in a big chair.

He fingered a long chain of pearls around his neck while he glared at their party's entry. Ching Shih smiled and offered a slight bow toward the emperor. From Natalie's vantage point, the Pirate Queen appeared smugger than anything. Jaiqing must have seen it as well.

"You dare to insult me in my home," he said in a low voice.

"Not at all, Emperor. I am greeting you as I was taught. After all, I am a woman of humble beginnings," Ching Shih retorted.

Jaiqing grunted and narrowed his eyes.

"Humble. And yet you stand here having stolen my Navy."

"Your Navy attacked my fleet. They lost. They surrendered. Nothing was stolen," Ching Shih said in an even tone.

"You have stolen much from the merchants here. Much of the royal treasury."

"This is boring," Ching Shih said with a roll of her eyes. "You asked for a parley. I am granting you one."

"You are *granting* me a parley? How dare you?"

"I do dare. I have the numbers to dare. Eighty thousand in my Navy with hundreds of ships. My force could crush you and sack this palace within a week. That gilded throne of yours could easily be mine with a snap of my fingers. I am granting *you* a parley because I am merciful. Now tell me, Emperor Jaiqing, what are your terms?"

The surrounding air thickened with tension. Some people do not believe emotions can weigh on the atmosphere, but Natalie did. Everyone in that room did. Hot anger radiated from the man on the throne. His small stature did not hinder his rage one bit. He glared at Ching Shih with a hatred that could set the palace ablaze.

"You are making a mockery of your Emperor," he said through gritted teeth.

"Everyone else will do so as well if a woman overthrows you," she said with a sly grin. "What are the terms of your parley?"

Natalie could see the Emperor's hands balled so tightly his knuckles turned white. He released one and jutted it toward one of his ministers. The man snapped to attention and retrieved a rolled paper from his robes. He handed it to the Emperor with the caution one reserved for feeding tigers.

"These are my terms," Jaiqing said as he unrolled the scroll. "Return my Navy. No more attacking Chinese merchant ships. Leave these waters now and never return."

"And what will be my payment?"

"Amnesty," he said in an angry breath. "Amnesty for you and all of your men. You may keep the spoils you have plundered thus far."

"All of the treasure. Spices, gold, jewels, everything?"

"Everything. Just return my Navy and leave forever. You may torment another country, but China is no longer your hunting ground."

The two faced off with unmovable eyes. Neither blinked as Ching Shih considered his proposal. Natalie held her breath as she looked from one ruler to the other. Jaiqing's mouth pulled into a thin line as he glared at the Pirate Queen. Ching Shih finally broke the moment as a calm smile spread across her face.

"We have an accord," she said with another slight bow.

"Fine," Jaiqing said sharply.

"In writing, of course," Ching Shih added.

"Of course."

The Emperor snapped his fingers, and his servant took the scrolled paper. He walked it over to the Pirate Queen timidly, and she snatched it from his hands. The man jumped back as though she tried to bite him, and Natalie heard Claude stifle a laugh behind them.

"One more thing," Ching Shih said.

"What is it?"

"I wish a treasure from you. A token of good faith," she said.

The Emperor glared at her with intense confusion. He seemed to stop moving with his mouth slightly ajar. Almost like he was a windup toy that lost its momentum. His eyes became darker than before, and Natalie feared what would happen next.

"A token?" he said at last.

"Yes. I want that golden elephant," Ching Shih said, pointing to an elephant statue in the room's corner.

The golden creature stood alone on a pedestal. It was about a foot tall, from feet to ears. Tiny designs and garniture wound down its legs and decorated its face. For such a small thing, it was gorgeous. Old and wonderful at the same time. It matched nothing else in the room, as if it came from another time and place altogether.

"You want that?" the Emperor asked.

"Yes, that is my price."

Again, he stared at her without a sound. There were no movements, not even a twitch. He was a broken toy once more.

"What's goin' on?" Natalie whispered to Claude.

"This is not what happened," Claude whispered back. "This did not happen in history. She never asked for that elephant. We beat his Navy, he asked for a parley, we took his deal, and we retired. That's what really happened. This ask is new. The Emperor does not know what to do about it."

"What about the fight outside?" Natalie asked.

"That did happen, but it was not because of you. I insulted the soldier's mother, and he attacked me."

Natalie thought about the sailors. Some seemed confused by her presence. Others barely regarded her at all. She was not supposed to be here, and only the goddess and her anchor child could recognize it. Well, them and Claude.

"Wait, why do you understand the history…." Natalie began.

"Fine! I will just take it myself," Ching Shih said, cutting off Natalie's train of thought.

No one stopped her. They seemed just as confused as the king. Ching Shih marched over to the elephant statue and beckoned Natalie. She looked at Claude for help.

"Go on, petite. The captain is waiting."

Natalie hurried over to Ching Shih and stared at the elephant. It truly was amazing. She knew nothing about sculptures, but even she could see it was old. Older than anything she had ever known. Older than the pictures in Nat's books.

"What's happenin'?" Natalie asked.

"This will get you to the Wise King. He will know better than I about what to do with you. If your goddess is here, the Wise King will know where."

"How will this elephant get me to him?"

"It was originally his treasure—one of many. Here, touch the statue," Ching Shih said, holding it out to her.

Natalie hesitantly reached out her hand. She placed it on the head of the golden elephant and readied herself for what was next. Nothing happened right away.

"Now, what do I do?"

"Give him my regards, young Natalie."

Ching Shih snapped her fingers. The world went white, and Natalie was gone.

CHAPTER TEN

Natalie's world rippled from shock as her body leaped from the world of China. For a moment, she wondered if she was on a ship again. The ground beneath her did not feel solid. She swayed blindly.

When she opened her eyes again, she found that her body truly was rocking back and forth. Not like the gentle rolling of the waves, but a jerking back and forth. The bright light temporarily blinded her, but once her vision cleared, she got a clear image of where she was. Natalie sat astride the back of a camel.

The land around her spun as Natalie fought to gain some sort of bearing. She tried to lay her eyes on a horizon, but dust blew in her face with a scorching wind, and she had to shut them against it. Her hand reached out in a panicked grab for something solid to hold. The only thing available was the golden elephant.

The statue tumbled quickly out of her hands. Natalie dropped off of the camel right after, as if their fates were intertwined somehow. Her body hit the ground hard, knocking the wind out of her. The camel made an agitated noise. She opened her eyes just in time to see the camel's hoof dropping over her head. She rolled away before the creature crushed her head with its back leg.

"You! What are you doing here?" shouted a man just above her.

Natalie sat up and took in her surroundings clearly for the first time. She was no longer in China. This place was scorched. Sand and sun and dry heat. Her lips felt chapped as she breathed in the desert air, and she smacked her mouth several times, trying to wet them.

"Answer me," the man said.

He was dark-complected. More so than Camille. More so than Claude. He might have been the darkest man she had ever seen. He wore layers of white and yellow. Flowing pants cinched at his shoes. A large maroon sash ran from his shoulder to his waist and ended at the hilt of a straight sword.

His hat was a mass of intricately folded bands of white cloth. Natalie had seen Camille wrap her hair similarly, but her style consisted of lots of colors and pretty braids. She had even done Natalie's hair up once, but it did not look as good as Camille's. This man's turban appeared to be purely to keep the sun from his head. Nothing flashy about it.

"Are you mute, child? Why are you dressed this way?" he barked.

"I… I am not from here," Natalie managed.

"Stand up," he said while offering her a hand.

She took it and stood. He was tall. So much so she no longer had to shield the sun to see him. He blocked out the sun all on his own. Another set of camels and a few mounted horses rode by. Each man stared at the odd girl. Each one was dressed like the tall man, more or less.

He placed a rough hand on her back and led her away from the procession of animals. She got a glimpse of what was coming up behind them. Hundreds of creatures. Camels and horses mixed with men and women. She blinked at the expansiveness of the caravan. It was massive, and she was grateful the tall man had moved her out of its path. It would be so easy to get crushed.

"Are you trying to steal?" he asked.

"What? No."

"Then why do you have that?" he asked, pointing at the golden elephant in her arms.

Natalie did not remember picking up the elephant, but there it was, back in her arms. She turned red all over.

"Oh, that. I didn't mean to take it," she said, meeting his eyes. "I'm not stealin' or nothin'. I swear. I don't even know where I am. Where is this?"

He eyed her suspiciously. She did not blame him, really. It must be a strange day indeed for this poor man. Some little white girl wearing Chinese clothes just drops in on his giant caravan. It was enough to confuse any person.

"Mali," he said.

Natalie did not rightly know where Mali was, but this looked an awful lot like the pictures of Africa in Nat's books. She assumed it was Africa rather than ask any more questions.

"I am here to see the Wise King," she said.

She tried to stand as tall as she could and speak with the authority Ching Shih seemed to command. It sounded a tad hollow, though, like a toddler pretending to play grown-up.

"You are here to see Mansa Musa?" he asked with a fair amount of disbelief in his voice.

"Yes! I am here to see Mansa Musa."

She puffed up her chest and spoke even louder. This seemed to work a little bit better. At least the volume hid her quivering voice. She suddenly remembered she was still holding the golden elephant. When she noticed, she thrust the statue out for the man to take. He plucked it from her hands slowly.

"I'm sorry. I ain't a thief. I swear."

"Alright, strange child. I do not know where you came from, but if anyone knows what to do with you, it is the great Mansa Musa."

CHAPTER ELEVEN

To look at a thing from far away is to take in its entirety. If one were to fly above a forest, you might see where the tree line ended and began. However, to be in the thick of a forest means you can only see a handful of trees, and it is incredibly easy to get lost. This is where the adage comes from. You cannot see the forest through the trees.

Natalie stepped back to take in the forest of Mansa Musa's caravan. While standing uphill, the rows of animals and people sprawled back for miles. However, when the tall man guided her into the thick of the procession, it was all she could do not to get lost in the camels and horses.

Every time Natalie moved to the left, the tall man jerked her to the right. If she held back to let a horse pass, he pushed her forward. It seemed nothing she did was right with him, and she shrank beneath his glare. All of his features were pointy and sharp, much like his attitude.

There was no mistaking the Wise King when they reached him. Like Ching Shih, he radiated power. It pulsed from him without effort. Natalie remembered Nat's struggle with the goddess' power and how awkward and troubled he was at first. This king had no sign of inadequacy. It was as if he had wielded the magic always.

He rode astride a massive white horse, which he slowed to a halt when they approached him. The horse wore white and maroon adornments with a golden bit in his mouth. It stomped the ground nearest Natalie as the king dismounted. She shrank away but kept her eyes trained on the king.

Mansa Musa wore silk robes to match his horse. Layers of white and maroon with dozens of gold chains around his neck. His turban wrapped around his head much like the tall man, but it was lined in golden thread with a spikey crown of rubies and emeralds perched on top. Natalie found herself unable to look away as the jewels glinted in the sunlight.

"Well, who is this?" the Wise King asked.

"A girl I caught trying to steal your golden elephant," the tall man said sharply.

Despite the tall man's size, he seemed insignificant compared to Mansa Musa. The king stood at least six foot six with broad, muscular shoulders. Natalie had never seen a man so large. The weight of his necklaces alone would pin her to the ground. When he stood straight, he blocked out the sun and created a shadow she could easily hide inside.

The great king bent down to get a better look, and Natalie cringed. To her horror, she realized the elephant was in her arms again. Natalie had no idea when she grabbed it. The case she was going to make for her innocence fell apart in seconds.

"You were trying to steal," he asked in a deep voice.

"No… your majesty. I weren't gonna steal it. I'm not…"

"You are not supposed to be here," he finished for her.

His voice was warm and kind. It was a stark contrast to the tall man, who spat at her with verbal venom. Mansa Musa smiled with soft eyes and placed a fatherly hand on her shoulder. It felt warm and heavy, and she relaxed under the comforting feeling it gave her.

"That will be all. I can deal with our guest from here."

"But… she stole," said the tall man.

"Do you question your king?" Mansa Musa said, returning to his full height.

"No. Never," the tall man said hastily, backing away from the massive king.

"Good. Leave us."

He bowed and skittered away, dodging camels and horses along the way until he vanished in the crowd. Even though the great king stopped, the procession continued on its way. It flowed the way of the tide without hindrance or free will.

Mansa Musa squatted to speak to Natalie face to face. Even with such a change in height, he still seemed massive. Not in a fearful way. He more favored the general ease of a gentle giant. Possibly a quiet beast, like a whale or an elephant. He grinned at her again and whispered.

"Now, child. You may speak plainly. No one can hear us."

Natalie took in a deep breath, grateful she had a moment to calm her panicked heart.

"I'm an anchor child. My goddess created the book of histories back in my time. He jumped inside, and we don't know what to do. Our world seems to be breakin' without him. There's a storm that won't quit."

"And how are you here?"

"I came inside the book to find him."

"Your mission is to bring him home?"

"Yes, sir. Oh, I mean majesty. Or is it excellency? Sorry. I don't rightly know. We don't have kings and such where I'm from."

"No kings?" he asked with a lift of his eyebrows.

"No… um… what do I call you?"

"Just Mansa Musa is fine."

"No, Mansa Musa. I live in America. Texas, really. But we don't have anythin' like that. We got a president, but he doesn't stay that forever."

"I have never heard of such a place," the Wise King said thoughtfully.

"Well, I don't reckon it's a place just yet. I don't know what year this is, but I guess that my version of America is pretty far off."

"Fascinating," he said, studying her attire. "And they dress this way in your America?"

Natalie became suddenly very aware of her clothes. She jumped a little as she took in her appearance. What a sight she was.

"No. This ain't how we dress. You are not my first goddess. When I first dropped in, I met Ching Shih. She's the one who found the elephant for me and sent me here to find you. She called you the Wise King."

Mansa Musa stood to his full height with a deep chuckle. It sounded like a muffled thunder rolling gently in the distance. He patted her on the back, nearly toppling her over. Natalie caught hold of one of his robes to keep from falling teacup over teakettle.

"Ching Shih. Yes, I can see why she sent you to me. She has no desire to slow down and take in a puzzle like this. The Pirate Queen loves to fight, conquer, and collect her bounty. I imagine she did not have much time for you."

Natalie looked up and down the caravan around them. So many people and so many animals. Everything appeared expensive, with gold adornments and fine fabrics. She stared at the golden elephant in her hand and spotted three more camels carrying sacks filled with similar statues—all gold and jewels.

"And what do you do with your bounty?" she asked.

Instantly, Natalie regretted the question. It sounded snide and shallow, even though it was not how she meant it. Luckily, Mansa Musa merely smiled down at her with warm eyes.

"Why, I give it away, child."

"You give it away?"

"Of course. Why hold on to something that can help so many? Do you know how many people that elephant could feed? Where did Ching Shih find it?"

"In a Chinese Emperor's palace," Natalie said hesitantly.

For the first time since they met, Mansa Musa looked troubled. Genuine concern crossed his face as he took in her words. She did not know the Wise King, but he seemed benevolent, and the idea of a rich man keeping the elephant appeared to genuinely upset him. His forehead wrinkled, and his eyes grew hard.

"That was never my intention. Why is it that gold always ends up with the rich?"

Natalie was pretty sure he was not asking her for an answer. After all, what did she know? She was just an anchor child who knew precious little about the world away from her window.

A deep, rolling boom sounded around her. The unmistakable clash of thunder before a crack of lightning. For a second, she thought it was the king laughing again, but when she looked up at him, his mouth was closed. In fact, he appeared apprehensive while scanning the skies above them. There was not a cloud in sight. It was a perfectly clear day with the sun radiating heat from above.

Another boom of thunder, this time louder. It was significant enough that half of the caravan stopped to look around them. Still nothing. They tentatively moved onward, but the king did not. He cast his gaze heavenward in all directions.

"That never happened. It is not possible here," the king said. He squatted again to face Natalie. His face was full of concern. "Something is very wrong in your world. You must tell me everything you know. Everything about your goddess. I fear we are all in grave danger."

CHAPTER TWELVE

Despite the massive number of people and animals around them, Mansa Musa and Natalie found the royal litter relatively quickly. Natalie had never seen such a thing. To her, it looked like a small house made of a tent carried on long poles. Men and horses lugged the thing along the road. They did not seem to mind their burden, and Natalie could not help but wonder why no one was using wheels to carry it.

"The Earth is not even, and the sand is unforgiving," the king said, as if reading her mind. "Do not worry. It is enchanted to weigh next to nothing. I would not have my people slaves to my bulky nature."

She gave a little nervous laugh, for lack of anything better to say. The king commanded his people to lower the litter so they might enter it. On the outside, the tent did not look big enough to house a giant king comfortably. Sure, he could fit inside, but it would leave little room for anyone else if they wanted to breathe easily.

Mansa Musa pulled back the flap and gestured for her to enter. Natalie walked through to find a vast room. Much like the captain's quarters of Ching Shih, the inside of the room was far larger than the outside would suggest. Apparently, goddesses really liked their space.

"Now then, we can speak plainly. Come meet my child," Mansa Musa said, closing the flap behind him.

Natalie felt the litter rise above the ground. It reminded her of the rocking of the ship, and she nearly fell over. The king steadied her, and they made their way deeper into the room. It was covered in plush, colorful rugs and bolts of cloth hanging from the ceiling. Natalie took a deep breath, smelling the earthy incense in the air. Unlike the oppressive heat on the outside, this place felt cool and inviting. It was as though the king had enchanted a constant breeze inside his home.

"Over here. He will be very excited to meet you," Mansa Musa said.

He led her to a back corner nearest his oversized bed. There, in a nook all to himself, sat a boy about her age. He was thin, lanky, and shorter than she expected. Given the large stature of his goddess, Natalie had prepared herself for a giant of a boy. But this one just looked like a regular kid. Perhaps even a little malnourished.

She reminded herself that the goddesses became whatever they wanted. Nan chose the form of an old woman. Ching Shih was a teenage pirate warrior. Her own goddess became a man—the man he always wanted to be on the inside. Perhaps Mansa Musa lived a scant life as a child and turned himself into something sturdy and formidable.

The boy sat on a pillow with a short table in front of him. He puzzled over a polished wooden rectangle with different-sized divots carved into it. Each depression had many jeweled stones inside it. The anchor child moved the pebbles around in a pattern Natalie could not read.

"He loves playing Mancala," Mansa Musa said in his booming voice. "What's your game? The one you use to divine the future."

"Chess," she replied.

"How fascinating. I do not know this game."

"I don't know it well either. Not the rules anyway. I just move the pieces around as they see fit."

The boy's head shot up as though just recognizing he had visitors. He fixed his gaze on Natalie, looking her up and down.

"You are not Chinese," the boy said slowly.

"No, I'm not," she said.

"But you are dressed that way."

"Yes, it's a long story," Natalie said.

"Yes, child. Please tell us your ailment. Perhaps we can help," the king said.

"Well, in my time, the world is… wrong. There's this storm, and we reckon it's because Nat's gone."

"Nat?"

"My goddess. He's somewhere in this book of goddess histories, but I can't find him. I don't feel him neither. Normally, I can feel him."

Mansa Musa and his anchor child exchanged curious looks. They stared for a long moment, having a silent conversation with one another. Natalie fidgeted in place, waiting for them to acknowledge her again.

"Is that why I heard thunder?" the boy asked.

"Yes, I believe so," Mansa Musa said. "If your goddess is in here, then you might be right. We could all be in trouble if you cannot find him."

"Can you help me? Can you feel him in here?"

"I do not sense him, but that is to be expected. We goddesses know of each other in here, but we rarely speak."

"Why did he go into this book of histories?" the child asked.

"Polly, his wife, died of a terrible fever. He sort of lost his mind, and we think he came here to find her in his own history and bring her back. But he's not back. He's been gone for weeks."

"Would that work?" the anchor child asked, turning to his goddess.

Mansa Musa rubbed his chin, staring thoughtfully down at Natalie. His brows furrowed, but he did not come across as angry. More pensive than anything else.

"I do not know," he said finally. "I have never heard of such a thing, but I also have not heard of creating a physical book made of the histories of the goddess. I suppose; theoretically, it could work. We cannot bring the dead back, but your goddess may have found a loophole around that restriction."

Natalie never thought about whether Nat could raise the dead. Years of living in the everyday world told her that sort of thing only happened in storybooks and motion pictures. But Nat was not supposed to do a lot of things. Enchant invisible windmills. Create an expanding house. Bend the laws of physics with a snap of the finger. But death? She wagered he could not pull that one off.

Suddenly, the litter came to an abrupt stop. Natalie tumbled to the floor as the tent lowered to the ground. When she stood back up, she felt relieved they were no longer moving. Her feet stabilized on the steady ground just below them.

"Ah! Wonderful. I forgot today is Friday. What a wonderful day for your visit, my child. Very fortuitous," Mansa Musa said.

His larger-than-life smile returned to his face. When he clapped his hands together, a small shock wave reverberated inside the tent. He stood even taller, towering over both children. For such an enormous man, he practically skipped to the flap in the tent.

"I will be delighted if you join me, child," he said.

In a flash of robes, he disappeared outside, letting the flap close behind him. Natalie turned to his lanky anchor child, who was rolling his eyes in the door's direction.

"What is he talkin' about? Why is he so happy about Friday?"

"Friday is when we stop. Friday is when we build. Friday is my least favorite day."

"Why?"

"He leaves me all alone. Favors his charity cases instead."

"What do you mean by charity cases?" she asked.

"Go after him. You will see for yourself."

He dismissed her with a wave of the hand. Natalie opened her mouth to say something more, but the anchor child was already enthralled in his pebble game. She ducked out quietly and raced after the Wise King.

CHAPTER THIRTEEN

Stepping out of the cool tent and into the sweltering sun was a shock to her system. The world was suddenly hot and bright and windy. Natalie's mouth dried in seconds. She rubbed her eyes to focus better.

As if reading her thoughts, Mansa Musa handed her a canteen made of thick animal skins. Natalie did not bother thanking him. She pulled the stopper and swallowed several big gulps of water. It tasted gritty, but she did not care.

Slowly, the horizon righted itself before her. Natalie wiped her mouth and handed the canteen back with a modicum of embarrassment. She had, after all, just acted like a wild animal in front of him. Mansa Musa did not seem to mind. He took the canteen back without a word.

When the world became clear again, she spotted a village about a quarter of a mile down the path. It sat downhill from where she stood. It was easy to get a good look at its size from her vantage point. Not quite as large as Amarillo, but definitely bigger than Tanglewood.

It appeared to be a bustling place. People moved in and out of the village, reminding Natalie of ants working tirelessly in unison. The few buildings she could see from her vantage point were small, mostly obscured by the enormous stone wall encircling the town. The urge to see more pulled her forward.

She suddenly realized she was by herself. Natalie turned around, looking for the Wise King. Apparently, he had gone forth without her. She had been so enraptured by taking in the village she had not noticed.

Natalie spotted Mansa Musa a few yards away. A mass of people surrounded him, and he threw out commands this way and that. How he kept everything and everyone straight was a mystery to her, but then again, he was a goddess. They could do just about anything.

"Bring the stones and wood we gathered to the village walls," he said, pointing to a group of men. "Collect some of the extra food and take it to the women of the village. They are less likely to hoard it," he said to a group of women.

Everyone nodded and bowed. They set off to work fast, seemingly happy to do the labor. The Wise King surveyed the village below with a grin on his face. It was almost as though he already owned the place, and he was inwardly congratulating himself on the victory.

Natalie sidled up to him and tugged on his robe. His smile never wavered as he turned his attention down to her.

"Are you conquering this village?"

"Oh no. I would never dream of such a thing!" the king said with some alarm. "You spent too much time with Ching Shih. I am not here to conquer. I am here to help."

"Help how?"

"In any manner I can. I find there is always a way to help people, especially those who have so little. This is my pilgrimage. It would be shameful not to grant charity to those who needed it on the way."

Natalie starred back down at the village again. It may have been bigger than Tanglewood, but it was definitely poorer. Even the ravages of the Great Depression could not compare to the poverty of this place.

Half of the houses did not have roofs. Merely ratty cloth stretched over crude walls. The few people she saw skitter inside the walls away from the massive convoy were thin and dressed in rags. Everything smelled of animal dung, and the children who ran after one another were covered in grime.

"I see what you mean," she said, nodding to Mansa Musa.

They heard huffing from down the road. Not the heavy breathing of the king's workers. No. This was the ragged puffing sound of someone out of shape and attempting to exercise. A squat man came trudging up the road and toward Natalie and the king.

"You there!" he shouted. "What is the meaning of your intrusion? We are a peaceful village and do not wish to fight. But if we must, we will defend ourselves."

"Brother!" Mansa Musa cried while taking the man in his massive arms. He hugged him, and the smaller man squirmed uncomfortably. "We are not here for violence. We are here to help."

"I am not your brother. Unhand me!"

The king released him but kept his cheerful smile all the same. The squat man spared a moment to stare at Natalie before turning his attention back on the king. He fixed his red face in a scowl.

"You are my brother because we are all brothers and sisters. Therefore, you are my brother. I will treat you and your people as such."

"And who is she? Your sister?" he snapped at the king and jutting a thumb at Natalie.

She was going to speak up to protest. Normally, she stayed away from confrontations, but the squat man rubbed her the wrong way, and he was not the least bit intimidating. She had sailed with dangerous pirates after all and could stand up for herself. Mansa Musa spoke up before she got out a word.

"Of course not. She is my child. That, I believe, is obvious," he said as that cheery smile of his faded from his face.

The squat man scanned her again. A little white girl in Chinese clothing compared to the large, dark Mansa Musa. He scowled and shook his head.

"I am not a man for jokes. From you or your little demon here."

"She is no demon," the king said.

Mansa Musa's eyes grew dark as he moved his substantial body between Natalie and the squat man. The sun's brilliance flickered in and out as he did so. Natalie looked upward to see a storm of clouds appearing out of nowhere in the sky. The great king clenched his fists, and the man cringed.

"I am Mansa Musa, the Wise King of Mali, and she is my child. Do you dare challenge that fact?"

"My apologies, Mansa Musa. I did not realize it was you," he said, sputtering like a weeping child. "Of course, she is no demon."

The storm clouds instantly dissipated, and the sun returned in full force. The Wise King slapped the back of the man's back in camaraderie. He let loose a deep, rumbling laugh.

"No worries, my brother. Now, tell your king what I can do for you. What is it you would like built in your village? A well? Perhaps a school? A library?"

"Well, I am the magistrate here, Your Greatness. You may give me the funds, and I will see to it that it goes in the proper directions."

Mansa Musa leveled a glare at the squat man, and he froze in place.

"I think not. My gold is not meant to go into your pockets. It is meant for the people."

"I am… the voice and leader of the people. What they wish I will provide."

He did not seem the least bit truthful, and Natalie scoffed audibly behind them. They turned to stare at her as she glared at the man. Natalie was not sure where this newly found bravery was coming from. Maybe being so close to Mansa Musa gave her courage. Perhaps she had run out of fear. Either way, she leaned into it.

"You don't talk like a person who's gonna build a school. You talk like a rich man wantin' to get richer. You sure look like you're doin' better than those folks down there. I'd wager you eat more in a day than they do in a week."

Mansa Musa barked with laughter. The man glared at her.

"I am here on behalf of the people, and I am the one who should distribute…."

"Enough of this," Mansa Musa said with a snap of his fingers.

The squat man froze mid-sentence. His eyes almost looked made of glass. They lost all emotion virtually. He stood before them like a chubby doll, waiting for the king to pull his string so he might speak again.

"You are to leave. Go to your home and stay there until our work is done and we leave your village," Mansa Musa said.

"Your will be done," he said mechanically.

The squat man turned on his heels and made his way back down the hill to his village. He did not stop for any reason, nor did he pant from the heat. The king had removed his free will. He was a puppet, at least for the time being.

"You found a streak of bravery, did you not," Mansa Musa said to Natalie.

"I just didn't like the man."

"I did not either," he said, offering an elbow out for Natalie. "Would you care to help me hand out gold coins to his people?"

"I would love to," she said with a smile.

Natalie looped her tiny arm inside the crook of his, and they walked down to the village together, allowing the squat puppet to lead the way.

CHAPTER FOURTEEN

From afar, the village appeared dingy and poor. When they got closer, it somehow got worse. The walls of the homes, which she had mistaken for stone earlier, were actually made of mud or dung. She could not tell which. Perhaps it was both.

The place stank of livestock, salt, and sweat. Everything was dry, baking in the sun. The streets were hard-packed earth with manure stamped into the cracks. Natalie tried not to cover her nose. She knew it would be seen as an insult.

The people were thin and sparsely dressed. While Mansa Musa and his people covered themselves head to toe to keep the sun away, these people barely had more than rags to wrap around themselves. Skinny children scattered away from them, hiding in alleyways as they passed. Several starving dogs and cats followed behind them.

"You can tell the nature of a place by how well they keep their children and animals," Mansa Musa whispered to her. "These people need food and clean water, or else nothing will thrive."

It all made Natalie even angrier when she thought about the squat man with his round belly and finer clothing. He obviously ate well while his people starved. There was no doubt where the money would have gone if Mansa Musa had given it to him the way he wanted.

Children, many her age or younger, peered out from the shadows, gawking at the sight of the mighty king and the small girl in Chinese clothes. That childhood curiosity was hard to squelch, even in the most dangerous of circumstances. She understood the draw of the unknown, and she stopped to wave at them.

There was a group of girls and boys nearby. All of their eyes grew to the size of teacup saucers when they took her in. A few boys poked the girls in the ribs, and they squealed in both fright and pain. The boys laughed and ran away and down the alley. A few of the girls chased after them. Not the smallest one, though. She could not be more than five, but she was the brave one who waved back.

"That one is a bit like you," the king said as he pointed to the little girl.

"Me? What do you mean?" Natalie asked.

"Brave for such a tiny thing."

"I'm not very brave," Natalie protested.

"I hear stories about your Nat. Nan whispers tales about him through time. Galahad, you call him. The one who made himself into a man all on his own. There is bravery there if I ever saw it."

"That's Nat. That's not me," she said sheepishly.

"Of course, it is you. You are one and the same. You must have that bravery in you at a young age. Besides, I can see it in your eyes," he said.

"You can?"

"Yes. You leaped into the unknown to find your goddess. That is brave."

"But I've been so scared ever since I left the farmhouse. This whole place is topsy-turvy to me. I can't even figure how I understand all of you. We can't be speakin' the same language."

"It is unknown to me too, but I will embrace a gift when I see one. Speaking of which," he said, reaching into his hip pouch. Mansa Musa pinched a gold coin in his fingers and brought it out to show the brave girl in the alley. "You child. Come here and collect a reward for your courage!"

The girl's eyes went wide. Natalie saw the gold glinting brightly in her eyes. Sparkly things were pretty. There was no denying the attraction of them, but gold meant so much more. Gold was beautiful, but it could also feed you. It could clothe your family and provide comfort and shelter. To this girl, the coin meant food for her entire family.

She scampered out of the alley's protection and approached Mansa Musa. She stood in place, shifting her weight from foot to foot as if deciding whether to take the offering. Her gaze flashed from the gold to the king and back again.

It reminded Natalie of the stray cats she fed at her childhood home. They were scrawny and hungry but unwilling to take the food she offered right off the bat. It took weeks of coaxing and multiple tins of sardines to get the cats to trust her. Such was the way of the streets. One had to weigh the reward versus the danger.

Mansa Musa tried to reach out to the girl, but she jumped three feet back. He smiled and tried to call her again, but she appeared frozen in place. A thought flashed into Natalie's head, and she took the coin from the king's hand. He released it without question. Natalie took a step toward the girl and out of Mansa Musa's shadow.

"It's alright. He's my friend, and I ain't a bit scary, am I?" Natalie asked.

The girl shook her head slowly.

"So, I think you can go ahead and take this coin here because I'm just a kid, too. Nothin' mean about me. You keep this and give it to your family. And if'n those other kids want coins, we got some for them too."

The girl stepped closer by degrees. Natalie knew better than to rush her. If she closed the gap before the little one was ready, she would get spooked and run away, just like a scrawny kitten. She held her smile, and eventually, the girl reached out a dirty hand and took the coin. It happened in a flash. She snatched the gold from Natalie's hand and bolted as fast as she could back down the alley.

"That is fascinating," Mansa Musa said as he moved to Natalie's side once more. "That was not how this went."

"What do you mean?"

"The history. *My* history. In the past, I offered the child a coin, and she refused to take it. I moved along to the well and handed out money there to the parents. But here, it is changed."

Natalie thought about the battle on Ching Shih's ship and with Claude. The would-be kidnapper she stabbed in the shin. The skirmish outside the palace because of her. Then there was the ghostly hand that appeared from nowhere. She was not supposed to be in China either, yet she was. Her presence changed history in small degrees.

"Because I am here," Natalie said.

"Yes. You changed this. Just by being here, you changed the way this happens in the book. Tell me, did you change anything in Ching Shih's time?"

"Well, the Emperor sorta stopped being able to speak when she asked for his elephant. The one she used to get me here. There was the kidnapper, too. Oh, and I made a friend on her ship. A pirate named Claude."

"A friend?"

"He jumped in the ocean and saved me. But I never was in China in the pirate days. Not in real life. I never met the real Claude. How can I change the history in here?"

"That is a good question. One we should ponder at length. But for now, I believe you have a promise to deliver," he said gently.

"A promise?"

Mansa Musa directed her attention back to the alley whence the little girl fled. There, standing behind her, were about a dozen more children staring at her longingly. The king passed her the pouch of gold coins, and she took it without a word. She had promised the children.

"This never happened either," the king said in her ear.

Chapter Fifteen

Natalie trailed behind the Wise King like a sardine in the wake of a whale. He swam ahead of her and parted the sea of people with ease. Had she been by herself, Natalie would have had to duck weave to get through. She reflected on how handy it was to have such a large friend with which to swim.

"Where are we going?" she shouted over his shoulder.

The village receded into the distance behind them. Mansa Musa led her back to his caravan of servants and gold. He had barely said a word since the little girl with the gold coin. Just patted Natalie's back and led her away.

"We are going to the woman's tent. My loyal servants will help you with your problem."

"My problem?"

"Yes. Your wardrobe. It is unbecoming of a daughter of Mansa Musa."

"I'm your daughter now?"

The Wise King whirled around and collected Natalie into his arms. She flinched in surprise, but when he held her to his chest, something changed. Mansa Musa held her like a baby in both arms. Her first impulse was to force her way to freedom.

He hugged her, and it felt inviting. Warm, but not the way the sun felt beating down on her head. Warm, like she was held. Someone had her. Someone protected her.

"I know when a child needs a hug. I know when a child needs a father, if only for a short while. There was a time when I was that child. If I can ease your thirsty soul for a few hours, it is my privilege to do so, my daughter."

Natalie gave up her fight. She shut her eyes and relaxed into the embrace. The anchor child had never been hugged so thoroughly. There were always roots and tables and chairs in the way, but here, in the wild world of Africa, she felt like she was held entirely for the first time in her life as an anchor child.

His exhale smelled like dates and salt. She did not mind a bit.

CHAPTER SIXTEEN

The women's tent stood as far away from the village as possible. Natalie could not tell why exactly. It was the most prominent structure by far and the first to be erected. Perhaps the Wise King wanted to keep an army of followers between the village of unknown threats and the women who served him.

When he threw back the double tent flaps, the picture in front of them threw Natalie off guard. It was hard to pin down what she expected. Some jeweled harem with half-naked concubines, perhaps? Like something out of *The Arabian Nights*. Maybe something grittier and raw, like what they encountered in the village?

This was something else entirely.

Lush carpets covered every inch of the floor. Rugs of every shape with elaborate patterns in maroon, black, and yellow lined the ground. In her mind, Natalie knew there was sand beneath her, but her feet did not understand that. They luxuriated in the plush fabric. It squished pleasantly beneath her boots.

Oil lamps hung from support poles and sat perched on low tables, giving the place a romantic glow in the twilight. Groups of candles clumped on ornate, golden trays. Some women congregated around the larger lamps while others milled about, doing chores with singular candlesticks in hand.

Several younger women moved this way and that with trays of food, stopping to serve the older ones sitting on tasseled pillows. Most had a purpose. Most had a job. Even the eldest of the women had minor jobs, directing the youngest girls or snipping the wicks off expired candles.

Unlike the books Natalie had read, no one here was half-dressed. No silky harem pants and sheer veils. The women looked much the same as they had in the caravan. Light dresses with sleeves and pants that covered their skin from the elements. A few had taken off the wrappings around their heads. When they saw their king, there was a collective gasp.

Everyone in the massive tent turned to stare at them. First at the king, and then down to Natalie. She shivered underneath her skin as the eyes of a hundred women focused on her. She shrank against the mighty king, hoping he might protect her.

"Mansa Musa! Exalted leader. What are you doing here?" a young woman said as she quickly moved in between the king and the rest of the women.

"Ah! Young Teshi. Look at how lovely you are becoming," he said with one of his jovial smiles.

"Thank you, Wise King," she said.

The girl's grin appeared too large for her face. Natalie could see her straining to hold it still. She was about thirteen, as far as she could tell. Even though Teshi's skin was quite dark, Natalie could make out a deep blush on her face. Almost like Teshi was holding pools of burgundy wine inside the skin of her cheeks.

For the life of her, Natalie could not tell why she was so tense. Then again, when she looked at the other women in the tent, they were just as uptight. Mansa Musa's smile had not done a thing to appease the crowd.

Suddenly, there was a flurry of movement in front of her—a fluttering of maroon fabric and gold. An older woman appeared in a blink, standing in between the king and Teshi. She seemed to be middle-aged, strong-bodied, and taller than any of the others. The woman crossed her hands over her chest and cast a judgmental glare over her pointed nose at Mansa Musa.

"Hello, Jasira," he said with a fresh smile.

"Mansa Musa, thank you for honoring us with your presence. However, you must leave. This is the women's tent," Jasira said with little softness.

"I do understand, of course. I have come to ask a favor," the king said, coaxing Natalie from his side. "This is my new friend and daughter. Will you please take care of her? Dress her as is appropriate for a child of mine."

Jasira turned her hawk gaze down to Natalie. She cringed beneath her scrutiny now that she could no longer hide from the terrifying woman. Just behind Jasira, Natalie spotted Teshi bouncing a little in place. She appeared to be excited.

"Of course, Wise King. We will do your will as always. However, you just must follow the rules, sire."

"Yes, I know. No men in the women's tent. Not even me," he said with a bow. "I leave you ladies to your ornamentations."

Before she had time to say another word to him, Mansa Musa ducked out of the tent, leaving her all alone. The only thing she caught from him was a laughing wink before the desert twilight swallowed him whole.

CHAPTER SEVENTEEN

There she stood, an anchor child facing off with a tent full of a hundred women. An eerie silence hung in the space between them as if every person held their breaths collectively. Natalie braced herself for whatever was to happen next. A rush of violence, perhaps? A mob of interest that would squeeze the life from her? She shook from the anticipation.

None of that happened.

Most of the older women turned away from her the second the moment ended. Half of the other women went back to their work, busily hurrying this way and that with trays of food or candles. Only the younger contingent honed in on her, and Teshi was their leader.

"Do as our king demands," Jasira said to the wide-eyed teenager.

"As you wish," Teshi said with barely contained excitement.

She closed the distance between them and took Natalie's hands in hers. Her smile was just as full as before when greeting the king, but it was not strained this time. This one was free with genuine excitement. She beamed at the anchor child as though she were a new puppy.

"What is your name?" Teshi asked in a bubbly voice.

"Natalie."

"Natalie! What an odd name. I wonder where our great king found you. Never mind. That does not matter. Please, you are our guest. Come with me."

Teshi gripped Natalie's hand and led her deep inside the women's tent. Everyone moved past her in a blur. Dozens of women and girls blended together in a steady stream of white, burgundy, and gold as she rushed by.

Most of the older ones paid them little attention. The younger ones, however, began collecting in their wake. Young girls from ages three to thirteen gathered in clumps behind Natalie, pinching her hair and tugging at her silk dress.

"Here we are. This is a perfect place," Teshi said.

They were in a far corner of the tent with dozens of oversized pillows. A group of excited teenagers awaited them in front of an array of mirrors and gilded chests. One of them jumped up and down in place when Teshi pulled Natalie into the middle of the gaggle.

"We are going to make you so very pretty," Teshi said.

"Thank you… I think. I'm not great at bein' pretty," Natalie said uneasily.

She longed for a pair of overalls and a boy's shirt at that moment. That was not to be her fate. Natalie knew there was no going back when they all began talking at once.

"What is she wearing?"

"I have never seen such a blue."

"We are going to make her so pretty!"

"She is so pale."

"Do you think she is sick?"

"Where did the Wise King find her?"

"Enough!" Teshi said over the rising din of the girls. "Our illustrious ruler has tasked us with making Natalie presentable. Let us do that. Enough gossip."

The murmurings did not go away. They just died down to whispers. Natalie was grateful. She could finally breathe.

A few of the older girls opened the chests around them while Teshi began stripping Natalie of her clothes. She grabbed for the undergarments while clutching an arm around her chest, but Teshi playfully slapped her hand away with a *tsk tsk* noise.

"We are all the same in here. Not to worry."

"I'm just… not used to any of this."

"You do not have women in your home? Where do you hail?"

"No, there're women. It's complicated. I don't know how to explain it to you," Natalie said. Then she thought of something odd about this whole thing. "Why don't you let the king in here?"

"Oh, that is a silly question. This is the women's tent."

"But he is your king."

"Of course. We serve him as anyone should. Mansa Musa is the great Wise King. The giver of wealth. We revere him as he should be."

"But he's not allowed in here?"

"No men are allowed in the women's tent. This place is just for us. Out there, we are daughters and wives and workers. In here, we are just women, and that is private and sacred."

"I don't reckon I get it, but it is kinda nice. You don't hafta worry in here," Natalie said with a renewed reverie for the place.

The night finally arrived around them, and the candles created a romantic aura that filled the tent with a dancing, breathing illumination. Spicy incense wafted like wispy smoke, traveling in between laughing women and squealing children. Natalie relaxed into the heady atmosphere and exhaled deeply.

By the time Teshi pulled the white dress over Natalie's head, she had forgotten she was naked mere seconds before. She pulled on the leggings and wrapped the belt around her waist with Teshi's help. Two more teenagers led her to a nearby mirror and sat her down on a pillow. Natalie stared at a near stranger.

Perhaps it was the lighting. Perhaps it was how the journey had worn on her. Perhaps it was the warped mirror. Either way, Natalie stared at a picture of her own face she did not fully recognize.

Her skin was tanner and dry. Her hair appeared oily and stuck to her scalp in places. Her brain told her that eyes did not change shape, yet here she was, looking deeply into eyes that seemed more prominent than before. Could she have changed that so much?

One girl sat in front of her with an oval tin in her hand. She dabbed two fingertips into the waxy salve inside and dotted it carefully along Natalie's cheeks. It smelled pleasantly of sandalwood and oil. She did not mind when the girl rubbed it into the rest of her face.

"There. That will help with the dryness." Teshi said, kneeling behind her. Natalie could see her in the mirror, hairbrush in hand. "Let us do something about this."

Teshi pulled out the two sharp sticks holding her hair in place. She handed them to the girl with the face balm, who gaped at it with two other girls. Natalie had half a mind to ask for them back, but did not want to sound rude. Not to these girls who were being so kind to her.

"Not to worry. We will put those in your pockets. A woman must always be able to protect herself, and those appear to be very sharp," Teshi said with a smile.

"You could have them…"

"Not a word. You are our guest."

Another girl appeared behind them and handed a cylinder to Teshi. She removed the top and tapped a handful of powder into her palm. With all the gentility of a sister, Teshi began applying the powder to Natalie's scalp. With every application of powder, Teshi pulled a soft hairbrush through Natalie's hair.

The transformation was surprising. The powder seemed to soak up the oil collected in Natalie's roots, bringing new life to her limp and damaged hair. With every gentle application, she appeared more and more herself. She smiled at her reflection.

Teshi finished brushing her hair. She worried the girl would stuff it inside a headwrap like the other women. That idea made her feel stifled and hot. Claustrophobic. Thankfully, she wove it into a simple braid down her back. Natalie smiled at the new her.

"There, that is better," Teshi said.

"Yes, thank you," Natalie said with an exhale of relief.

A girl about her age appeared beside them. She held a large tray of food and offered it to Natalie. When she peered over the rim, she only recognized one thing. Rice. The rest looked like some kind of berries and reddish, kidney-shaped nuts.

"Food for you," the girl said.

"Thank you. What are these?" Natalie asked.

"These are kola nuts. Always served to new and honored guests," Teshi said. "Please eat. I will finish with your things."

Natalie smiled and tucked into the food. It was not a feast, but she was grateful for it. The nuts were a little hard to bite down on, but she did so without complaint. When Natalie got to the rice, there were no utensils to use. A quick glance around the tent told her that the other women ate rice with their fingers, so she did the same.

"Now for the adornments," Teshi said when Natalie finished the plate.

"What? No. I don't need anythin' fancy. Please."

"No daughter of Mansa Musa can walk through the world without something. We all have adornments because of his love and devotion. Please, I will be insulted if you do not accept."

"I don't want to insult you. You've been so nice."

"Then you will accept. Here, the children chose this for you."

The girl with the face balm returned, holding something oval on a pillow. She handed it to Natalie with great reverence, bowing as she placed it in her hand. It was a golden bracelet with the most familiar pattern along the outside. A green, jeweled snake weaving all the way around.

Natalie took the trinket, and the world began twisting around her. The ground pitched this way and that, making her slant her body to stay upright. It was a good thing she was seated, because she might have fallen over otherwise.

When she looked at the other girls for a sign of what was happening, they peered at her, concerned. The world was not moving for them. Teshi's face was full of concern. She reached out to touch Natalie's arm, but decided against it.

Her vision tunneled as she turned back to the bracelet. It haunted her somehow. This was a mistake, she thought. It could not be the same bracelet as before.

"Are you alright?" Teshi asked.

"Where is my dress? The blue one I had on," Natalie said breathlessly.

"It is right over there," she said, pointing to a blue heap by the mirror.

Natalie scrambled across the carpet to the dress and immediately started fishing inside the pockets. There it was, still where she had left it. She had tucked it in her pocket when Ching Shih gave her the dress. The golden bracelet with the snake. Her entire entourage fell silent when she pulled the original bracelet out and held it up to the new one.

At first, she thought it had to be a coincidence. Surely they made lots of jewelry that looked the same. There could only be so many styles and decorations. However, when she inspected them side by side, they were identical. The same pattern. The same slight flaw near the snake's eye. The same thinner pinch of gold near the tail.

These bracelets were not similar. They were the same.

It was not until Teshi spoke Natalie realized the whole tent had gone quiet again. Every woman in her sightline stared at her—some in disbelief and some in fear.

"Where did you get that?" Teshi asked.

How could she tell them a floating hand appeared in a wall and dropped it? That would not make sense to these admirable women. It did not even make sense to her, and she lived through it.

"It is time for you to go," said a stern voice above her.

Natalie peered up to see Jasira standing next to the mirror. She wanted to apologize to her for being a disruption. If the anchor child could go back in time and hide the bracelet, she would. Everyone feared her now. Why had she not kept the bracelet secret to herself?

"The king is outside waiting for you," Jasira said.

"I'm sorry. I didn't mean…"

"You shall not keep him waiting," Jasira interrupted.

"My apologies," Natalie whispered. "Thank you, Teshi. I appreciate all of your help."

Teshi smiled at her, but the joy in her eyes was fabricated. It broke a vital bone in Natalie's chest to see the girl suddenly so afraid of her. Teshi gave her a small wave as Jasira rushed Natalie from the tent. Every eye watched her leave, and no one said a word until the woman pushed her safely out into the night.

CHAPTER EIGHTEEN

By the time Mansa Musa and Natalie made it back to his tent, Natalie felt three years older. She barely had the energy to raise her eyes from the ground, let alone meet anyone's gaze. The sound of the cheerful laughter from the women's tent faded into the night behind her, hammering home her otherness in this world.

"I believe we need to examine this," Mansa Musa said as he led Natalie to the back, where his anchor child sat. He held both of the bracelets in his hands and examined them with the interest of a scientist. "Your presence here is changing the story. The book is creating a new history around your interactions with us."

"Seems to be that way," Natalie said wearily.

She threw herself on top of a pillow on the floor. The chopsticks in her pocket stuck to her side, and Natalie had to shift to get comfortable again. Mansa Musa and his anchor child paid her no mind. They passed the bracelets back and forth between each other.

"If that is true, who knows what is happening to your goddess. He may be lost in an alternate reality of his own history. If he intended to come here to return his wife to your time, and he has not done so, something may have happened. Something that never happened before."

"What do you mean?" Natalie asked.

"I mean, he may have been injured. He may be held hostage. He might have died. We do not know. This is unprecedented, and the rules are not established. Tell me, did he have any enemies in his history?"

"Enemies? No. Everyone loves Nat. He's a good man."

"Think hard, young Natalie. Perhaps not the normal enemies in your world. Ones that could cross over to this realm. Powerful people."

"I can't think of…"

Her sentence died in her throat. Natalie tensed her entire face, trying not to panic. An entirely new chill took over her body. One that cold-soaked her very bones.

Violence. The horrid creature, Violence, was here inside the book.

When Nat struggled with his new identity as the goddess, his emotions became so powerful they split apart. First, it was Fear. Nat's sense of fear manifested in a shriveled version of himself. Fear was not a threat, but when joined with his other emotion, Violence, they created a terrible enemy. Violence pulled Fear inside himself to birth the creature known as Fiona.

Fiona wreaked havoc on the *Canyon Cathedral*, a sanctuary for witches of all kinds. She kidnapped poor Delphia and cut off her arm. She even tried to take Nat's goddess powers for herself. Nat prevailed when Calliope forced him to create *The Goddess Stories* book, where he went inside to get the wisdom he needed to truly wield his power.

Nat fought Fiona and won. He ripped Fear and Violence apart, destroying Fiona in the process. While he welcomed Fear back inside his body, Violence was banished inside *The Goddess Stories*. Nan vowed they would hold him there for all of time.

Now, Nat was missing somewhere in the book. If Natalie was changing the story in small ways, she imagined Nat's intrusion would rock the boat even more. What if Violence escaped and stole the powers? What if he was holding Nat hostage?

"You have not answered me, child. Yet, I see your mind is racing," Mansa Musa said.

"I'm sorry. Just thinkin' about an enemy we have in here. It's Nat's manifestation of rage and malice. We call him Violence, and Nat trapped him in a cage inside the book. If somethin' were to happen, and Violence got out, it would be bad for everyone."

"I see. Then we must get you to someone who can find your goddess."

"Who?"

"There is someone who deals in maps. She is our resident builder, you might say. Keeps blueprints of everything."

"She knows where everything is? How do we get to her?"

"Well, I know a way, but it means we will have to skip ahead in my own story to get there. Tis easy enough. Brace yourself."

Mansa Musa raised his considerable hand and snapped. It cracked in the air like the boom of fireworks the second after you see the sparkles. The sound reverberated down to Natalie's bones.

The world shifted. The light moved. All around them, the sun seemed to rise and set a dozen times. It was as if the days flew by. A whole sun cycle lasted mere seconds. It made Natalie nauseous, but she held steadfast in her resolve not to vomit.

Everything stopped, and she was happy about it. Mansa Musa stood proud and solid. When she turned to the other anchor child, he too appeared queasy. His color blanched, and he held a hand over his mouth. While Natalie did not wish the queasiness on anyone, she was mildly grateful it was not just her.

"There. We are here," the king said.

"Where?" she asked.

"Egypt. You will love it here, and it is the best place to find our builder," he said with another one of his broad grins.

Mansa Musa walked toward the exit and bade her follow him. Natalie took a step, but something caught her arm, stopping her. She turned to see the anchor child's hand clasped around her wrist. His eyes locked on her with great intention.

"Be careful," he said earnestly. "Mansa Musa made himself large to command men and promote peace. He does not realize how many enemies he has made over the years. Ones who whisper behind his back. Especially in Egypt."

"But he's the goddess. They can't really hurt him, can they?"

"Probably not, but they can hurt you. Stay close to him. If you are changing the story, they might see you as a good target. Something to kill in order to upset the king."

Her breath caught, and she froze in place. Natalie had almost been kidnapped once. She did not want it to happen again. What if she could not get away next time? Another idea occurred to her. What if the same thing had happened to him as well? There were significant costs to being the anchor child of a famous goddess. Natalie had born witness to that.

When she jumped inside this wretched book, she never thought she would face so much trouble. She had been thrown into the ocean, pitched into a pirate battle, dropped into an African village, and ostracized from a tent full of women. Now, she had to contend with Egyptian conspirators.

"Here. Put this on. You will be less conspicuous," the boy said, handing her a maroon cloak. "Your skin will give you away as not belonging. This will help."

Natalie felt numb all over, but she did as she was told. Her heart pounded so hard she was positive he could hear it.

"And the bracelets. You need to wear them."

"What? But why? They scare people."

"If this came to you twice, you must keep it," he said.

"We don't know what it means."

"You will never know what it means if you do not take it with you."

"Fair point, I reckon," Natalie said.

She slipped the bracelets on her wrists—one for each arm.

"Good. That's better," the boy said as he looked her over. "I bid you farewell and good luck. May your journey be short and fruitful."

"Thank you."

She did not know what else to say or do. Did they shake hands? Was that rude? If it were up to her, she would hug her brother anchor child.

Fear made her body tremble all over, and she wanted someone to hold her the way Mansa Musa had earlier that day. That all-encompassing embrace reassured all the fearful bones in her body. Anything to squeeze her terror away. Anything to fill the empty parts of her belly that wanted desperately to go home.

In the end, she gave him a stiff bow. He returned it. She left the tent quickly before she started crying. Now was not the time for that. She had to be brave. She had to be strong. She had to find Nat before something terrible happened. If it had not already.

CHAPTER NINETEEN

Egypt was not what she expected. All of her books described great pyramids amidst a vast desert. A dry wasteland where the sun baked everything in sight. A place of sand and scorch. When she stepped out into the world, a vibrant metropolis greeted her.

The massive caravan made camp along a great river. It was the Nile, Natalie imagined. She had no notion of other Egyptian rivers. Along the banks, the Earth was fresh and green. A sea of reeds rustled like waves along the opposite bank. Palm trees shot into the air as if stretching toward the sun. The only palm trees she had ever seen were on Nat's postcards. Natalie had no idea they could grow that tall.

A mass of people moved around them—more than just Mansa Musa's caravan. Merchants called from their stalls, women rushed by chiding unruly children, and workers lugged their heavy loads in a steady stream of humanity. It was as though Egypt was a heart, and the people moved as the blood coursing in its veins.

"Where are we?" Natalie asked.

"The great city of Thebes. Come, child. We have someone to meet," the Wise King said, patting her on the back.

"I'm afraid you'll lose me in the crowd," she shouted up at him, trying to be heard over the din.

"Then come up here!"

With one swoop of his arms, he lifted Natalie off her feet. She flailed in the air for a second before he placed her on top of his shoulders. Her eyes flew wide, but she balanced herself on her new perch. Her hood flew back, uncovering her bare head to the sun. Suddenly, she found herself above the crowd and feeling exposed.

Natalie fumbled a bit, trying to figure out what to do with her hands. When the big man moved, she would have to hold on to something. The nearest option was his turban, but that felt wrong somehow.

"No worries, child. You may hold on to my head. It is not a sin," he said.

She let out a sigh of relief and grabbed ahold as gently as she could. Of course, when he began walking, she gripped tighter. Mansa Musa chuckled beneath her, and she felt the rumble from beneath her rear end.

Both the king's men and the residents of Thebes stopped what they were doing to watch the giant man, clad in gold, who carried a little girl as though he were a beast of burden. Everyone stared at the white girl in fine clothes, riding astride a king. Natalie wished she could shrink down and hide in his turban, like in *Alice in Wonderland*. Perhaps getting lost in the crowd would have been less conspicuous.

"Here," Mansa Musa said, handing a leather pouch up to her. "Hand these out to people as we walk. It will make you popular."

"I… I think I'm already popular," she said as the stream of people locked eyes with her.

"Very well. It will make you beloved then."

Natalie opened the pouch to find it filled with gold coins. She plucked one out and tossed it to a woman with two children clutched to her skirt. Her oldest child caught it mid air. When the woman saw the treasure Natalie had given, her eyes welled with tears.

She continued to toss coins to the people, always aiming for those who looked like they needed it the most. The mothers, the beggars, and the malnourished. Her tosses were not always accurate, but she hit her targets more often than not. She enjoyed this feeling of benevolence, like she was helping people. It was a slight comfort in a topsy turvy world where she felt so afraid much of the time.

It did not take long for the crowd to hone in on the strange girl doling gold out to the public. Dozens of people veered off their normal paths to crowd around her. Arms shot into the air, begging for a taste of her charity. They swarmed Mansa Musa, and she was genuinely afraid he might get crushed to death.

"Make a path!" the king boomed.

His words forced a shock wave throughout the crowd, and they did as he said. No longer did the masses push against them. Instead, they parted to allow the king through. He passed them with a kind wave.

"Thank you, my brothers and sisters. There is more gold with my people near the river. You shall find our charity there," he said with a pleasant laugh.

Everyone cheered in unison. Many praises rang out for the godly king and his strange child. Natalie breathed in a sigh of relief.

A great crackle of electricity shattered the peace. Thunder followed close behind, shaking the ground. It rattled Natalie so much she slipped from Mansa Musa's shoulders. Luckily, he caught her before she hit the ground.

The cheers silenced abruptly as the people turned their attention skyward. Natalie did the same, but there was nothing. No clouds and no rain. Only the ever oppressive African sun loomed over them. The king and Natalie shared nervous looks.

"Go, my friends. Collect your reward on this fine day!" Mansa Musa said.

Slowly, the crowd moved along. First in ones and twos, and then, by the dozens. Natalie pulled him down to her level to whisper in his ear.

"That did not happen, did it?" she asked. "I mean, in your history."

"No. I think it is coming from your world."

Natalie pictured the farmhouse back home. The faces of Camille and Vivian flashed into her mind. She remembered how nervous Camille was watching the tornado appear and disappear in the distance. She usually controlled the weather, but this elusive storm was beyond her. That alone scared Natalie more than anything else. She had to find Nat soon.

"I think we need to hurry. Who are we supposed to meet? How do we find the builder?"

"Well, in my history, the men we need to see will approach me at any moment."

"What men?" Natalie asked.

"They work for the Sultan's Magistrate. He wants an audience with me."

"What will he do with us?" Natalie asked.

"I honestly do not know, little one. In my past, I declined the meeting. After all, it was not the Sultan asking for an audience. It was only a magistrate and an arrogant one at that. Kings do not bow to such people. But this time, I will say yes to the meeting so that we might gain access to the builder."

"What if he tries to kill us?" Natalie said with a squeak in her voice.

"Not to worry. You are with the goddess. No one will harm you."

He patted her shoulder and nearly knocked her off her feet. Her knees felt like they were beating together. She jutted her arms outward to regain her balance.

Natalie did not have long to get her bearings. There was a commotion in front of them. Something was coming her way. When the crowd parted, a new feeling of dread took over her. Three men dressed in fine robes approached Mansa Musa.

The surrounding peasants gave the men a wide berth. Natalie could tell why. Their scowls could melt glass on a cold day. Something about the group's demeanor reminded her of the sailor in Ching Shih's time. The one who tried to kidnap her.

"Mansa Musa," said the tallest one. "Our great ruler has sent for you."

"Now, I do doubt that, brother. Your great ruler is Sultan an-Nasir Muhammed, and he resides in Cairo at the moment. I know this because I recently ate a fine meal with him."

"The ruler of Thebes. Our Magistrate, Nefer-Webben. He bids you come to pay tribute to him," another man said. He had three long scars running down the side of his face. "You must kiss his feet and beg for permission to enter his city."

Mansa Musa smiled. It was not his genial grin or the one he used to make Natalie feel at ease. He smiled the way parents do when their children try to talk back to them in public. The king was a few minutes away from grabbing the scarred man and swatting him in the streets.

"I do not think Sultan an-Nasir Muhammed would agree that Nefer-Webben is the ruler of anything. And I do not bow to him or anyone else," he said in a deep voice. When he locked eyes with Natalie, he continued. "However, I will have an audience with your magistrate. It has been a long journey, and I would love to thank him for his hospitality in this wondrous city."

The three men seemed shocked into silence. Their mouths hung ajar, and they exchanged curious looks with one another. The scarred man, in particular, struggled for words. Mansa Musa chuckled as he watched them.

Natalie figured this was the part that he changed. His agreeing to meet the magistrate was new, and the men did not know how to react. Much like the Emperor, their faces went blank. The tall one opened and shut his mouth a dozen times, not finding the words.

Another loud boom shook the city of Thebes. The shockwave sent Natalie to the ground. Her rear smacked the dirt hard, and she scrambled to get back up. Most of the people cowered, and several women screamed. A few babies wailed. Yet again, there were no clouds in the sky.

CHAPTER TWENTY

Mansa Musa and Natalie followed the trio of the magistrate's men through the spidery streets of Thebes and toward what appeared to be a giant wall. It was not until they passed through the gates that Natalie realized there was another entire city inside.

She had assumed the previous bustling streets and stalls made up the city. There were so many people living and working outside the walls who clamored around Mansa Musa's people. That section alone was undoubtedly more extensive than the previous village.

Inside the walls, there were grander homes, stone-built shops, and people wearing more elegant clothes. The scent of sandalwood incense wafted on the air, which was far more pleasant than the smell of sweat and livestock where Mansa Musa had parked his caravan.

This was where the wealthier people were. The ones with power. The ones who kept everyone else on the other side of the walls.

It seemed they walked forever, moving upward steadily as they did so. Natalie was getting tired from the constant push, and beads of sweat rolled down her back. She was immensely grateful when they reached their destination. A massive temple flanked by guards.

They moved past the men, who were armed with dramatically curved blades in their belts. Natalie could see their muscles tense as the group neared them. The largest guard stared down at Natalie with a suspicious scowl, but one guide waved him off.

"These are guests of the magistrate. Let them pass."

The guards nodded, and Mansa Musa led the group through the entrance. When they walked into the temple, Natalie gasped. Unlike the ragged streets outside the wall, this place was clean, beautiful, and pristinely decorated. She sniffed the air, expecting to detect something, anything, that might give away what sort of place this was. There was nothing. The room was odorless, save for the slight hint of candle smoke. It unnerved her more than the stench of manure or sweat.

Tall columns flanked each side, painted red and blue, with spiraling hieroglyphs from bottom to top. Natalie did not know what any of it meant, but she could pick out universal images. Birds, cats, women, men, and gods with dog heads. It was a language unknown to her but so engrossing. She nearly tripped over Mansa Musa's feet, looking at it all.

Next stood the sphinxes. At least, that was what she thought they were. Natalie had read about them in Nat's book, but there were not any pictures. To be fair, it would be quite the undertaking to capture the magnitude of a sphinx. A woman's head on a lion's body. The sphinxes sat in a row, larger than life ought to be.

As Natalie walked beneath one of them, she stared helplessly up at the stone sculpture sitting upon its tall pillar. The creature was a marvel for so many reasons; the size, the skill, and the pose. Every sphinx sat in a posture that was both perfectly at ease and downright intimidating. They made her think about Nat, and the thought made her want to cry.

"This way," barked the scarred man when he saw her lag behind.

Natalie jumped to attention and hurried to catch up. Much to her surprise, Mansa Musa grabbed the scarred man by his shoulders and lifted him from the ground. His feet dangled like a child's beneath him.

"You will not speak that way to my daughter," he said in a deep growl.

"I… I did not mean…"

"She is worth a dozen of you. Apologize."

"Yes! I am sorry. Please put me down," the scarred man said frantically. The king dropped him to the floor, and he turned to face her. "I am sorry. Truly sorry."

"It's alright," Natalie said.

What else could she say? It seemed to be enough. Mansa Musa nodded to the man, and he hurried ahead to meet up with his cohorts. The Wise King waited for her to catch up before he spoke.

"Now is a good time," he said in a low voice.

"A good time for what?" Natalie whispered.

"For you and I to escape," he said, smiling at her like a kid who just stole a candy bar. "I think that will teach him to monitor us. Let us be off."

"Wait. You didn't really want him to apologize to me?" Natalie asked.

A terrible thought hit her. She wondered if Mansa Musa defended her only to get away from the magistrate's men. What if it was just a ruse? That stung a touch, and she was not sure why. Maybe because she wanted someone as impressive as the Wise King to hold her in that high esteem. Now she wondered if he meant it at all.

"No. He needed to apologize. That was genuine," he said, leaning down to meet her eyes properly. "You *are* worth more than a dozen of him."

"Really?" she asked.

"No, that is not true either. You are worth closer to five dozen, but I do not think he can count that high."

Natalie snorted, and the king laughed. Not the booming, hearty laugh he usually did. After all, they were trying to ditch Magistrate's men. But it was an honest laugh, and she was grateful to hear it.

Mansa Musa took Natalie's hand and led her away from the main corridor, weaving in and out pillars. Natalie's head swam as they ducked through anti-chambers, side-stepped guards, and created a mild ruckus when they stumbled into the women's bathhouse. Finally, the king stopped in front of an enormous doorway bookended with tall columns inlaid with gold leaf writing.

"Here we are," he said proudly.

"Where are we?" Natalie asked.

"The library of Thebes. Well, one of them. This one houses some of the most ancient of their writings."

He marched inside, and Natalie followed in his wake. Despite the high sun of the day, the library was nearly as dark as night. Multiple stations held candles burning down milky beeswax. The scent of ash, paper, and glue hung heavy in the air. The library felt different from anywhere else they had been so far. She liked it because it felt like home.

Natalie breathed easier almost instantly. After all, there were few places in the world as peaceful as a library. Even fewer still that could make a reader feel at home no matter how far they wandered. Books meant safety.

"The builder is in a library? I don't understand," she said.

Mansa Musa ran his considerable hand along the isles of scrolls and drawers, reading their markers as he did. She could not understand what any of the words said. They were different from the hieroglyphs. No pictures of cats or birds at all. The king seemed to know what they meant, so Natalie stepped back and waited.

"The builder is here in a sense," he said as he paused in front of an isle made entirely of drawers. Mansa Musa nodded to himself, took a candle, and bade Natalie follow him. "She is not with us at this time. No, far from it. She was a long time ago. Yet she is still here."

"I don't reckon I follow."

He illuminated the label on a long drawer and set the candle down on a sconce next to him. He lifted the golden handle. It looked so tiny in his hands. For a second, Natalie was worried he would break it. When he pulled, the drawer gave easily and silently. Natalie let out a breath she was unaware she was holding.

She peered inside and was surprised by what she found. There were sheets and sheets of thin copper. Each one had Egyptian writings etched into it as though someone hammered every point. These were the hieroglyphs she had seen on the columns. The pretty pictures.

Mansa Musa thumbed through them gingerly. When he finished reading one, he would gently lift and place it on the other side of the drawer before moving on to the next one. Finally, the Wise King settled on a particularly tarnished one. He brought it under the candlelight for her to see.

"Do you know what this is?" he asked.

"Hieroglyphs?"

"That is true, but these are special. Do you see how a circle surrounds these?"

Natalie examined the place where he was pointing. Sure enough, there was a grouping of pictures surrounded by what looked to her like a lasso.

"That denotes a name. A very royal name. I was hoping I would be able to find her here. They erased so many of her statues and writings, you know. All because she was a woman."

"Who?"

"Hatshepsut. Our builder."

"Our builder?"

"Yes. She was a pharaoh when women were not supposed to be so."

"What about Cleopatra?" Natalie asked.

"Oh, she was much later, and Cleopatra was not one of the goddesses, no matter how much she wanted to be," he said with a grin, like there was a funny story behind his words.

"How is finding this copper thing gonna get the builder to help us?" Natalie asked.

"I am afraid this is where you and I part ways, little one. Hatshepsut will help you from here, but I have to send you to her time the way Ching Shih sent you to me."

"But… but you're not comin'?"

Natalie felt a great well of emotion force its way upwards through her diaphragm. The pressure brought the beginnings of tears to her eyes. Sadness choked her, making the next breaths come out in a series of quick gasps.

Mansa Musa had been a friend to her. Almost like a father, really. That was not a simple thing to throw away for a girl who had never had a father. She thought about how he hugged her, and the tears came freely. Natalie felt so stupid and small.

"Now now there, child. It is not farewell forever. It is farewell for the moment. We goddesses relive our lives here as many times as we like. You are forever a part of my story now. I will see you often."

"But I won't see you," she said, blinking back tears. "It won't be this version of me."

"You must continue your journey. You must save your world. No, you must save *our* world. Once you do that, you may visit me in the book as often as you like."

"Do you promise?" she asked, sounding every inch an eight-year-old girl.

"My dear, of course. My word is solid. I will see you again," he said.

"But… what if I can't? What if I fail?"

Her breath caught in between words. The horrible precursor that always led to uncontrollable weeping. Natalie forced it back down, but a few more tears made their way through and rolled down her cheek.

"My Natalie, that is an impossibility. Not at all in the realm of truth. You, my child, are exactly what we need and more. No question."

Mansa Musa opened his expansive arms, and Natalie flung herself inside them. He wrapped her in the warmest hug she had ever felt. The world turned into velvet, and it enveloped her in a soft embrace. She breathed in the smell of sun and sandalwood in his robes and dried her tears. Before she thought twice, Natalie reached across and kissed the great king's cheek.

"Now then," he said as they released each other. "Be the goddess child I know you are, Natalie. Touch the name in the circle and save us all. I am counting on you."

He smiled at her again, but she could tell it was to cover the tears welling up in his own eyes. She focused her attention on the copper plate in front of her before she lost her nerve. Every ounce of her being wanted to stay with Mansa Musa, where it was safe. But she could not. The Wise King was right. It was all up to her.

Natalie reached out and touched the name of Hatshepsut and left the Wise King. All she could was hope it was not forever.

CHAPTER TWENTY ONE

Again, white light surrounded her. It was so blinding it made her ears ring. That made no sense to her. How could something you see make your ears hurt? Why was it possible for one sense to invade the others?

The floor seemed to drop beneath her feet, and Natalie floated for an instant, weightless in oblivion. When she finally felt ground beneath her feet once more, it met her with a jolt. Gravity nearly toppled her backward as the world caught up to her.

When the light dissipated, and she could see clearly again, she found herself nearly nose to nose with a girl. They both gasped, and Natalie hopped back. The two girls took in each other with mouths agape. Their expressions were near mirror images of each other—shock with the afterthought of fear.

The girl stood about Natalie's height and looked about her age. That was where the similarities stopped. The girl was muscular and tan, with dark eyes that seemed almost too large for her heart-shaped face. Black eyeliner rounded each eye, making them appear even bigger and intimidating.

She had a shaved head with some sort of black wig on top, even though it was not any kind of hair Natalie had seen before. It was coarse and braided into an extravagant fashion. Each braid held several blue and gold beads. When she turned her head, they flashed in the sun. It reminded a little of Claude's hair, but his beads were never so delicate. These looked expensive.

There was no need to wonder who this was. At least, not to Natalie. Like recognizes like. Even though they were from different parts of the world and other parts of time, she knew her sister. This was, without a doubt, a fellow anchor child.

The girl's face turned indignant as she took in Natalie. In her arms, she clutched several scrolls, and she squeezed them as she tensed. She opened her mouth to say something but was interrupted by a man who nearly pushed Natalie aside.

"There is no room to add a fourth column where you drew it," he said to the anchor child without a greeting. "It will not work."

His words were short and curt. There was not a drop of respect in them. It was that condescending type of talking adults did to children and small men did to women. The anchor child glared in his direction.

Natalie turned and took in the insulting intruder. She did not know what the situation was, but there was no reason to talk to anyone with so little regard.

The other anchor's nostrils flared. Her face set firm, and she jutted out her chin in defiance. She opened one of her scrolls with great urgency and pointed to a series of rectangles and circles on it. Then she pointed a finger into the distance.

It had not occurred to Natalie until that moment that they were standing on the top of a tall set of stairs. She did not dare count them all. One glance told her it would make her dizzy. Taking in the world around her nearly had her toppling over her own feet.

The staircase sat on top of a tall wedge of stone. An entire desert spread below them, alive with people working away.

Natalie followed where the child was pointing and saw the expansive building behind her. The columns went for what seemed like days, holding up not just the level they stood upon but the level above it. A double-decker monument rose larger than she could take in from her vantage point.

The child again pointed to her scroll and then the building, this time with more force. The man rolled his eyes and crossed his arms over his chest. Disdain etched itself into every line of his considerably worn face.

"This is the truth. I am not asking. I am merely telling you now what I will tell the workers. There is no other way."

He attempted to turn away from the fuming anchor child and leave, but a voice stopped him in his tracks. It exploded from somewhere behind them with the force of one of Ching Shih's cannons. The man halted mid-step and turned back around.

"You dare give orders!"

The voice came from behind the two anchor children. Natalie nearly jumped out of her skin. There had not been a person there seconds before.

The tone was steely and full of menace. Even though it sounded feminine, there was no doubt the power inside those words. Words to be feared. Words of a goddess.

When Natalie turned to see the speaking goddess, she found an Egyptian woman more beautiful than anyone she had ever seen. As far as Natalie could tell, she stood about average height, but her demeanor made her appear taller. Her heart-shaped face mirrored her anchor child's, but hers had been sharpened and refined with maturity.

Her dress was simple and white. It left her arms bare and hugged her curves down to her knees. She wore a golden belt that synched her dress together at the waist. Long cords with red and blue beads dangled from its knot. An elaborate necklace nearly covered her chest. It was gold, with blue and red jewels cascading outward in a radial design. She had circular earrings to match.

Those dark eyes startled Natalie all over again. They were large and outlined in black. The paint fanned out from her eyes as if they had wings. Golden makeup accented the color and lined the underside of her eyebrows. Her head was shaven like the child, but her wig was longer with fine, elaborate braids.

This had to be the builder goddess, Hatshepsut. Looking at this creature, no one could deny her divinity. Judging by the change in the man's demeanor, he certainly did not.

"No… No, your exalted one. I would never," he said, fumbling for words.

"Yet, that was what you were just doing."

"I was just telling your child that there is not enough room for a fourth column where it is drawn. That is all."

"There is room because I drew it," the goddess said firmly.

"Yes, but…"

"Are you saying that I am incapable?"

Intense fear flashed in the man's face. Natalie might have felt sorry for him if he had not been such a jerk minutes ago. She spared a brief fantasy about what he would look like as Hatshepsut's new pet.

"No, your exalted one. I only meant that we measured the area for the latest columns, and there is not enough room for four."

"*You* measured?" she asked.

"Yes, I did."

"That is troubling because I measured as well. I measured it twice, and I decreed there is plenty of room."

"But… it won't fit," he said in a tiny voice.

Hatshepsut folded her arms over her chest calmly and leveled a look at the man. He shriveled beneath her glare. Natalie did not blame him. Anyone would. She was not sure who was more intimidating, Ching Shih or Hatshepsut.

Suddenly, the goddess dropped her hands to her sides and balled them into fists. Then she roared. Not just a scream. It was a full roar.

For an instant, her beautiful face transformed into that of a lioness. A blue and gold headdress with a coiled snake in the middle flashed on her head, and two expansive wings thrust outward from her body. Rubies and sapphires were stitched on every feather of her wings and every inch of the headdress.

It took less than a second for the goddess to transform herself from a beautiful Pharoah to a gilded, cat-faced angel. Her new image lasted for the time it took her to finish her devastating roar. Just like that, it disappeared.

Natalie struggled to keep her footing, but the man was not so fortunate. The rage of the goddess's roar focused solely on him, and he stumbled backward to get away from it. He cowered on his knees with his hands up in a prayer position. His knees shook beneath his weight.

"I am sorry, my goddess. Bast, please forgive me! I will make it work. I promise," he said.

"You will, or you will die," she said, crossing her arms over her chest again.

The man uncovered his face, and when he saw Hatshepsut was again a woman, he rose to his feet. Natalie suddenly noticed that the sound of hammering had stopped. There were no conversations. Everyone nearby had stopped to watch the goddess in the act.

Hatshepsut and her anchor child appeared nonplussed about the spectacle. She gazed down at the child and nodded some unspoken direction to her. The child rifled through her scrolls, and when she found to appropriate one, she held it out for the man to take.

He stared down at the little girl with her petite frame and sharp chin pointed at him. There was no saving face, and he knew it. His bald head flushed red as he took the scroll with the building plans like the whipped dog he was.

"Consider your will done, my goddess," he said.

"Good. Now leave," Hatshepsut said.

The man slunk away as fast as he was able. She barely noted his passing. He was but a fly in her royal ointment. Natalie's heart filled with instant respect for the pharaoh.

It was not until the anchor child pointed her out that Hatshepsut noticed Natalie's presence, surprising since she stuck out like a sore thumb. She did not want the terrifying goddess to notice her, but things had to move forward. She needed her help to find Nat.

"You," the goddess said, taking in Natalie and her clothes. "You are new. Not on any of my charts. You do not belong here."

"I… uh… was sent here," Natalie said, not knowing how else to respond.

"Who sent you here?"

"A friend…" Natalie began. She scanned the people around them. Many pretended to work but were obviously listening. She needed to be careful about what she said. "A goddess friend of yours."

The goddess and the anchor child glared at Natalie. She could not tell whether it was out of suspicion or just plain curiosity.

"You are displaced," Hatshepsut said. "I loathe displaced things."

"I came here on a quest," Natalie said, trying desperately to get her story out. It sounded dumb to her ears. Quests were for books and fairy tales. Yet, it was the best word for her situation, so she continued. "My goddess created this book of histories. He jumped inside a few weeks ago and hasn't come back. I came in here to get him."

"You are… an anchor child," she said.

"Yes, I am."

"Yet, you have no roots."

The goddess turned her head to stare at Natalie's feet. She dutifully lifted them to show the complete lack of roots. Hatshepsut's child starred just as closely.

"I don't seem to in here. I can't reckon why. But that's not important. I have to find my goddess. The world outside this book is fallin' apart."

As if on cue, three significant cracks of lightning shot through the sky simultaneously, despite it being a perfectly cloudless day. The following thunder shook the ground beneath them, knocking several workers off their feet. All turned to look at the goddess as if to check if it was her doing.

For the first time, Hatshepsut appeared unnerved. Her child gaped up at her, and she gave her a curt shake of the head. Again, Natalie felt like they were having a conversation all to themselves, without words. She wondered if people felt this way when spending time with her at the farmhouse.

"You stay here," she said to her child. "Keep the men working. Make them do it as we planned. No insubordinations."

She nodded fiercely at her goddess. Much to Natalie's surprise, Hatshepsut smiled and patted her child on the head. It was the first time she saw the goddess appear gentle. When she turned on Natalie, the smile vanished.

"This way, strange child," she said as she took Natalie's hand. The goddess led her toward the larger entrance to the vast temple. "We must find the place you belong."

Natalie followed Hatshepsut without a word. Her hands were warm and strong. She had the sensation of a fox with its foot caught in a trap. If she tried to move, surely the goddess would take it with her and not think twice.

CHAPTER TWENTY TWO

Hatshepsut led Natalie throughout the temple like a water moccasin weaving effortlessly across a still pond. She moved as though she had no skeleton. Grace with the illusion of a lack of bones. Even her steps were soundless, like a serpent. She glided with every footfall while Natalie clomped like a mule behind her.

The place was amazing—an unfinished wonder. With Mansa Musa, Natalie had seen what an Egyptian temple looked like when it was finished, and seeing it now in progress was no less impressive. She wondered how these people could walk around and not be in awe.

Laborers dashed this way and that lugging stone and wood. Women crisscrossed the pillars with food baskets on their hips and clay jugs of water balanced on their heads. Children followed their mothers, clinging to their skirts and carrying baskets of their own.

Natalie noticed something important. As Hatshepsut moved through the temple, people reacted to her differently. The women would stop what they were doing and bow to the Pharaoh Queen. Their children followed suit. However, most of the men continued on their way. A few bowed slightly, but many averted their eyes and ducked away from her. If Hatshepsut noticed the disparity, she did not show it on her face.

She finally released Natalie when they reached an entranceway decorated in blue and red paint. Blocks of colors and symbols lined the stone door, telling some story Natalie could not understand. That was not the first thing a person would notice about the door. In fact, Natalie could only see part of the writing because a giant sphinx was blocking the way.

Not a beast carved out of stone, as she saw before. An actual living, breathing sphinx.

The creature was enormous. Even seated, the sphinx was taller than any man. Mansa Musa would have to look up to face her. A lion's body with a fierce woman's head and eagle-like wings. She had a necklace and black hair cut, much like Hatshepsut, and her wings were the same blue and gold.

The sphinx glared down at three men. They did not appear to be laborers. Their clothes were too refined for that. Natalie could not hear what they were saying as they murmured frantically to one another. The beast snarled, bearing the bottom of her formidable fangs.

Natalie froze. If Hatshepsut had not pulled her forward, she might have permanently planted herself in that spot. If she could have willed new roots to grow in that moment, she would have. Anything to keep her distance.

As they got closer, the men's words became clearer.

"It has to be the sun. I am telling you."

"That does not make sense. What about the three at night? It is an injured dog."

"You are both wrong. The answer is a table, a stool, and an easel."

"It cannot be three answers!"

"You are both ridiculous."

"What is your answer!" roared the sphinx.

The three men jumped in unison as if just remembering they were standing in front of a creature who could devour them in seconds.

"What is happening here?" Hatshepsut said.

The men jumped again as the Pharaoh Queen appeared next to them. Natalie scanned their faces and found pure fear. There was something else as well. Guilt. Like a group of children caught doing something they were not supposed to.

"Most exalted one! We are here as your humble servants as always," said the smallest man. "We are here to view your plans, of course. So that we might anticipate the next phase in building."

Natalie did not know who this was or what station he held, but she knew a liar when she saw one. He reminded her of the squat man she and Mansa Musa encountered outside the first village. Hatshepsut crossed her arms over her chest, and Natalie echoed her position.

"You are not allowed in my private room. All of you know this," Hatshepsut said flatly.

"Many apologies, our most exalted queen. We thought you would be happy if we collected the next set of plans and prepared in advance."

"Liar," the sphinx said with a growl.

The small man stepped backward and cowered with his comrades. To see them now, any person might think they were afraid. Mere cowards caught with their hands in the cookie jar. But there was something else there, too. Something more sinister behind their eyes. Something dishonest. Natalie did not trust them one bit, and neither did the goddess.

"Do not make the mistake of thinking I am naïve. I know what you want. I know what you are doing. You and your cohorts want to spy on me and my plans. You wish to undermine me. That has always been your game. You and the priests."

"Never! I assure you…"

"Enough of the lies. I put my pet here for this very reason," Hatshepsut said, gesturing to the sphinx. "How am I supposed to get anything done when my people are undermining me?"

"Never, my queen! We are your humble servants."

"Yes, my humble servants. Then, by all means, answer. If you are worthy of my confidence, answer her riddle. Only those who are worthy can manage it."

Everyone turned to look at the sphinx. When the beast smiled, it somehow appeared even scarier than when it snarled.

"What goes on fours in the morning, on twos in the afternoon, and on threes at night?" she said.

The three men put their heads together and whispered. Each one twitched nervously this way and that. Finally, the small man stepped forward. Natalie saw his hands shaking.

"An injured dog."

"Incorrect," Hatshepsut said.

The sphinx stood so suddenly that everyone jumped back except the goddess, who pulled Natalie close. She roared ferociously into the men's faces and opened her wings. They screamed and made to run away. Hatshepsut's pet swiped at them with one mighty paw, launching the small man across the vast room. The men lifted their comrade and made a hasty retreat.

Once they were out of sight, the sphinx stepped over to her master and rubbed her massive head against her shoulder. It was the same gesture of love any house cat would grant their favorite human, but on a giant scale. Hatshepsut rubbed the beast's head and patted her back. The sudden affection was a little jarring after the burst of violence. Natalie pictured the sphinx as a larger-than-life attack dog.

"May I eat one of them next time?" she asked.

"Perhaps, dear heart. I will let you know."

Chapter Twenty Three

Hatshepsut finished petting the beast. After another round of head butts, the sphinx stood and moved away from the doorway. She did not seem to notice Natalie at all besides a passing glance. Perhaps she took her cues from the goddess. Perhaps it was because Natalie was so small and not a threat. Either way, she was immensely grateful the creature did not point her anger in her direction.

Once beyond the sphinx, Natalie found herself inside a large chamber filled with crisscrossing planks of stained wood. The diamond-shaped openings they made were filled with scrolls and copper sheets. In the center of the room stood a large, rectangular table with many drawings and writings on them.

It felt vaguely like the library back in Thebes, except it was not bathed in darkness. Far from it, in fact. An opening in the back of the room let in a bright rod of light. It illuminated the papyruses on the table.

Natalie craned her neck to see the writing on the pages. Several were long and needed heavy stones to weigh down their corners. Otherwise, they would curl up and blow away. Some papers were barely more than strips of scratch. On all of them, Natalie recognized the strange pictures she had seen in Thebes.

The goddess slammed her hands down on the table. It shattered the calm Natalie had been luxuriating in mere seconds before. She looked up to see the terrifying figure the worker had seen. The great queen flashed her jeweled wings with her cobra headdress. A great roar broke free from her mouth as her face transformed into a black lioness.

Natalie screamed and stumbled backward, nearly taking the drawings on the table with her. Hatshepsut advanced on her slowly, like a cat who intended to play with her catch.

"Who sent you," she growled deeply. "Which of the priests sent you here to spy. To disrupt my plans. Was it the ones who sent those morons outside?"

"What?"

Hatshepsut grabbed a chair that was in between her and Natalie and flung it into the corner. It splintered into a dozen pieces as it crashed against the wall.

"The priests. Which one sent you here?"

Natalie's heart beat hard in her chest. She found it difficult to catch a good breath. She steadied herself on a shelf of scrolls and get her words out.

"No priests! I swear. Mansa Musa sent me!"

Hatshepsut stopped in her tracks. Her face fell and returned to that of a human's. Her wings dropped and evaporated into thin air. The headdress flickered out of existence. She gazed upon Natalie with all sense of malice melted away.

"The Wise King? He is the one you were talking about?"

"Yes," Natalie said breathlessly.

"Did he say why he sent you to me?" she asked.

Natalie drew in a few more heaving gasps and tried to calm her heart. Her mouth was so dry it might as well have been filled with cotton.

"He said you were the builder. The one who charted out where everyone goes. He said you might know where Nat is."

"Nat?"

"My goddess. He's missing."

Hatshepsut no longer appeared scary, nor did she seem all that angry. Her demeanor was more curiosity than anything else, followed quickly by determination. The goddess turned to her volumes of scrolls without another word.

As the Pharaoh Queen paced back and forth, Natalie marveled at the collection, running her fingers over her different scrolls and maps. There were so many charts. Natalie had no idea how she could make heads or tails of where everything was.

"When is it that you live?" she asked over her shoulder.

"Nineteen forty. We live in America."

She turned around and stared at Natalie. Her face could not be more perplexed than if Natalie said she was from the moon. For an instant, she wondered if she recorded time the same here. After all, Jesus was not a person yet. There was no B.C. or A.D. What sort of reference might she have for a number like nineteen forty?

"America?" Hatshepsut asked.

She began sifting through her papers again, flinging scrolls out on the floor when they were not the ones she was after. For someone who seemed so organized, the builder goddess was indeed making a mess of things. Natalie ventured a question.

"So… you believe me?"

"Of course, I do. Mansa Musa's time is not for centuries. No priest spy would know of him. If you know him, you are one of us, and your story must be genuine."

Some previously unknown muscle in Natalie's chest relaxed when she heard those words. It was a part she had not realized existed until then. She was definitely out of the woods now. Well, as far as Hatshepsut was concerned. The great lioness goddess would not eat her alive for being a spy or feed her to her sphinx.

"Ah, here," Hatshepsut said, pulling down several sheets of rolled papyrus. She took them to the rectangular table, being sure to side-step the broken chair. She laid them out on the table in one long line, using stones to hold down the corners. "This is the timeline of the goddesses. I have tracked us all."

Natalie took in the massive timeline. Other than some long lines with branches here and there, she could not make sense of it. The long paper held more hieroglyphs and odd writing.

"Can you read this?" Hatshepsut asked when she noticed Natalie's curiosity.

"No. I'm sorry."

"This is where it began," she said, pointing to upper right-hand lines and pictures. "This is the original goddess's reign. It is the oldest."

Hatshepsut traced her finger to the left along a sold line. It was the longest line by a wide margin. There were minor tick marks and writing all across it, like annotations or labels. Natalie assumed they connected with the years she reigned and other turning points, but who could tell with a language made out of birds and feathers.

The thick line continued with large slashes that seemed to be of varying widths. Each one had its own scribbling of writing, depending on how long it was. At the end of the page, the line died off. Almost as though it faded away rather than ended. A jumble of pictures accompanied that part. Hatshepsut's finger hovered over it as she read the words.

"America," she said slowly.

"How do you know all this? I mean, if Mansa Musa ain't been born yet, how do you know about him?"

"It is what I do. We all know about one another in an abstract sense, but I map and build. I gaze ahead and record the lineage of goddesses. Some are interested in such things. Others are too absorbed in their own reigns."

"Then how did you not know Nat or me?"

"I cannot say. It does not make sense. Something... has changed. Look here," Hatshepsut said as she pointed to a section of the timeline. It had spidery branches forking outward from the central line. She moved to a different area where the same phenomenon was happening. "I did not draw this."

"What is it?"

"Changes. Something is changing history. This part is Mansa Musa's time. It is much changed. And this one is Ching Shih's time."

The goddess took in Natalie and her fine African clothes. Her gaze cast downward to the two identical bracelets on her wrists. She nodded as if it confirmed some theory she was forming.

"The one that is the most altered is this one at the end. The one where you said you hail from. This America."

Natalie leaned over the table and reached out to the symbol that marked her home. Something deep in her gut made her want to touch it. She missed her friends, and the longing for them was overwhelming.

When she tapped her finger ever so lightly at the end of the line, red ink flowed outward like a blossoming rose of blood. Natalie and Hatshepsut leaped backward as the mark spread into the size of a silver dollar.

"Something is very wrong," the goddess said.

"I know what it is. I know what is changin' the history. I know what is causin' all of this."

"What is it?"

"It's me. I'm making it happen. I'm gonna kill us all."

CHAPTER TWENTY FOUR

Hatshepsut grabbed a rag and blotted the ink before it spread more than it had already. Natalie turned her hands over to see if there was a wound on her finger. Anything to explain where the red originated. She found none. When Hatshepsut threw the rag and hit Natalie in the face with it, it knocked her back to reality.

"That makes no sense. Are all children from America this idiotic?"

Natalie planned to answer, but she found no words. How did one respond to that? It was certainly not what she was expecting.

"This is not your fault. You say your goddess created a book with all of our histories inside. Then, he jumped inside?"

"Yes."

"You are only here because he has not come back, and you are looking for him."

"That's right."

"Then, this is not your fault. It is his. You are doing your duty. True, your presence here seems to be creating these little ripples. Changes I have not seen before. The thunder is definitely strange. Possibly problematic."

"That's happenin' everywhere," Natalie interjected. "In Ching Shih's time and Mansa Musa's time too. I think it's because of the storm."

"What storm?"

"Ever since Nat left our world, there's a storm that keeps comin'. We have a witch who's good with weather magic, and even she can't control it. It's gettin' worse every day. I think it might be leakin' into these histories."

Hatshepsut's lips tensed, and her brow furrowed. It looked strange on such a beautiful face. Natalie had seen her serene, intent, and terrifying, but never nervous. If this Pharoah Queen was worried, what hope did she have to fix it? The notion set her teeth on edge.

"I don't know what to do. I hafta find Nat and take him back to my time."

"Can you not sense him? My child and I are always linked."

"Normally, yes. But I can't feel Nat at all in here. Mansa Musa thought you might could see him on your maps. He says you're the builder."

Hatshepsut took in a deep breath and let it out silently. Her shoulders slumped as she leaned on her elbows. Natalie wondered if anyone had ever gotten to see her tired or vulnerable. It must be difficult living as the Pharaoh Queen with no one but your anchor child to talk to. Natalie pitied poor Hatshepsut, the goddess who could not let her guard down.

"That is the thing that creates legacies," Hatshepsut said at last. "Building, I mean. Smaller rulers war. They seek their fame on the battlefield. They measure their value in the conquered. What they never realize is that the blood they spill soaks into the ground. It mars the plants. It disappears and sows future aggression. But to build something that lasts. Well, that is real power. That is a true legacy."

"This temple is your legacy."

"Yes. This and many more. People will come here to pray and marvel. They will read the writings. They will know my name long after I abdicate."

Something Mansa Musa said before popped into Natalie's mind. He told her that the people tried to erase Hatshepsut's name from history. All because she was a woman pharaoh. Natalie wondered what that meant. Did they chisel her name from monuments? Burn papyruses that told stories about her?

Natalie took in the lovely, if not tired, Pharaoh Queen in front of her and decided not to tell her. There was no good to be served by relaying that information. Nothing could be changed. Not for the better or the worse. Not now.

She changed the subject before her tongue tripped over itself.

"Why did you think I was a spy?"

"The priests do not favor a woman pharaoh. I am one of the first and the longest-reigning. You saw the worker who tried to defy my orders? The spies outside the door?"

Natalie nodded. She recalled the worker and how sure he was until he got the full wrath of the winged lioness. She pictured the spies whispering to one another like conspirators. A shiver ran up her spine.

"That is constant. It is difficult for any ruler. There are always demons in the shadows, but it is worse for a woman. Luckily, I am the goddess, and the workers know it. It takes a formidable power of will and might to change the tapestry of an empire. The priests fear me, but they are always looking for an angle to take over. I must stay vigilant."

"But you are the goddess. You could just as easily kill them," Natalie said.

She thought about Ching Shih. Her men followed her without fail. No spies whispered behind her back because she would kill them in the open and be cheered for it. Murder did not bother the Pirate Queen. It seemed to be the currency of the high seas.

"If you water your seeds with blood, your crop will be rotten," Hatshepsut said. "I want their respect. Unfortunately, it comes from fear in the beginning. They will bend over time. This is how you build to last."

Footsteps thudded down the hallway, heading toward them. Hatshepsut stood at attention with her back straight and her chin held high. The pharaoh's mask returned to her face, and Natalie felt a tad sorry for it. When the intruder entered the room, it was a woman. She was dressed in all white, much like the goddess.

"Pyhia? What are you doing here? How did you get past my pet?"

"My queen, I answered her riddle, of course," Pyhia said with a bow.

"You answered it?"

"Yes, my queen. She asked what goes on fours in the morning, on twos in the afternoon, and on threes at night? The answer is man. When we are young, we crawl on all fours. When we are adults, we walk on two legs, and when we are old, we walk on a cane. Three legs."

Natalie anticipated an angry queen. The fact that someone broke the code of her sphinx had to be troubling. That was not the case, however. Hatshepsut smiled and beamed with pride as she took in the woman. It was hard to tell what she was to the Pharoah Queen, but they seemed close enough for respect.

"Very smart of you, Pyhia. Well done. Why are you here?"

"More offerings from your alter, my exalted one," she said as she laid a large basket covered with a cloth on the floor in between them.

It was the first time Natalie noticed the bundle. Perhaps it was the shock of having a stranger interrupt them so unexpectedly.

"Forgive my intrusion, but it was beginning to overflow. Plus, the little one kept escaping."

"Little one?" the goddess asked.

They drew nearer, and Natalie spotted something small moving underneath the cloth. A tiny, muffled mew broke the silence. Another, more persistent meow followed. Hatshepsut pulled back the shawl to reveal a tiny black kitten perched on top of a pile of palm fronds, painted stones, and idols woven from cloth and beads. Many resembled the great goddess herself. Some were fashioned to look like the sphinx.

A regal smile flashed across her face as she gazed down at the bundle. Natalie's heart nearly broke watching the queen's reaction. It was as if no one had ever given her such a gift in her life. Hatshepsut reached down and plucked the mewing kitten from its basket and held it to her bosom. The creature pawed playfully at her earrings.

"From the children," Pyhia said as an explanation.

"Thank them for me," Hatshepsut said.

The goddess nodded, and the servant left, bowing until she was out of the room. Natalie took the bundle of offerings as Hatshepsut lifted the kitten to her face and lightly nudged her nose to its nose.

"The children?" Natalie asked.

"And the women. They leave me offerings and gifts. This is the first time I have been granted a kitten. I will tell them how pleased I am. Perhaps they will send more."

"I thought you had to be scary to get their respect."

"I have to frighten to get the priest's respect and some of the workers. They must be reminded I am the goddess. Not the children. You see, child, that is why you build."

"I don't understand."

"The thing you create is not made in a day. It is forged through the years. The truly magnificent accomplishments take a long time. These priests… they are today. Those children are tomorrow, and tomorrow is all I truly care about."

CHAPTER TWENTY FIVE

Hatshepsut snuggled the kitten a bit more before she set it down on the stone table with all the maps of the goddesses. It immediately ran toward the nearest marble and batted it around, knocking loose one corner. The goddess returned it with all the patience of a mother.

"Now, back to your Nat," she said.

Natalie was happy to be getting back to the task at hand. Every second she spent here was another second Nat was still lost. It was another second before Camille and the others had to fend off the terrible storm heading their way. The world needed a goddess. That was what Mansa Musa said. That was what everyone said.

"So, you can't see where he is now?" Nat asked.

Hatshepsut scanned the maps again, running her fingers this way and that. Occasionally, she would stop over one of the spidery branches cause by Natalie's intrusion. When she finally stood back up, the Pharaoh Queen did not appear pleased at all.

"No. I cannot see him."

Natalie let out a long sigh and tried to hide her disappointment. She was terrified and exhausted. Mansa Musa told her that this queen, the builder, would find him for her. Now, she did not know what to do.

"I do have a theory," Hatshepsut said.

"Really? What is it?"

"You see this extra line here," she said as she ran her finger down a particularly long fork in the timeline. "It runs down to this large swath of time. It is the second-longest reign of the goddess. The only one longer was the original goddess."

"Why is this line important?"

"Can you not see? It is still moving."

Natalie leaned in as close as she could with the edge of the table pressing against her stomach. A lock of hair fell free from her braid, and the kitten batted at it. Natalie petted the creature as she focused on the line. There it was. No mistaking. The line was moving by degrees toward the extensive timeline Hatshepsut mentioned.

"How is that… possible?"

"How is any of this possible? But here is the significant part. The place where that line originates is right here. Right now. It is coming from this moment in time."

"So it is tellin' us where to go next?"

"This is what I believe," the goddess said.

"Are you sure?" Natalie asked in a broken voice.

The temple trembled as a new barrage of thunderclaps sounded outside. Natalie ducked as though the ceiling might cave in. The kitten hissed, scampered off the table, and hid behind a row of shelves. Hatshepsut stood tall and firm even though the sky sounded like it was ripping apart.

The room grew dark, and the atmosphere grew heavy with moisture. The blast of sunshine that illuminated the room vanished. Natalie found it difficult to breathe in the wet air around her. She suddenly wondered if it could rain indoors.

"We do not have enough time for speculation," Hatshepsut said.

Natalie stood back up, trying to match the goddess's stature. It was a poor copy, but it made her feel somewhat stronger. When lightning struck outside, she heard several people scream over the sound of the downpour. Hatshepsut stood tall, refusing to flinch. There was no mistaking the nervousness in her eyes.

"We must send you to this timeline. My map is telling me that is where to go, and there I shall send you. I just hope he knows how to help you, young anchor child."

"Who?"

"Put your hand here," the goddess said, placing Natalie's hand on the timeline in question. "Hold your breath. This might be disorienting."

"Wait! Where am I going?" she asked frantically.

"Tell the artist I send my regards."

Hatshepsut touched one elegant finger to Natalie's forehead, and the whole world flashed out of existence. Yet again, Natalie fell into nothingness.

CHAPTER TWENTY SIX

She did not seem to fall the way she had before. There was no dropping involved. That was a pleasant change, at least. It was more of a sense of leaning forward. Natalie was not a fan of having her stomach in her throat, but she also hated getting halfway stuck inside a stone wall, which was where she found herself when the world came back into view.

The first thing she felt was the shock of it all. Once her brain caught up to that notion, all Natalie could focus on was the squeeze. Her face, arms, and left shoulder were free, but the rest of her body felt like it was caught in a vice. A vice that somehow clamped every inch of her body at once.

Panic spread like cold tendrils through her spidery veins. It began in the skin of her legs and traveled to her arms and the back of her neck. As all terror does, it seeped into her very blood, and by the time it pumped into her heart, she knew there was nothing else to do but scream.

Natalie lashed out like a cornered animal, clawing at the stone with her hands. The more she tried to move her unmovable legs, the worse her panic became. Her breath came out far too fast and short, but somehow, she could not get enough oxygen. Everything went all swimmy in her brain.

"Easy, child. You must calm your breathing if I am to ever get you out of there," said a smooth voice near her face.

Natalie opened her eyes and tried to focus on the person. She had been in such a panic she completely missed another human being standing directly in front of her. Her eyes felt hot and full of tears, but the blurry colors sharpened into a person—a man.

"Okay. That is a start. Tell me your name."

The cadence of his voice calmed the worst of her nerves. That still left quite a few parts of her trembling in terror, but he was correct. It was a start.

"My… my name is… Natalie," she said, while trying to catch her breath.

"Natalie. Good. A fine name. I am Felix. It is good to meet you. Now, let us figure out how to get you out of this wall."

He took her right hand in his left one and squeezed. His hands were rough and warm. It covered them in something slightly sticky, but Natalie could not tell what. She blinked away a few more tears, and he became clearer. An average-sized man of about middle age. He had olive skin and mousey brown hair with grey streaks on the sides.

"There, you can see me. Good. Focus on me. Listen to my words."

"Okay. I think I can do that."

"You are not stuck," he mumbled.

"But I am."

"No. You are not. You only think that you are."

"I am stuck! I can't move."

The frenzy in her blood kicked up again, and Natalie thought she might truly lose her mind this time. She squeezed the man's hand as hard as she could, and to her surprise, he squeezed right back. His pressure calmed her just enough to get her fear under control.

"I want you to close your eyes and take a deep breath. A breath so big you could fit an entire sunset inside your lungs. Do it with me," he said.

He did do it. The man took in a huge, loud breath, and Natalie mimicked him. She filled her lungs with as much as she could. It was hard, since only her right lung was technically free from the wall.

"Hold it in," he said while keeping in his own air. "Now, let it out and say, 'I am not in a wall!' Just as loud as you can."

"I'm not in a wall!" Natalie yelled with everything she had in her body as she let out her breath.

To her surprise and delight, about half of her body came free. She was only trapped to her waist now. The shock nearly knocked her out. She drew in several giant helpings of air now that both of her lungs were free, and relief flooded her system. There was a way out.

The man smiled at her. He was still holding her right hand, but now, he took her left one as well. Natalie locked eyes on her savior, intent on doing whatever he said.

"Okay. Again. Deep breath in. Hold it. I am not in a wall!"

"I'm not in a wall!" Natalie yelled again.

Her body moved further. Now, she was only encased up to her shins. Felix had to put his hands under her armpits to keep her from falling forward and snapping her legs. There was no need for direction this time. Natalie knew what to do. Together, they took in a deep breath, held it, and screamed in unison.

"I am not in a wall!"

Natalie's legs broke free, and Felix caught her in the air. He spun her around and placed her gently on the cobblestones beneath her feet. She put her hand over her chest, willing her heart to calm down. It was not listening very well, but it was better than the panic she felt minutes ago.

"There you are. And look, you did not even mess up the mural I was painting," Felix said as he gestured to the wall.

Natalie looked up at the spot where she had so recently been imprisoned. There was a painting taking form. Currently, there were a lot of drawings and blocks of color, but when she stepped back, she could make out an alley with a man standing before a wall covered in colors. Some sort of creature was clawing its way out of the wall toward him, and his arms were up.

"I see I have it wrong, but it was close," he said.

"What do you mean?"

"The mural. I paint what my visions tell me. I saw this creature coming out of a wall that I was working on. I painted that vision in order to meet the creature, and the creature ended up being you. How fortuitous."

Felix turned on her with a pleasant smile. He focused when he took in her eyes entirely, and she shrank a little under his sudden scrutiny. She tried to look at her hands but saw they were covered in yellow and red paint. It was on her arms as well. Then she remembered. Felix's hands had been sticky. Sticky with paint.

"You are an anchor child. You are... not supposed to be here," he said.

"Yes, I know," Natalie said.

"But my mural said you were coming."

For the first time, Felix appeared genuinely confused. She did not know the man's standard expressions, but he did not seem to wear confusion easily. Being a long-lived goddess, she wondered if he ever got confused.

"Hatshepsut asked me to give you her regards," Natalie said, not knowing what else to say.

She did not think it was possible, but Felix's face turned even more confounded. She struggled to repress a giggle. Luckily, the soreness in her ribs helped her with that mission. A quick stabbing at her side made her suck in her breath.

Felix opened and closed his mouth a few times before finding his voice again.

"Well then, allow me to bid you welcome to Roma. I believe you should come back to my home with me. We have much to discuss. Perhaps procure you some new clothes."

When she gazed down at the white robes, they were smeared with streaks of paint from where Felix had caught her. She felt suddenly self-conscience, as though the paint labeled her the creature from the painting. Again, she breathed in deep the sensation of otherness. A stranger in a strange land.

Natalie's stomach rumbled, adding insult to injury. She realized she had not eaten since leaving the women's tent. It was impossible to tell how long she had been in the goddess book. The years and days skipped by her like a stone on a pond.

"I am certain my wife can help with that as well," he said as he wrapped one heavy arm around her.

Natalie leaned into his embrace. Her mission had not changed. She knew it was only a matter of time before the storm found her here as well, and this would not be a safe haven for long. At that moment, she was just grateful to be free and hoped the artist could help her.

Plus, dinner sounded pretty good.

CHAPTER TWENTY SEVEN

The streets of Roma wove in an unrecognizable maze. Natalie's mind swam as Felix led her past vendors, homes, and late-night revelers. Each street smelled different somehow. Just when she got used to the aromatic scent of the spice merchants, they would take a turn and be accosted by the incense and perfumes of late-night social houses. In one corner, the heady odor of yeast permeated the air, only to be followed by the tang of fresh blood from a butcher.

"You should probably not look inside," Felix said, hurrying her past a house full of barely-dressed women.

They turned a corner and nearly slammed into three soldiers. They wore white and red uniforms with metal armor fitted together with leather straps. Their metal helmets matched the swords on their belts.

"You! Watch where you are going," boomed the lead soldier.

"My apologies, Centurion," Felix said with a theatrical bow. "It is completely our fault, and I bid you farewell and goodwill."

"Wait. I know you," the centurion said.

"I assure you are mistaken," Felix said.

"No. I am not. You are that scribbler. The one who paints our Emperor in such a dishonorable manner."

"That may be. I see you know my work," Felix said with a smile. "To be fair, if Nero did not want to be drawn as dishonorable, perhaps he should behave better."

"You painted him kissing a bull and calling it his mother!"

One man behind the lead soldier struggled to stifle a laugh. The other jabbed him in the rib. He covered the insubordination with a sudden coughing fit.

"You dare call him simply Nero?" the Centurion asked, ignoring his soldier.

"I do. Does he have another name?"

"You will address him as Nero Claudius Caesar Augustus Germanicus!"

Felix laughed heartily, unaware the man clutched his hand over the hilt of his sword. Standing there, laughing in the face of danger, reminded her of Mansa Musa. It made her instantly feel closer to the bizarre artist.

"That is truly a mouthful, Centurion. I believe I will continue to paint his name as Nero. Much easier."

"Not if we stop you here and now! And this," he said, turning his attention to Natalie. "Is this one of your little helpers? One of your child scribblers. Best we teach her what this sort of work will get her."

The centurions reached for their swords but were not fast enough. Felix snapped his fingers, and they froze in place. The grin never left his face. Natalie waved her hand in front of their faces, but not one of them blinked. The head centurion had tears forming in the corners of his eyes, but did not budge.

"I do not particularly like people threatening me. I especially do not like anyone who threatens a child. Obviously, you lot are not art aficionados. Perhaps if you create some scribbles yourself, your opinion about my kin will change."

Natalie saw sweat beading on the soldiers' brows and run down their bare calves. One was trying desperately to say something, but he could not move his mouth.

"What was that?" Felix asked, moving closer to the man.

Again, all the centurion could manage was a croaking whimper.

"You wish to try out your drawing skills?" Felix asked theatrically.

He smiled and winked at Natalie. She tried not to laugh, but it came out as a snort and a giggle.

"Well, why did you not say so earlier? You should go to my painting spot. There, you will find paint and brushes for all of you. Go forth and write how you truly feel about Nero all over the walls of Roma. Be sure to paint the bull's testicles larger than our daring leader's."

Felix snapped his fingers once again, and the men began blinking. They slumped against one another for an instant, trying to regain their balance. It did not last long. As soon as they righted each other, the trio hurried away from them. Felix and Natalie watched them leave, retracing their path to collect the art supplies.

"That didn't seem real fair," Natalie said with another snort.

"No, but it was fun. Besides, they are not fair with others. Why should I be fair with them? Let us be off now. I am famished. My wife will be anxious to meet you."

CHAPTER TWENTY EIGHT

Felix's home was not what she had expected. To be fair, Natalie had little knowledge about Roma and how the people lived. She reckoned Felix would have a grand villa, or one of those palaces held up with columns similar to Hatshepsut's temple. Something with servants, bustling with activity. The only part she got right was the activity.

The goddess led her through the winding, complicated streets of Roma. They ducked down alleyways, and he hurried across any principal thoroughfares to avoid the soldiers roaming the streets. When he threw back a hatch that resembled nothing more than a cellar door, she stared at him, speechless.

"This is my home," he said with great exuberance in his voice.

"This?" she asked, pointing down the ladder. "There's a house in there? It doesn't look like more than a larder or somethin' like it. Do you live in a root cellar?"

"Oh Gods, no," he said with a laugh. "Surely, this is not the first time you have seen this type of magic."

Natalie had, of course. The farmhouse back home had been cloaked to appear like a dilapidated mess, but it was expansive and lovely inside. Likewise, the *Canyon Cathedral* hid their sanctuary under a lake bed, with only a rusty boat as a doorway. Not to mention the homes of Ching Shih and Mansa Musa worked the same way.

"No better way to keep greedy masses from coveting what you have than to disguise it as something they do not want. Come along. In you go."

Felix gestured for Natalie to go in first, and she descended the ladder into the darkness. She wondered how he lived in the dark. How did his family manage? As she stepped lower and lower, the room got brighter and brighter. As soon as Felix threw the lid shut above them, the sound of laughter wafted up from below.

Natalie reached the last step amidst a frenzy of activity. She was forced to back against a wall. Otherwise, she might have been trampled. Everything whirled around her in flashes of color. When things slowed down and she fully took in the scene, there were far more kids than that. If she dared to count, the number would be fifteen, at least.

Felix landed on the floor with a gentle thud. As soon as he did, the entire household went silent. Every eye turned to take him in, and there was a collective inhale among the gaggle.

"Father!" they all screamed in unison.

The barrage of children ran to him at once. Natalie flattened her back against the wall to avoid the crowd. Felix threw his arms wide and took in their affection, laughing and kissing the ones he could reach.

"Yes, my children. Yes! It is good to see you all as well. But here, I have someone for you to meet. This is Natalie," he said as he gestured to her.

Fifteen sets of eyes trained on her, and for an instant, Natalie was terrified they would rush her the way they rushed Felix. Instead, they hit her with a barrage of questions.

"Who are you?"

"Did my father make you?"

"Do you paint?"

"Can you be my sister?"

"Can you be my brother?"

"Are you magical?"

"That is enough, children. Natalie is hungry and does not have time to answer all of these at once. Make room. Make room. We are off to the kitchen."

Half of the children cheered, and the other half groaned. All moved aside so Felix could lead Natalie away from her wall. She was grateful to be freed, but the claustrophobia of it all followed her into the house proper. Children flanked her left and right. Two of the younger girls picked at her clothes in wonder.

Felix's house was as expansive as Natalie imagined. It was just hidden underground. They passed through seven rooms before making it to the kitchen. Each one housed more children. She wondered if Felix had more than one wife.

One group of older siblings sat around a square table and painted pottery. Vases and jugs the color of red clay stacked along the wall. Children painted designs and scenes of battles using black paint. Gladiators raised swords high over beasts, centurions lined up with shields against enemies, and women bowed to various goddesses with offerings.

Several of the girls stared up at her from their work, but most kept at it. Two of them stood up with excited looks on their faces and followed the crowd.

In another room, five young children gathered around a lit hearth. They moved small, colored tiles around on the floor. It reminded Natalie of the way she liked to put together puzzles at home. The pieces themselves were not much, but when you put them together, the image was revealed.

Their puzzle was coming along nicely, and Natalie could almost make a face in the colors. One with freckles. One that seemed vaguely familiar. Felix hurried her along before she could make it out.

The kitchen smelled of warm bread and olives. Natalie tasted the tang of salt in the air, and it made her stomach growl all over again. She swiveled around to see if anyone heard it that time, but the place was so noisy, no one noticed.

"There's my loving wife," Felix said as he opened his arms toward a tall woman slicing figs.

She placed her knife beside the chopping board and turned to greet her husband. The woman was tall and thin. Not skinny the way Natalie was, all knobby knees and elbows. She was not powerfully built like Hatshepsut and Ching Shih. She was not young, nor was she old. Her bosom drooped, and her neck was crossed with aging lines.

If Natalie were to assign a label to this woman based on appearances alone, she would simply call her a mother. No pretense or the falsehoods of face paint. A woman as steady as the Earth beneath her.

She stood tall and stable with a warm smile and a babe swaddled to her chest in a series of wraps. Part of her dark hair was tied in a bun on her head. The rest drifted down below her waistline, where a toddler tugged on it. Not a wince crossed her face. Not a moment of chiding.

Had she not been in that kitchen and married to the goddess, Natalie would have thought she was perfectly normal. A loving mother in the service to her children.

"My husband," she said.

They embraced one another, careful not to smash the sleeping baby on her chest. She whispered something to the toddler, who was begging for his father's attention. Felix lifted the boy on his shoulders, and the child squealed with glee.

Natalie never had a real family. Not one like this, anyway. There had never been a bustling house full of siblings and cousins. No mother and father. Just Mamaw. She wondered how many of these large families were this happy.

"Oh, you have brought a guest, Felix. Why did you not say so?"

"Is it… alright? That I'm here, I mean," Natalie said.

"Of course! We have plenty of food. I would have offered you a seat and a drink straight away. Come here, child. All of you, release her clothes. The poor thing looks half-starved."

"Natalie, may I present my wife, Laidi," Felix said.

"Nice to meet you," Natalie said.

She was not entirely sure how Romans greeted one another. A bow felt too formal, but nothing was far too little. Natalie wished, and not for the first time, the rules of greeting one another were universal. She ventured a handshake. Laidi took Natalie's hand, wrapped it around her elbow, and led her to a vast table.

In a flash, the starving anchor child was sitting on a bench with a plate of food. Hearty bread, olives, figs, and salted oil. She felt like she might cry from happiness.

It was rude, the way she dug in right there. She also reckoned that she did not much care. Even though time remained an intangible thing in the book, Natalie felt like she had been traveling for weeks. She wondered if it had been weeks or mere days since she left. In the same vein, how much time had passed in Tanglewood?

Her view was suddenly filled with Laidi's smiling face. Not too close to be intimidating, but close enough to get her attention. Natalie snapped to attention and struggled to remember some sense of manners.

"I'm… so sorry. I didn't thank you. I must be just a sight."

"No need for that," Laidi said with a pat on her hand. "I merely wanted to make sure you were alright. Everything tastes fine?"

"Oh yes. It's just wonderful. I don't wager I've ever had bread this good. Not ever."

"How wonderful. Aurelia, our guest is giving your bread high praise!"

Now that Natalie was not quite so focused on food, she could fully take the rest of the kitchen. A wall with four giant brick ovens stood just twenty yards away. Suddenly, the heat registered on her face. It was as if the ovens had waited for attention before allowing her the courtesy of warmth.

A golden-headed teenage girl stepped into view. She was all smiles and elegant features, like her mother. She wore an olive green dress that cinched at the waist and hung loosely around her chest. It tied on her shoulders, leaving her arms bare. Natalie tried not to stare when she noticed the black soot stains from her fingertips to her elbows.

"How grand! I am always excited to bake for new people," Aurelia exclaimed. "Wait there. I have some sweet buns in the oven right now. Nearly ready. I just have to turn them."

Aurelia hurried to the furthest oven and shoved her hands straight inside. Natalie nearly cried out to stop her, but it was too late. Much to her surprise, the girl did not scream. She did not recoil in pain. Aurelia turned a clay baking tray a half rotation before removing her hands. No injuries to be seen.

It occurred to Natalie that the girl was a witch. She perked up and fully took in the surrounding children. Two boys played in the corner. One levitated a series of stones in the air for the other to snatch. Three children about her age chased one another in some game of tag. They vanished in and out of walls. An older boy commanded bull horns to grow from his head as he playfully scared a gaggle of girls.

This was not just a home. It was a school just like *Miss Camille's Home for Wayward Children*. A place where witches learned. Natalie exhaled, and a tiny laugh accompanied. She could not help it. For the first time since she left Tanglewood, she found a place that felt like home.

CHAPTER TWENTY NINE

When Aurelia brought her a sweet bun, Natalie thanked her and ate with manners. The raging hunger was gone, and she felt relieved to be among witches. Aurelia looked like she wanted to stay and chat with her, but Laidi motioned to the other empty mouths around the table.

"So, Natalie. Where are you from?"

"I... um..."

She scanned the kitchen, looking for Felix, but he was nowhere in sight. Natalie was not sure how much she should tell Laidi. The last thing she wanted to do was scare her or frighten her children. The storm would find her eventually, and the idea set her spine so rigid it hurt.

"Oh, do not mind me. I am terrible about prying. It is the cost and reward for being a mother."

"How many children are here? If that ain't too personal."

"About thirty. Oh wait, I keep forgetting the baby," she said, stroking the child's head. "Thirty-one, it is."

"That's a lot. They ain't all yours, are they? I mean ones you birthed."

"Oh gods, no. Twenty are mine. The rest are orphans. Oh wait, I am forgetting the baby again. Twenty-one are mine."

"How... is that possible? I never heard of someone birthin' so many."

"I always wanted a large family, you see," Laidi said with a sparkle in her eye. "When I met Felix and learned magic, one of the first things I taught myself were incantations of childbirth. Why worry about the anguish of childbirth if you do not have to?"

Natalie stared at her bug-eyed for a long minute. She searched desperately for something to say. Anything that made her sound more intelligent than she felt.

"I didn't know there was such a thing," she said finally.

"Of course! There is a spell for just about anything. I will teach it to you before you leave. Now, you may think you are too young to be thinking about that sort of thing now, but you will thank me when the time comes."

Natalie's spine went rigid. She balled her hands in her lap and pressed her lips together. The anchor child did not feel angry. Laidi meant well. She was more nervous about how to proceed with the conversation.

How could she unwrap the complication that was her life in a brief chat? An anchor child who was a girl to a goddess who was a man. What magical words would be sufficient? She surely did not know them if they existed.

Luckily, she did not have to. Laidi took in her body language and softened her gaze. She peered deeply into Natalie's eyes with all the hope and love of a mother. For an instant, Natalie thought Laidi might take her in her arms, and a part of her desperately wanted that embrace. There has never lived a person who did not yearn for a mother's hug.

"My dear child," Laidi said as she squeezed Natalie's hand. "You will not be thanking me for that spell, will you? That is not in your cards. At least, not as they are in front of me."

Suddenly, a tremendous boom sounded above them. The walls of the underground villa rattled, causing several children to scream. The older ones beckoned the youngest into groups, where they held one another for comfort. One tiny voice after another wailed.

"Is it a quake?"

"It is raining outside!"

"There was a flash."

"How many flashes?"

"Where did that come from?"

"It was so sudden!"

"What is happening?"

The baby at Laidi's chest whimpered with all the commotion. She stood and began bouncing the child to soothe it. Laidi never broke her gaze with Natalie, and she could read every rapid expression on her face as they came. There was worry, fear, calm, strength, and back to worry again. None of her looks included blame, and Natalie was grateful for it.

There was a collective breath of relief when Felix entered the room. He was by his wife's side in seconds, and she tucked her head into his chest. Felix rubbed the newborn's head gently, and the baby's whimpers faded away.

"What is happening, husband?"

"I am not sure."

Of course, Natalie knew. She knew so thoroughly that when the second boom came from above, she did not jump. Not a flinch in her body. She could taste the electricity in the air. After all, it was meant for her. Only when the tear splashed on her white knuckles, did she realize she was weeping. Once she started, it was hard to stop.

"Felix, Laidi, I'm so sorry."

"What are you sorry about, child?"

The two gazed down at her. Not just them. Every eye in the room trained on Natalie, and the air grew still. Anticipation frazzled everyone's nerves, making Natalie's eye twitch.

"It's here for me."

"What is here for you?" he asked.

"The storm. It found me. You are all in grave danger."

CHAPTER THIRTY

Their footsteps echoed through the stone hallways of Felix's unground villa. Her feet padded furiously to keep up with his wider stride. She panted for air but did not stop for a break. There was no time. They both knew that. This world was at stake.

It was only the two of them now. Felix left the children with Laidi back in the kitchen. When the storm kept coming, they gathered around their mother for protection like goslings tucked under a wing.

Natalie's stomach sank like molten lead into her guts as she ran away from them. This was all her fault. Her presence brought it here.

Soon, she and Felix were all alone, hurrying past mural after mural in an empty wing of his home. No one was here. Not much light either. They were still underground, and this area was barren of all but a few light sconces. Felix held a flaming torch in front of himself as he scanned the walls, looking for something unknown to her.

"Felix… I'm sorry," Natalie began when he let her take a breath.

"No. I forbid you to do that," he said.

"Do what?"

"Take the blame for something you did not do."

"But it's following me," she protested.

"You came here to find your missing goddess. You were sent here by Hatshepsut to find me. Nothing is your fault. You are trying to save everyone. I see that, and I need you to see it as well."

"How do you mean?"

"Reject this guilt. It is unfounded. You are not the reason for the storm," Felix said, placing his hands on her shoulders. "Your goddess is. He left your world. His absence is bringing the storm. If you fail to find him in here, it will not matter where we go. The world will be destroyed."

"What… what can I do? I've looked all over."

As if on cue, they both looked away from each other and toward the nearest mural. It was a gorgeous mosaic of a battle on the high seas. Multiple ships blasted away, cannons exploding and men jumping into the sea. It was not until she noticed the ribbed sails and the red flags that she recognized the main ship. It was Ching Shih's flagship. Natalie had been to the exact battle on the wall.

"You know this place?" Felix asked her.

"Yes. I was there. Right there. It was the first place I saw when I jumped into the book. Nearly drowned to death."

"The Pirate Queen's vessel," he said in a whisper, as if to himself. He turned back to her with an earnest look on his face. "Tell me, where did you go? Where have you been in our histories?"

Natalie knew she should answer him. After all, he was staring right at her, and she had nothing to hide. Yet, she found herself without words. All she could think about was the mural. The beautiful ship painted in hundreds of colored tiles in front of her. It was intoxicating.

Something deep inside pulled her toward the mural. It felt akin to the invisible tether she shared with Nat. That unperceivable tie that connected immortal flesh with immortal flesh. The ship grabbed that leash and called to her.

"Natalie? Can you hear me?"

She could, but it did not stop her. She was in a trance. Her feet moved her toward the wall without her knowing. It was as if her body took over while her brain went for a swim. The mural just got closer and closer, and before she knew what was happening, she had reached out a hand.

"Natalie, stop!"

Before he could grab her, Natalie reached a hand into the mural. It disappeared inside the image like the wall was not made of stone and mortar. The line of reality around her hand blurred, and her hand passed straight into a different world. She peered through the portal to see the deck of Ching Shih's ship.

There was the vague sensation of someone's grip around her waist, holding her body in Roma, but all she could focus on was the feel of the salty wind on her skin. The smell of gunpowder singed her pores. She spotted a girl twisted on the floor with a large man looming over her. He had her wrist behind her back.

Suddenly, Natalie broke free of her trance and realized what she was staring at. The girl was her. The version of herself when she first arrived in the book. This was where the evil soldier tried to kidnap her.

She reached out to stop him, and he released her doppelganger. Something inside her gut went cold when he turned and met her eyes.

"What trickery is this?"

When he grabbed her hand, Natalie recoiled. She pulled hard against the man, but it was like trying to jerk free from a vice. He yanked hard, nearly toppling her back onto the deck of the Pirate Queen's ship.

Natalie knew her head crossed over when the wind blasted against her ears. She was momentarily deaf. He nearly had her. One more good yank and she would be back on the ship, back in the battle.

Natalie turned to her other self and pleaded with her eyes for help. The other anchor child stared wide-eyed back at her without an ounce of recognition. Then, she remembered the cannon smoke and how it obscured her vision when she was the frightened girl on the deck of the ship.

Of course, she did not recognize herself. This already happened. If she had not made the connection the first time around, nothing would change.

Felix wrapped his arms tighter around her. He laced one across her shoulder and wrenched her free from the man in the mural. Natalie suddenly fell backward, away from the high seas and into the warmth of Felix's mural hall.

When she gazed down at her arm, she realized the snake bracelet was gone. The one on her left wrist was still there, but the other one had been left somewhere in the future on the deck of a Chinese pirate ship.

CHAPTER THIRTY ONE

Natalie could not stop staring at her wrists. She slowly turned the bracelet with her fingers, taking in every detail of the one she had left. This bangle somehow existed as two identical pieces of jewelry. One was given to her by Teshi, and one was given to her by herself. Yet, it was the same—a loop like a snake eating its tail.

For the life of her, she had no idea what it all meant. All she knew was that it made her head ache to think about it.

"Natalie, can you hear me?"

"What?"

When she finally focused on her surroundings, she saw Felix kneeling over her. He took her hands and helped her to her feet. His eyes were kind and worried.

"What just happened? Why did you do that?"

"I just... I don't know. I reckon I was just pulled there," Natalie said.

"Pulled there?"

"Somethin' just pulled me to the mural. I can't say why. But I lived it already."

"Live it already?"

The anchor child felt helpless. She desperately wanted to explain herself better. She wanted to tell Felix about the bracelet, but she barely understood it herself. The words jammed in her throat, making it hard to breathe.

"Take a moment. Think through this. Talk when you are able," he said gently.

Felix rested his hands on her shoulders. They felt solid and comforting, even when the next wave of thunder shook the hall.

"I was there first. The pirate ship. Ching Shih. Just then, the mural pulled me back. It was almost like it wanted me there. It don't make sense."

Suddenly, an awful realization hit her. Natalie grabbed Felix's arms and stared into his eyes in horror.

"Oh God, Felix! Is Nat there? Has he been there in China this whole time, and I missed him? Is that why I keep gettin' dragged there? What if somethin' happened to him? I have to go back!"

"Wait. Breathe, Natalie. Hold on," Felix said as he placed a hand on her cheek. "Nat is not there. Ching Shih would have known, or you would have sensed him. You were already there once, and he was not there. I need you to think for me. Where else have you been?"

Natalie forced her breathing to slow. She focused on Felix's eyes as he gazed compassionately into hers. One by one, the words came through.

"Well, I reckon Ching Shih was the first. Then she sent me to see Mansa Musa since he's the Wise King. He didn't know where Nat had gone off to, so he sent me to Hatshepsut. Said the builder might know where he was. Then, she sent me to you."

"But the one the book sent you to was Ching Shih?"

"The book? I 'spose so. Everyone else has been passin' me around."

"I think I might have an idea," he said.

"What idea?"

Felix took her hand and led her through the open hallway. They passed about a half dozen other murals. Most whizzed by in an unrecognizable blur. A few of them she knew. There was the kind face of Mansa Musa with his convoy of gold. One of the grandest murals was of Hatshepsut and her elaborate temple. None of those murals tugged at her the way the pirate ship had.

She saw others she did not recognize as well. A beautiful island princess with her easel. An African man in some royal uniform she did not recognize. A disheveled sailor on the high seas.

"Felix, I don't understand. Where are we going?"

He stopped and turned to her. His eyes looked a tad wild in the torch's glow. It was disconcerting. Felix must have read Natalie's face, because he took a deep breath and composed himself.

"I need you to tell me why your goddess came here," he said.

"Because he... lost someone. His wife."

"He left because of his grief."

"He went inside the book to find her in his history, but somethin' ain't right," she insisted.

Felix stood up straighter. A calm enveloped his face, and every muscle relaxed. It looked like someone had poured warm cocoa all over the inside of Felix's brain, and now he was leaning into the comfort of it.

"I think I understand now. It makes sense why the book sent you to Ching Shih first."

"Really? Why? She acted pretty darn happy to pass me on."

"Natalie, do you know why I have lived longer than most?" he asked.

It was not a question she expected. She searched her brain for words to answer with, but found none. She opted just to shake her head instead.

"I have chosen a simpler life. You see the kings and queens out there. The warrior pirates and the boastful. None of them can hold the price of this power for very long. No matter how much they conquer or build, it is not enough. They have this amazing power, and when it cannot provide the satisfaction they want from it over and over again, they choose death as a release."

"I don't think I understand," she said.

"I lasted the longest because I chose the humble life of an artist. I wanted to fill my life with children and teach them everything I knew. I spent so many years happy in this great home I made for us. But the price for that happiness was my immortality. Eventually, I will lose Laidi to old age, just like I did the three wives before her. I outlive every single child in that kitchen."

Moisture collected into the corners of Felix's eyes, and his face flushed. The shock of that thought kicked the anchor child squarely in the chest. She pictured the tiny baby Laidi held in the wrap around her body. The idea of Felix watching that child die of old age did not make sense.

Natalie's mouth went bone dry. Any comforting words she might have found died on the desert of her tongue.

"It is the way of the goddess. I bore it longer than most because I created people to bear it with me. I was happy far more than I was not. My children lived rich, full lives. But there is a reason most of us do not walk around like this," he said, holding out one arm.

Natalie gasped. The skin of Felix's arm transformed. Large swaths of paint strokes in all the shades of his skin slashed this way and that. She had seen this with Nat when he allowed anyone to see it. It was the immortal paint the old gods painted the first goddess. The magic from which all their power originated.

"Showing our colors is raw and difficult. Some camouflage it like I do, and others wear things like gloves," he said with a knowing nod.

Of course, she knew this. Natalie knew about Nan, the goddess who gave the power to Nat. She wore gloves all the time—dozens of them in every color of the rainbow. Nan never went without them. At least, not until the end. Her end.

Technically, Natalie had never met Nan. She could not be created until the old goddess died. However, she knew Nan from Nat's memories. He loved her more than he ever admitted, so Natalie did as well.

Nat, too, wore gloves for a good while, but his reasons were purely because he did not know any better. Nan told him the goddess could not be touched, and he took her at her word. It turned out, in true Nan fashion, she omitted a few key details.

Then it occurred to her. All the goddesses she had met since she dropped into the book were gloveless. They did not hide away from the people. Well, most of them. The one outlier was Ching Shih. She wore gloves.

"There. Now you see it," Felix said.

"I thought Ching Shih wore them because she was a pirate."

"She may have fought and conquered like a ruthless queen, but she did so under a weight of grief. Her husband died, giving her the power of the goddess, but there was not enough gold in the Orient to drown out her sorrow. Sometimes, the ones who yell the loudest are the ones who are the most injured."

"Then, why did the book send me to her? Nat wasn't there."

"I think the book sensed the grief. It sent you to the nearest goddess with a broken heart. From there, we have all been trying to help you in the worst way. With good intentions, of course. But you do not need a wise man or a builder. You need to follow the grief. It will lead you to your Nat."

"But how do I do that?"

"Well, I have an idea about that, but I am pretty certain you will not like it."

CHAPTER THIRTY TWO

Much to their surprise, a spindly boy was waiting for them when they reached the mural. He sat on the floor, barely lit by his torch, lining up tiles by size and color on the floor. He did not look a bit confused to see them when he met Natalie's eyes.

"I've been waiting for you," he said.

"You figured this out long before I did," Felix said with a slow smile.

"I heard the commotion when the girl came in," the boy explained. "I knew what she was right away. I had Alexander and Saxon help me back here."

"You are his anchor child," Natalie said.

"And he is far smarter than I at times. There is much to be said for the quiet ones."

The realization pulsed inside her head like a light bulb struggling to come to life. He knew her the moment she entered Felix's home. He picked her out, recognized her journey, and plotted the following steps before she even noticed his existence. Natalie suddenly felt entirely inadequate by comparison.

"Only sometimes," said the boy. "And this is the mural you need."

Felix and Natalie turned their attention to the image in front of them. It was beautiful. A scene of a series of pyramids surrounded by a thick, lush jungle. They were not the pyramids of Egypt. Those were smooth, perfect lines—pristine geometry placed in a sea of sand.

These pyramids were made of white and grey stone, with creatures etched into the sides and stairs running to the top. Steps ran up a steep slope, climbing to the summit. Buildings of various sizes sprouted from the tree line here and there.

The colors of the image floored Natalie. She wondered how it was possible to make something so lifelike using only painted bits of ceramic. The mural easily stood fifteen feet above her and twenty feet end to end.

"What is that place?" she asked in wonder.

"It is the center wonder of the Mayan empire. Copan," Felix said. "If we are going to send you on the path of following grief, that would be the next best place to go."

A sudden foreboding settled into her belly. It felt hard and heavy. Almost as if she swallowed a stone, and it refused to pass. Something felt terribly wrong about this Copan, despite its beauty.

There was the other feeling as well, similar to the Chinese mural. Something deep within her gut reached out to the image in front of her. Natalie did not want it to be true, but Felix's theory must have some weight to it. Why else would she be so compelled to a place she dreaded?

"So, you've been here? You know this Copan?" Natalie asked.

"No. It has not happened yet. Not in my time anyway."

"Then how do you know 'bout it? How do you know all these goddesses enough to make murals about them?"

"It is one of my abilities. I can see into other histories. At least, enough to paint them."

"Then how come you can't see Nat? Why ain't there a portrait of him here?"

"I haven't seen him yet," Felix said.

"What about Nan? She was the goddess before him. I bet if I could find her, she would take me to him."

"We have not seen her yet either," the anchor boy said.

Natalie took in the mural again. The stone was still there, promising her something terrible was going to happen. She drew in a frustrated breath and let it out in a huff. She wanted to cry. She wanted to hide there. She wanted to go home.

A deep rumble shook the villa. Even though they were underground, Natalie could hear the explosion of the lightning above them. Three more hits, and the roof of the ceiling cracked above their heads, showering dust down on their heads.

"There ain't much time," she said.

"No. I am afraid you must go," Felix said with a face full of remorse. "I hate to send you away and alone, especially to that place, but there is nothing more to be done. Hopefully, when you are back on track, the storm will leave you be."

Nothing he said made Natalie feel any better, but she knew he was right. She nodded and stepped closer to the mural. She stuck her hand out to test the water, so to speak. Her fingers disappeared into the wall.

"Wait!"

They all turned to see a girl running toward them. Her blond hair flew behind her in a golden curtain. Her arms were sooty and black up to her elbows. Natalie recognized her immediately.

"Aurelia? You should be with your mother. What are you doing here?" Felix asked.

"I cannot let her leave this way," she said, and turned to address Natalie directly. "If you are going to move on, you cannot go in those clothes. Here, take this. It will be better than what you are wearing."

Aurelia held a bundle for Natalie. She took it hesitantly and opened it. Inside was a simple shift dress with a sash to wrap around the waist. It was olive green and cut similar to Aurelia's. The material felt light and soft.

Natalie did not know what people in Copan wore, but this had to be better than the paint-splattered African garb Mansa Musa had given her. At least she would be less conspicuous. Plus, all the layers of her current dress did not breathe well in the heat.

Felix and his anchor child averted their eyes as Aurelia helped Natalie into the clothes with all the care of a sister. Even though Natalie was never fond of dresses, she was grateful this one covered her modestly. She felt a tad less alien wearing it.

"I also brought you this," Aurelia said as she held out a small chunk of bread. "Who knows when you will be able to eat again."

"Thank you so much," Natalie said.

She took the gift and slipped it into her pocket. She also transferred the sharp hairpins. The bracelet she kept on her left wrist.

Another crash from above, and the walls shook so hard it nearly knocked Natalie and Aurelia off their feet. The anchor child threw his arms over his head to protect himself from the falling dirt. Somewhere in the distance, they heard screaming.

"Go, Natalie. Hurry!" Felix yelled.

There was no time left to lose. Like it or not, she had to go. Natalie turned away from Aurelia and ran straight for the mural. Hesitation could cost lives. She leaped without looking and tumbled straight into the painting, vanishing from Roma forever.

CHAPTER THIRTY THREE

She half-expected the blinding light again. If not that, then some sort of momentary feeling of transition. That was not what she got. Much like when she first entered the book, Natalie went straight from one reality to the next. She leaped into the wall and tumbled directly into an unknown land as though she merely hopped through a door.

Natalie hit the hard-packed earth on one knee with her hands bracing her weight. She drew in a deep breath as the landscape righted itself before her. The air filled her lungs, heavy and wet. Heat radiated from the sun above as though it were closer to the ground here than anywhere else. Not even Egypt felt this sweltering.

Sweat beads broke out all over her body and soaked the shift dress Aurelia gave her beneath the arms and down the back. Natalie was grateful not to be wearing the other clothes, but she felt terrible about ruining it so quickly.

A small structure greeted her mere yards away. It appeared man-made, with carvings of strange serpents winding themselves around the doorway. Pale bricks stacked around the snake's body, each one carved into oddly shaped human heads and skulls. Some had fangs, and others stuck out curled tongues.

When she heard a commotion coming her way, she ducked inside the strange place. At the very least, she would be out of the elements.

It was hard to tell who was more surprised. Natalie, or the small artist inside. They both jumped away from one another like each was a venomous snake. The artist dropped her chisel and reached for her knife. Her eyes were wide with fear.

"No! Wait. I ain't gonna hurt you," Natalie said frantically, holding her hands up in the air.

"Who… are you?" she asked, slowly lowering her weapon.

The artist woman did not drop the knife, nor did she stick it back in her belt, but Natalie still considered it a victory. At least she was not in imminent danger any longer.

"I am here for the… goddess?"

Natalie was not sure who the goddess was here, but if history had taught her anything, it was that worshippers followed the goddess no matter where they were or what their name was. Perhaps just asking for a goddess would be enough for this peculiar woman to direct her in the right direction. Natalie was exhausted.

The artist moved closer to her to get a better look. As she did, Natalie could return the favor. As far as women went, this one was tiny. Just over four feet tall, Natalie reckoned. Her head was thin and elongated from her hairline to the crown. It was painted with red paint along her forehead, behind her ears, and along her shoulders.

She had a mass of black hair pulled tightly back and fastened at the back of her head in a series of knots, with green feathers flaring out. Her skin was tan, if a touch of red, and her light brown eyes probed Natalie's for some sort of answer to her presence.

She wore a skirt of sorts. It was black with white flowers that wrapped between her legs. Her yellow and red top wrapped her bosom beneath her arms and flared away from her waist. Natalie had never seen anyone like her. There was so much color. She could not stop staring.

"You are here for the festival, then?" she asked Natalie.

"Festival?"

"If you are looking for the goddess, then you must be here for the festival," she said.

The woman put her hands on her hips. She scowled at Natalie, looking impatient.

"Um… yes. That's why I am here. The festival. Where is it?"

"The great pyramid. Everyone will gather there."

"Where is that?" Natalie asked.

The woman crossed her arms and peered at Natalie as though she were the dumbest person alive. Apparently, everyone knew what and where that was. She did not want to be pegged as any more of an outsider than she already was.

"I am not from here," she blurted. "I've made a pilgrimage here to find the goddess, and uh… observe the awesome power."

This seemed to be enough of an explanation for the artist. That, or perhaps she did not have the patience to look further into the matter. Both were easily possible. Either way, she relaxed her accusations and decided Natalie was no threat.

"The festival will be there," she said, pointing out of the temple and to the left. "The parade will be by shortly. Just join in and follow everyone to the pyramid."

"Thank you," Natalie said.

The woman made some approximation of a shrug and turned back to her artwork. Natalie had not noticed it until that moment, but the temple walls were sculpted just as well as outside. The only difference was these pictures were also painted. Bizarre, knotted designs curled around the figures of people and animals. Jaguars, snakes, and monkeys.

In between the creatures, some symbols might be words. They were laid out similar to the Egyptian hieroglyphs Natalie had seen with Hatshepsut. All in rows, like there was some sort of rhyme and reason. She desperately wished she could read them.

"What is that you're making?" Natalie asked, pointing to the wall.

"This is the history of the exalted one. The goddess. Eighteen Rabbit. I am adding to it. But please do not tell anyone I am here."

"Why not?"

"Woman are not encouraged to sculpt," she said with a frown.

"That is why you don't want him to know?"

"No. That is why I do not wish his advisors to know. I want this to stay secret from Eighteen Rabbit because he will not be pleased with what I am making."

"What are you making?" Natalie asked.

She sincerely hoped the woman would not look at her the way she had earlier. As if she had three heads and only one had a brain. Luckily, the artist pressed on with no sort of skepticism.

"It is the story of his wife and child. Normally, we do not sculpt such things. Only triumphs. But she died in childbirth, and I thought that should be recorded. She was a good ruler. A beacon for us all. I liked her."

"If that's so, then why wouldn't Eighteen Rabbit want you to draw her story?"

The woman stared blankly at Natalie for a hard moment. She barely blinked, and Natalie shrank under her gaze.

"You really are not from here, are you?"

"No."

"From where do you hail?"

"I... um... somewhere far."

They were interrupted by the burst of raucous laughing just outside the entryway. It happened so suddenly Natalie thought it was a clap of thunder. She jumped nearly an inch in the air, whipping around and searching for lightning. Surely the storm had found her, she thought.

There was nothing but a dense herd of people merrily walking past, laughing and carrying on. A constant flow of skin and color marching past.

"It is the parade," the woman explained as she placed a rough hand on Natalie's shoulder. "If it is Eighteen Rabbit you seek, follow them. They will lead you to the festival."

"Are you not joining?" Natalie asked.

"No. I do not like these types of festivals. I will stay here and finish my work. The queen would have wanted that of me."

"You mean Eighteen Rabbit's wife?"

The artist said nothing. Her only answer was in the heartbroken look that crossed her face. Without a word, she turned her back to the anchor child and went right back to her work.

She thought about calling out for a farewell, but she did not know the woman's name, and there was no good way to do such a thing when you did not know a person's name. Instead, she made her way to the doorway of the temple and joined the procession of revelers.

CHAPTER THIRTY FOUR

The mass of people swept her up and carried her away like an ocean current made of bodies. They were not the nicest smelling bodies, either. Natalie took in the scent of sweat, sun, armpit odor, and sun-dried dirt. She was packed so close to the others she took in their rotten smell of ruined teeth and gums. This had to be a time before dentists.

Then she realized she must not smell like a rose herself. After all, she had been dunked in the ocean, dragged through a desert, covered in dust, and thrown into a sweltering jungle. She had not bathed since Tanglewood. Perhaps it was an appropriate camouflage for herself. Natalie could hide in their shared body odor.

When the group became used to her presence, they relaxed their ranks, allowing more room for her body to move independently. She breathed a little easier when her feet began doing the navigating for her. Plus, she could better see her party-goers now.

Natalie felt like she had been sucked into an exotic flock of birds. Most of the people wore huge headdresses made of white and black feathers. Some even had feathers down their backs and shoulders. When they danced about, the feathers bounced, making them look like an odd species of half-plucked birds.

Many wore little more than sashes around their waists, barely obscuring their most private of body parts. Natalie blushed. Some wore skirts similar to the woman she met earlier. Others fastened capes with gold and precious stones around their shoulders. All of their clothes were dyed in shades of green, blue, red, and white.

The most interesting parts of their costumes were the lavishly decorated belts and jade necklaces. So intricate and fanciful with feathers and beads. Natalie enjoyed hearing the jangle of the beads clicking against each other as the revelers danced around her.

Everyone adorned themselves in swaths of red and white paint. Many had the elongated head of the woman she met in the temple. Others had strange body modifications like stretched earlobes and bone hooks threaded through their lips. Natalie wondered how they did it or how they ate.

The lot was merry. They sang some song she did not understand to a tune that was utterly foreign to her. She had to duck and pivot to avoid the whipping feathers as the people sang and danced around her. Their happiness was infectious.

Natalie smiled for the first time since sitting at Laidi's table. In the back of her brain, a little voice reminded her why she was there. It whispered horrifying words of warning. That stone of foreboding in her gut still sat unmoving. Yet, she clapped along with their strange song.

The trees ended suddenly, and the entire mass of Copan revealed itself to them. It was even more magnificent in person than in Felix's mural. Not just one pyramid. There were several buildings with climbing staircases. Each one was filled with party-goers cheering and singing.

It was easy to pick out the parrots, even with all the commotion. The world around them was a vast jungle, and the bright birds stuck out like red and blue gems flying in a sky of green. They cawed and swooped down among the people, seemingly unafraid of humans.

The current of people pushed along, all moving at the same pace. Everyone appeared to be heading toward the same spot with no genuine sense of urgency. Natalie traveled with them past an enormous building that looked like many rectangular slabs stacked on top of one another.

There were relief pictures sculpted into the side of the walls—terrifying images of warriors, eagles, and jaguars devouring human hearts. A mighty staircase led to the top, but it was so intimidating, Natalie wondered how anyone had the stomach to climb the thing. A steep slope stretched high, reaching toward the sun.

To move beyond the temple, they had to weave in and out of rows of columns. They did not look Egyptian or Roman. No, these were elaborate and not meant to hold anything but their own weight. Each pillar stood tall and proud. Each column appeared to be carved by hand. The designs and shapes swirled this way and that, forming images of hands and weapons and animals.

Natalie had seen nothing like it before. These were not the clear-cut images of Egyptian hieroglyphs, nor were they easily identifiable like Felix's murals. The anchor child found it difficult to pick out any focal point in the chaos of the sculpture. It was not until she saw the face in the front that she realized these were the portraits of people. Important people, she reckoned, judging by the size and intricacy of each pillar.

The crowd kept trying to pull her back into the parade, but she held her ground long enough to stare directly into the twisted, carved face. Something inside her gut told her this was the goddess. This was Eighteen Rabbit.

There would be no dwelling on that thought for long. One woman in the crowd grabbed her hand and dragged her back into the laughing party. She continued onward with the image of the goddess's statue still lingering in her mind.

A perfectly flat, green field hosted some sort of sporting game. Two teams that were painted different colors kicked a ball and ran at one another. A series of multilayered, stone seats perched on each side where fans sat and cheered for their favorite team. Natalie could not tell what the game was, but the fans jumped and cheered when one player bumped a small ball off his hip and into a hoop at the end of the field.

The people nearest Natalie grabbed her arms and pulled her away from the game. They dragged her toward a different crowd, spinning her around while laughing. It made her dizzy, but Natalie laughed again.

One woman held Natalie's shoulders and shouted to someone out of her sight. She could not make out all the words. Just the basics. The words "here" and "new player." The singing and laughter drowned out everything in between.

"What's happenin'?"

No one answered. The woman pointed at two men nearest her, and they hoisted Natalie on their shoulders. It was disconcerting at first, and the feathers pricking her rump were not pleasant, but Natalie felt happy. The people below her seemed to be pleased to see her. It was a pleasant reprieve from all the danger.

Another song picked up, and the masses joined in. More hands moved to support Natalie's weight, and they started moving her along the top of the crowd. She soon realized they were carrying her toward what could only be described as a stage. It was a flat plateau of land with several people in costume, dancing around and leading the song.

The players clapped wildly when the crowd delivered Natalie to them. They placed her gently on the stage, and Natalie waved with appreciation. Two of the actors rushed forward, dancing in a circle around her. She smiled. It was all great fun.

"Quiet, good people! Please give us room to speak!"

The voice came from a new actor. He was older than the rest and wore a splendid white cape covered in white and green feathers. There was an air of authority around the man, and when he spoke, the people quietened.

"Thank you! We are so pleased to perform our play for you. Enjoy the show, and do not forget to sing along," he said.

Everyone cheered as he exited the stage with a theatrical flourish. The other actors made to follow him. Natalie followed suit, but she was stopped by the female player dressed all in yellow and black. Natalie thought she resembled a bee.

"Not you. You are chosen!" the actress said.

"What does that mean?"

"It means you are the star. Get out there!"

The bee woman gave Natalie a gentle shove. Before she knew what was happening, Natalie found herself alone in the middle of a stage with a hundred Mayans staring at her. It felt like the women's tent all over again. Everyone gaped at her in anticipation.

It was the first time she had seen them quiet. They watched her intently, and she had no idea what to do.

Time passed strangely. To Natalie, it felt like minutes standing there in front of all those awaiting eyes. In reality, it was probably only a few seconds. She opened her mouth to say something. What she would say, she did not know, but it felt like she should try.

"Um… hello?"

Just then, a miracle happened. Before she could get out another word, a new actor burst on to the scene. The crowd went wild when they saw him enter. Natalie turned to see the biggest man she had seen since she arrived in Copan.

He wore no shirt with yellow and red cloth wrapped around his legs. There was a red belt about his waist, with one sash hanging low over his groin. The tip of the material nearly hit his calf. A white cape hugged his shoulders with huge jade fasteners and necklaces.

The most exciting thing about the costume was the hat. A great, green serpent's head jutted out from his headdress. Its feathered tail ran down his back like the creature was scaling him. Unlike many of the partiers, his face was not painted. Then again, he did not need to with a crown like that.

"My people!" he shouted as he threw his hands in the air.

The crowd roared with applause. He motioned his hands downward, and they quietened. Natalie wondered for a moment if this was Eighteen Rabbit, and he was using magic to command the people in the audience.

When she gazed into the face of the man, she knew he was not a goddess. He did not shimmer with power. He was merely a human with an excellent gift for crowd work.

"Are you ready for our show?"

Again, they cheered with great vigor.

"As we wait for our true Eighteen Rabbit to perform today, I, Kawoq, will play our great ruler for you. In the most humble of ways, of course."

"Hurray for Kawoq! Hurray for Kawoq! Hurray for Kawoq!"

The actor turned to Natalie and gestured to her with both hands. He strode across the stage theatrically, making it to her side in only three leaps.

"What is your name, little one?" Kawoq asked her quietly.

"My… name?"

"What are you called?"

"Natalie is my name."

"Strange name, but who am I to judge," he said with a smile.

"I… uh… guess so?"

Kawoq faced the crowd again as he patted Natalie on the back. She nearly fell over from the force of it, but righted herself.

"And this is Natalie! She is here to play the sacrifice!"

"Hurray, Natalie! Hurray, Natalie! Hurray, Natalie!"

CHAPTER THIRTY FIVE

Natalie felt a squirm in her stomach when she replayed his words in her mind. Her eyes flew open in terror, and she tugged at his cape. When he met her eyes, they seemed kind enough, but it did little to calm her apprehension.

"Not to worry. It is only a play."

"A play?"

"Play along with us."

That made her feel better, but the unease of being spontaneously cast in a play did not go away completely. It reminded her of those dreams where you go to dinner naked, or you had to take a test without knowing the subject. All she knew about her part was that she was the sacrifice. That sounded awful.

Suddenly, there were two other actors on either side of her. They were the ones who led the singing earlier. A woman and a man. Both appeared to be little more than teenagers.

"And presenting your royal guards!" Kawoq said, pointing at the two of them.

Natalie peered desperately at the girl.

"What do I do?" she whispered.

"Do not worry. We pull a child from the crowd every time. There is nothing to your part. Just follow along."

She nodded, but felt little better.

An ear-piercing roar came out of nowhere. Well, at first, it seemed to come out of nowhere. Natalie's first inclination was to look at the sky for the storm. While she gazed upward, everyone else was watching Kawoq. The roar had come from him.

"I am the great Eighteen Rabbit!" he yelled with such bass it shook the floor. Natalie doubted his lack of magic. "All bow before me!"

The actors pulled Natalie to the ground, and they bowed together. She only stood back up when they did.

"The sun is nearly high, and my great celebration is upon us. Soon my great work will begin."

"But great king, have the stars foretold of this day?" said the male actor.

"I have foretold it, and I am your living god. The stars bow to me!"

The man and woman pulled her down on her knees again. They bowed together.

"All hail, Eighteen Rabbit!"

"All hail, Eighteen Rabbit!" the crowd repeated.

"Bring me my sacrifice," he said as he pointed to Natalie.

The two actors pulled Natalie from the ground and hurried her across the stage. They pushed her in front of Kawoq and took two steps backward. Kawoq glared down at Natalie, and she tried not to panic.

It was only a play; she reminded herself. Only a play. It was not real.

"With you, I have reached the pinnacle of power. No one is above me. I have moved the very mountains to mine the stone for my great temples. The sky weeps when I command it. Now, with your death, I will ascend above the stars! To stars, I will fly to rule everyone from above!"

He raised his hands into the air, and the crowd went wild. The two behind her cheered as well. Natalie could not keep her heart from pounding.

"It's just a play," she whispered to herself.

"Guards! Take her to the holy temple and hold her down!" Kawoq said.

"Yes, supreme ruler! All hail, Eighteen Rabbit!"

The man and woman grabbed her arms and lowered her to the ground. Natalie panicked. This did not feel right. Everything in her body told her to run. The guards grabbed her wrists and ankles and pinned her to the ground. Natalie pulled against them, trying to wriggle free.

"The sun is at the height. Now is the time!"

Kawoq pulled a knife from his cape and held it in the air. The blade glinted in the sunlight as he focused on Natalie with a terrifying face full of violence. The crowd went stark still. Everyone except for Natalie. She struggled harder to break free.

"For immortality!" he yelled to the sky.

Kawoq crossed the stage with his knife held high. He knelt next to Natalie, swinging his fist downward in an arc. It all happened so fast. Natalie yelped and braced herself for the impact. With her pinned, there was no way the blade would miss any vital organs. She arched her body as far as she could.

The world silenced. Only the heavy breathing of the actors who knelt around her filled her ears. It took a few hard seconds to realize she was not hurting. Natalie opened her eyes, prepared to gaze upon a bleeding wound, but there was none. No knife protruding from her gut. Nothing.

When the world stopped spinning, she saw Kawoq's fist holding the knife on the ground by her side. He missed her completely.

The actress unrolled something from beneath her skirt. It was a stone wrapped in red cloth. Several strips of red fabric dangled from it, making it almost look like an octopus. Kawoq slipped her the knife and took the stone. The audience saw none of this since Kawoq's cape obscured the switch.

He rose slowly, pulling the stone from the ground dramatically. Now Natalie understood the point of the octopus. The way Kawoq lifted the tone made it look like he was tearing out Natalie's heart. The strips of red cloth resembled blood and sinew.

She felt sick. While knowing she would not die was a relief, her part in the play felt wrong and gross. The heat did not help matters. Natalie no longer fought against her fake guards. She was not supposed to be, she reckoned. She might as well lay there dead and collect herself.

"At last!" yelled Kawoq. "Eternity in the stars. Rejoice, my people!"

The crowd roared to life. Natalie had not realized how quiet the onlookers were until they started clapping again. Some began singing songs again. Others called out the actors by name like they were celebrities.

"Thank you, everyone!" Kawoq said. "Now, let us thank the star of the show. Young Natalie!"

The actors released her arms and legs. The female whispered into her ears.

"You did really well! So believable. I truly thought you were scared for a minute."

"Yeah, me too," Natalie said wearily.

They hoisted her to her feet. The world felt a bit wobbly, as if she was still on Ching Shih's ship, casting this way and that. Natalie struggled to stand up straight. Luckily, Kawoq pulled her into a hug. She leaned against him and tried to smile for her new adoring fans.

After about a minute of praise, the people began filing away. They were off to some other attraction, Natalie assumed. Perhaps there was a meal that accompanied whatever this festival was. The thought of food was decidedly not appetizing to her.

"You did so well," Kawoq said as he released her.

His face was back to being kind. Natalie kept her footing by focusing on his hairline. It was like watching a steady horizon to keep your balance.

"Thanks," was all she could say.

"I am serious. If you ever want a job, just let me know."

"That's real nice of you, Kawoq, but I don't reckon the theater life is the right one for me."

"Suit yourself. I am here if you change your mind. Enjoy the rest of the festival."

"Thank you."

Natalie hopped off the stage and walked away as fast as her wobbly legs could carry her.

Chapter Thirty Six

Of course, they could not deny the main attraction. The colossal pyramid of Copan loomed above all, reaching into the sky. It was as though it were trying to kiss the sun. Natalie reckoned it had to be around seventy feet tall or more. It was hard to tell from the bottom. Staircases led to the summit on all sides.

Along the edges of the staircase were hieroglyphs. At least, that was what they looked like to the anchor child. Flat images carved into stone in repeating patterns, just like the ones she had seen before.

Directly in front of the stairs was another one of the sculpted pillars. Now that she knew what to look for, Natalie recognized the face on the front. It was Eighteen Rabbit, the goddess.

Groups sang their separate songs, and people milled about, waiting for something. They called this a festival, but everything she had seen felt like appetizers for something bigger. Kawoq and his actors hinted it had to do with Eighteen Rabbit. If he was the goddess, she had to find him.

The crowd cheered in unison, and it startled her back to the present. For a terrible moment, she felt like she was back on the stage again, with Kawoq rushing at her with a knife. Of course, that was nonsense, but her heart raced all the same.

Just as soon as the bursts of noise came, it dissipated. Some unseen force in the masses commanded attention, much like the actors had. Natalie heard no one's voice. No booming declaration.

The crowd's silence spread like a ripple in water. It began near the stairs and radiated from there. Natalie was not sure what drew their attention, but everyone turned in unison. They spoke only in hushed whispers. When they all applauded, she focused on the focal point.

A procession of important people parted the crowd. Their robes were fine and clean. They wore jewelry of jade and gold. When they passed the masses, they held their noses to the sky. To seem above the commoners or because of the stench of the crowd, Natalie did not know.

Behind them strolled the goddess. There was no mistaking him. He walked with an air of authority, even though he wore less than anyone else. Just a simple, white skirt with a gold and jade belt around his waist. It matched the elaborate necklace that hung low on his chest.

His head was elongated like the rest of the Mayans, but there were no bone piercings or body paint. The feathered headdress was simple and elegant. It shot one perfectly white feather straight into the air with a cascade of more delicate feathers in a minimal spray down his back. The goddess stuck out in the crowd not because he wore more but because he wore less. He did not need to. All bowed to his glowing power.

The crowd hushed as he walked past them. Natalie weaved through the bodies, trying to get a better look. Perhaps if she could catch Eighteen Rabbit's attention, she could explain what was happening. He would stop whatever this was and help her.

She felt the body paint smear on her skin and dress as she squeezed through the colorful people. Tiny pinpricks of feathers stabbed her skin. Some even attached themselves to her clothes. Natalie pressed onward, ignoring the discomfort.

When she wriggled her way to the front, Eighteen Rabbit was at the bottom of the hieroglyph staircase. He turned to his people and raised his hands in the air. Everyone cheered wildly, and a slow smile spread across his face. Kawoq indeed was great at imitating him.

Despite the grin, Eighteen Rabbit did not look happy. He was in pain. Natalie knew the signs. His brow pinched, and he blinked hard. Natalie could see moisture pooling in the corners of his eyes, but the king wiped it away with a simple hand gesture. He swallowed hard several times as he tried to compose himself.

No one seemed to notice but Natalie. Everyone cheered as he raised his hands in the air yet again. When he did, Natalie saw the ornate knife fastened on his belt. Something in her gut flinched. It was the same thing that told her to bolt.

"My people! Thank you for coming. We are on the precipice of a new era. A great and prosperous time! To receive our due riches, we must do as we always have. A sacrifice to the gods!"

The crowd erupted around her. Natalie was the only one standing stark still. Her knees felt weak, and she feared she would collapse right there.

"I must ascend to the stars. There I will find our new riches!"

The people around cheered and cried his name. One woman nearest him wept as she reached for him. She crawled on all fours toward the ruler. Two somber-looking men forced her back into the crowd. The king did not seem to notice.

"Bring out the sacrifice!" Eighteen Rabbit yelled over the din.

Natalie could not tell where the new group originated. Not from her vantage point. It was nearly impossible to see very far with this many people, but she heard the screaming girl before she laid eyes on her.

It was not a typical scream. The sacrifice sounded almost gagged. Natalie listened for words but heard none. Just a lot of grunts and stifled shrieks. Then, she spotted the girl and understood.

Two armed men carried the girl on their backs. Each one had a firm grasp on her ankles and wrists, careful not to let her touch the ground. She jerked and kicked, trying to break free. Her choked screams fell on unsympathetic ears, and Natalie knew why.

This was an anchor child. *His* anchor child. A being who could not speak to others. Someone who could not plead her case. Someone so vulnerable she could not run away, no matter how much she wanted to. This was the sacrifice.

CHAPTER THIRTY SEVEN

The red dress the anchor child wore fell loosely around her like she was already bleeding. Already dead. Already an offering. She thrashed and spat, but nothing helped.

Natalie moved away from the hive of people. She ran to the procession and tried to reach for the squirming child. There was no plan per se, but she had to do something. Natalie had to save her.

One guard smacked Natalie aside with minimal effort. He might as well have been swatting at a fly. She landed hard on her rear end.

When she tried again, the anchor child locked eyes on her. A heartbreaking look crossed her face. Like recognized like, and the child pleaded with her in the language only the anchor children understood.

This time, a different man intervened. He was not preoccupied with wrangling a defenseless girl to her doom. The guard grabbed Natalie's shoulders and held her in place. She struggled to break free, but he was too strong.

"No! Stop. Let go of her. She's just a kid!" Natalie shrieked.

Her protests got lost in the din. The masses drowned her out. What could she do when an entire city was hell-bent on sacrificing a little girl? What if they decided she was next?

Natalie swallowed that thought. Eighteen Rabbit led the priests around him up the stairs. The two guards holding the anchor child followed behind them. All around Natalie, the people chanted and sang some shared song she could not understand. She heard the girl let out another choked scream and knew she had to do something.

With one quick thrust of her foot, Natalie jabbed her heel into her captor's foot as hard as she could. His leather sandals were little protection against her boots, even though she was significantly smaller than he was. The guard released her with a grunt, and Natalie scrambled away from him.

Several other guards grabbed at her clothes as she raced between them. One found purchase on the hem of her skirt, but one hard elbow in the eye made him let go. He jumped back and cursed.

None of the partygoers seemed to notice the drama. Every eye focused on the royal procession, which was already halfway up the pyramid at that point. Natalie ducked the last guard and raced up after them.

Her breath came hard and fast. The heat made it hard to draw in a lungful of air, and she panted like a dog. It got worse the higher she went, but she had to move forward. There was no turning back.

So many steps. Every time Natalie felt she was almost there, another dozen seemed to appear beneath her. Briefly, she wondered if this was magic or if it was merely a marvel of architecture. After a while, she took the steps on all fours like a monkey.

By the time she reached the summit, the party was nowhere to be found. The chanting continued all around her, but now she could hear it above her as well. She spotted a crude ladder resting on the side of the wall. It led to the very top of the pyramid.

"That's where you are," she said aloud.

Natalie raced to the ladder and climbed it as fast as her weakened arms could manage. The structure was wooden poles held together with long strips of leather. It probably would have felt sturdy enough if she were still on the ground. Up this high, her heart raced as she clung to the rungs. Her breath came in ragged huffs.

Her brain told her not to look down. Of course, she did the opposite. It was human nature, after all. Do the opposite of good sense in cases of intense fear. When the anchor child peered down at the world below, bile rose in her throat. The vast crowd below swirled in her vision. The ground appeared to swell and recede, growing closer and farther away in waves.

She turned her gaze upward and swallowed down the sick burning her esophagus. The wild wind pushed against her body, but she made her legs continue to climb. Freezing there on the ladder, halfway between Earth and Heaven, was not an option.

She pulled herself to the top and saw the poor anchor child tied to a rectangular slab altar. Even from where Natalie stood, she could see the girl's roots taking hold. She could not run away even if she was free to go. Those roots held her firm.

Eighteen Rabbit stood over the girl with his weapon poised over his head. It was not like any kind of sword she had ever seen. It looked more like a long paddle than anything else. When she stared harder, she noticed the blades. Seven sharp, obsidian blades fanned out of the club's edges—one large on top and three on each side.

The priests and guards chanted along with the masses below them. Their eyes were closed, so they were unaware of Natalie, but Eighteen Rabbit saw her. He locked eyes with her and hesitated.

This was her only chance. She had to reason with him. They could be alone at that one moment. There was no escape for his anchor child without his permission.

"Please, stop! Don't do this. You don't have to sacrifice yourself," Natalie pleaded.

His eyes were wild as he took her in. They both knew to kill his child meant he would die too. It was the rule of the goddess. They both lived, or they both died—no one without the other.

Natalie spotted the doubt on his face. She saw the large paint strokes covering his skin and knew he was not trying to hide anything. Maybe he never did. His paint made him look more vulnerable than before.

Eighteen Rabbit held his terrible club in the air long enough that one of his priests opened his eyes and spotted Natalie. Apparently, the deed should have already been done by then, and they had not expected to hear a girl's voice. The others followed suit, and she found several angry faces glaring down at her.

"Sire, what are you doing?"

"This is your decree."

"The child is the ultimate sacrifice."

Eighteen Rabbit gazed down at his anchor child, who was weeping. Tears ran down her face and wetted her tangled hair.

"You don't have to do this," Natalie whispered. "Just let her go. I know you are sad. I know you lost your family, but you don't have to die."

The vulnerability in Eighteen Rabbit's face turned into grief. Wracking, sobbing grief. Sorrow that could break a goddess. That grief turned into rage, and that rage turned into a terrifying smile of insanity. He raised the blades into the sunlight and plunged them down in a horrifying arc.

Natalie knew what was about the happen before anyone. She had seen the play. Hell, she had *been* the play. No one understood what this really was. They did not know what would happen if a goddess tried to kill their anchor child.

Her legs started moving before she told them to. She rushed forward, even though she knew there was no way to make it in time. The anchor child let out a choked scream, and the blades fell upon her.

An explosion rocked the world. One that upended reality and scorched the Earth. Natalie flew backward and fell into the timeless ether below.

CHAPTER THIRTY EIGHT

She was certain she died. The shock of the explosion pounded inside her chest and knocked her off her feet. Natalie fell for what seemed like an eternity. Perhaps that indeed was what death felt like—just falling forever. If that was the case, she had died so many times already.

When her back hit the hard ground, it knocked the wind out of her. Natalie gasped for air as she clutched her chest. The pain reverberated through her bones like vibrations from a tuning fork. It was excruciating.

"Well, I reckon I ain't dead," Natalie said through wheezing coughs. "Can't imagine there's this much pain in heaven."

"I saved you. Open your eyes, child," said a voice above her.

Natalie blinked a few times and focused on the figure standing over her. With her blurred vision, all she could see was a dark woman against a gorgeous blue sky. Not a cloud above her. She sat up to better see the person, and her breath caught.

The woman was a marvel. She was dark like Mansa Musa, but not like him at the same time. Her skin appeared more like a series of tiny jewels than anything else. Her black hair hung in long ropes adorned with jeweled beads. She wore a golden skirt to her ankles with a myriad of golden necklaces that covered her chest.

This creature radiated power and importance. She stood tall with the air of someone completely at ease with herself in the world. Without being told, Natalie just knew that this was the original goddess. The one the old gods turned immortal in the beginning ages of humanity.

"I... um... don't know how to address you, your highness. Is that right? I'm sorry. That can't be right," Natalie said.

"I am no more than your goddess. We are all the same. You are a part of me as much as I am a part of you. Flesh and flesh."

"What happened?"

"See for yourself."

Natalie looked around and tried not to scream when she took it in. She found herself in a strange place. To the left was the Mayan city of Copan. Well, what was left of it.

Bodies littered the ground—hundreds of them. Every reveler was sprawled out, unmoving. The blast spared no one. Just piles of painted bodies and feathered headdresses littered the ground.

The silence felt sickening as a quietened world surrounded them. It was not just the lack of songs and dancing. No parrots cawed in the trees. No insects buzzed in the wind. Nothing but the ghastly quiet of the recently dead. That breath the world drew in to mark the passing of so many souls.

To her right stood the original goddess in front of a place that looked very much like Africa. Not the Africa Mansa Musa had shown, or Hatshepsut for that matter. This was the Africa she had read about in books. Majestic savannahs with baobab trees and an oasis surrounded by water.

The contrast between the two places was stark, like standing in between Heaven and Hell.

"How did this happen?" Natalie asked, frozen in her personal limbo.

"Eighteen Rabbit killed his anchor child," the original goddess said with little emotion. "He believed if he did, the reign of the goddess would end. The grief would end."

"But it didn't. If it did, there'd be no me, no Nat, no other goddesses that lived after this."

"The power of the goddess cannot be destroyed. It is only transferred."

"But who?"

The original goddess pointed one long finger toward a small temple. Natalie recognized it as the place where she met the artist. The one who was sculpting the tragic story of Eighteen Rabbit's wife.

Copan had been host to a boisterous party mere minutes ago. Now, the only sign of life was the labored breathing coming from inside the temple. Natalie gasped as the artist woman limped out of the temple and collapsed onto the ground. She crawled slowly away from the epicenter of death, gasping as she did so.

"She… she survived?" Natalie asked.

"The next goddess."

"But there's no anchor child. How can she be the next one?"

"As I have said, it is impossible to destroy the goddess's power. In this case, Eighteen Rabbit's suicide forced power away from him. It settled inside the first living host it could find. This was the host."

Natalie stared at the artist, trying desperately to crawl away. She was the last survivor and needed help. Instinctively, Natalie made to help, but the goddess put one glistening arm up to stop her.

"She cannot see you now. There is no way to help her," she said.

"What happens to her?"

"She lives a full life. It takes almost twenty years for the goddess's power to manifest inside her body fully. Since the transfer was not direct, the anchor child did not emerge until much later. She takes that long to find the words of the Gods inside her mouth. During those years, the Mayan people suffered from plague and famine. A once-glorious civilization murdered by one suffering person. It was an apocalypse for their people."

"The suffering... it's... why I'm here. Felix said I had to follow the grief to find Nat. If that's true, then why are you here?"

"Your goddess is suffering," she said simply.

"Do you know where he is?"

The goddess regarded her. Those eyes of hers resembled golden marbles than human eyes. She smiled faintly, like she knew something terribly sad, but did not want to tell her. She gestured away from the Mayan catastrophe and toward her beautiful savannah.

"You may walk with me," she said simply.

In front of a baobab tree stood a structure Natalie had not seen before. It was an elaborate cage made from twisted roots. They wove together to create a perfect trap. She wondered if it was for some unique bird, given how much beauty laid in its design. Even though it was wood, the cage appeared just as strong as any metal.

Natalie moved closer when she saw something moving inside. No, it was not something. It was someone. There, sitting inside the root cage, was Nat.

Chapter Thirty Nine

Natalie nearly jumped out of her skin. She raced to the cage, wrapping her fingers around the wooden bars. Nat had his head in between his knees with his fingers digging into his scalp. He looked like a poor, pitiful version of himself. All dirty fingernails and oily hair.

She did not know why he was there, but she had to get him out.

"Nat! Oh, Nat, I found you. I gotta get you home. There's a storm comin'. Camille can't control it. It's comin' because you ain't there."

At first, he said nothing. His body merely rocked slightly back and forth. When Nat spoke, it came out raspy and raw.

"I'm hungry," he said in a soft voice.

"What?"

"I'm so hungry," he said as he raised his head. His hair was shaggy and longer than she remembered. It hung on his face, obscuring his eyes. "They never feed me here."

"They don't? Why? Why are you in a cage?"

"Please, I'm so hungry," he said.

Natalie suddenly remembered the chunk of bread in her pocket. The one Aurelia had given her before she left Rome. She dug inside her dress until she found it. Natalie held out the bread for Nat to take.

Everything happened in a sharp flash.

Nat reeled on her, his hair flipping back so she could fully see his wicked, terrifying eyes. He lunged at the bar with a feral shriek. Two clawed hands slashed at the bars as he tried to grab desperately at her outstretched arm.

Her hand still hovered over her pockets. Without thinking, Natalie grabbed the hairpins and stabbed them into Nat's arm. Much to her horror, it did nothing to stop him. Those claws slashed at her face, regardless of the blood oozing from his new wounds.

Luckily, the original goddess was quicker than anyone. With a gentle hand, she grabbed Natalie and pulled her out of reach. The bread dropped to the ground. Nat clawed and snarled at them both like a rabid dog. He reached through the cage for the bread, but the goddess kicked it away.

"Feed me! You heartless shrew. Feed me!"

Natalie stood, stunned. It took her a few minutes to realize what had happened. Nat tried to attack her, and the goddess saved her. Once she could process and think clearly, she finally spoke.

"That ain't Nat," she said numbly.

All the happiness and relief she felt at finding Nat melted away. Her good pals, fear and dread, came back in full force.

"This is a partial truth," said the original goddess. "This is Violence. Your goddess's manifestation of Violence. I am sure he told you about this creature."

"Yes, I know this creature," she said with a scowl.

Natalie stared at the beast in the cage. Now that she saw his face entirely, she wondered how she could have ever mistaken him for Nat. Violence's eyes were wild and bloodshot. He frothed at the mouth, snapping this way and that at nothing in the air. His body hung like a bony corpse underneath his baggy clothes.

"What's happened to him?" Natalie asked.

"We starve him here. It is the best way to weaken such a creature."

"Monsters! I call you all monsters!" Violence screamed.

"It seems... wrong," Natalie said, wincing at Violence's face.

"It is the only way," the goddess said simply, as though that were enough of an explanation.

"But what if I'm supposed to be here talkin' to him?" Natalie asked. "Felix says Nat is here somewhere in grief. I have to follow the grief. Ever since I started doin' that, the storm has left me alone."

"The storm is still there. Perhaps not as you follow the grief, but it is back in your time. It will destroy the world if you do not bring your goddess back."

"How come you can't find him in here? Why can no other goddess find him in here?" Natalie asked in exasperation.

The original goddess's face pinched in a pained expression. It looked odd on her beautiful face.

"I am not sure, and that makes me nervous. I know all things, yet I cannot see him. This book he created is unusual. The rules are unclear, but I have a theory."

"And that is?"

"It is because he is not dead. We are here at the end of our stories. Everyone in here has decided to die and passed on the power. Your goddess is not dead. Perhaps that is why we cannot see him."

"And the storm?" Natalie asked.

"The universe has always had a goddess. Our power is knitted inside the very fabric of time and space. The storm is the universe trying to fix itself. Your Nat has found a way to remove the power without killing it. If this is not rectified, there will be another apocalypse," the goddess said.

"Like what happened with Eighteen Rabbit?" Natalie asked in a quivering whisper.

"Worse. The power found a host. The universal balance was restored. If your Nat does not return, the world cannot right itself. Everything will crumble, including the other timelines."

"Good!" spat Violence as he raked his claws along the bars. "End your precious world. Finally, Nat is doing something worthwhile. When he came back, I told him where to go. Now, I hope he's trapped forever!"

Natalie noticed the goddess's back straightening. She turned toward Violence with an air of malice. Even though the goddess was not an enormous being, Natalie cringed under the weight of her power. She approached the cage with all the energy of a hungry lioness. Violence did not bat an eye.

"You have seen Nat?" the goddess asked.

"He came here. Drawn to me, I guess. Looking for Polly."

"And where did you send him?"

A crooked smile flashed across Violence's face. Normally, Natalie would tremble under such a glare, but she was getting mad. Not just mad, but enraged. He knew where Nat was, and he was toying with them.

"Somewhere he would never find her. Somewhere he would never leave," he said.

"Where is that?" the goddess asked.

"Why should I tell you?" he snapped.

"Because you'll die too," Natalie said. Her fists clenched at her sides. "You would rather keep us guessin' while the whole world gets destroyed? Eventually, the storm will rip this book apart. That means you die too!"

"Ah, but my dear child," he said with another crooked smile. "I'm dead already. As long as I'm locked away, I'm as good as dead. But if someone were to let me out…."

"Name your terms," the goddess said without hesitation.

"No!" Natalie shrieked. "You can't just let him out. Nat put him in there for a reason!"

"Silence, child. Your betters are talking," Violence said as he eyed the original goddess. "My terms are simple. Release me from this cage, and I'll tell you where I sent Nat. Odds are he's still there."

The goddess eyed him with no emotion on her face. For the life of her, Natalie could not tell what she was thinking. Whether she was for or against was a complete mystery.

"Good luck finding him without me," he said with a bit of shrug.

"Very well," the goddess said. "I will release you."

"No!"

She raised one golden hand and snapped her fingers. There was no debating. The root cage disintegrated into a circular mound of sawdust on the ground. No more barriers and no more bars. Violence was free.

CHAPTER FORTY

The sky above them darkened, turning a sickeningly green hue. All the oranges and purples of the land putrefied into the most diseased shades of blue and grey. Violence looked at the circle of dust around him and laughed maniacally. His twisted smile spread far too wide to be human.

He briefly turned his attention to the pins sticking out of his arm. It was as if he had only just remembered they were there. Two porcupine quills jabbed deeply into his flesh. Violence yanked them out swiftly, barely registering the blood seeping from the wound.

When he set his eyes on Natalie, he looked hungry. Not just for food. For more blood and pain and suffering. It was so disorienting to see a version of Nat that was this menacing. She moved her weight to the balls of her feet, readying herself to flee.

"How… how could you let him out?" Natalie asked the goddess.

She did not look in Natalie's direction. She never took her gaze away from Violence. Her stare was still that of the lioness, solid and waiting for her prey to twitch.

"Now, you will tell us where you sent Nat," she said evenly.

"Sure, why not," Violence said with a shrug. "There's no harm now that I'm out. I sent him to Nan. I saw where she went after she imprisoned me here. I knew if he went there, he'd never get out. He missed her so much, you see. Not to mention, Nan's little secret."

Violence made a show of fake shock on his face. His expression twisted into a menacing laugh that sounded like a demented giggle. It seemed to rumble deep into the ground, vibrate the soles of Natalie's feet, and reverberate into the surrounding air.

"Wait? What secret? What are you talkin' about?" Natalie asked.

"Oh, sweet child," Violence said, moving closer to her. "You have no idea. You think I'm a monster. I don't come close to your precious Nan."

Violence changed his body slowly. He hunched over, keeping the creepy smile on his face. His arms elongated, and his hands expanded with sharp nails. When he walked, Violence used his claws to tear at the Earth beneath him like a terrifying ape.

Before she knew what was happening, Violence was on top of her. Natalie fell to the ground to get away from his snapping teeth. He laughed maniacally as his eyes sunk into his face. When his smile pulled toward his ears, those white teeth of his sharpened to that of a wolf's.

"No! Get away from me!" Natalie screamed.

"I thought you were looking for Nat," he said in a voice that crackled in the air. "Here I am. This is about as close as you are gonna get!"

Natalie crab-walked backward as fast as possible, but Violence grabbed one of her legs and yanked her closer. She could smell his rancid breath as his mouth opened wider than any human should be able. Natalie covered her face and braced for an attack.

Suddenly, a hand closed around the back collar of her dress. With one smooth yank, Natalie was pulled backward and away from Violence's terrible jaws. She scrambled to her feet and saw the original goddess standing next to her. Her face revealed no emotion.

"Thank you for your honesty, Violence," the goddess said.

She snapped her fingers, throwing Violence backward. The cage roots grew back in a flash. They tore the ground, raising up and up over the ashes of the family before them. He was trapped again in mere seconds.

The land returned to the colors of life—all the warmth of the sun and the trees.

It happened so fast, and Violence did not have time to react until it was too late. He screamed and tore at the bars. The great beast's features dissolved, and he turned back into a starving, shriveled man.

"No! Liar! You are a liar!" he yelled at the goddess.

The original goddess was in his face in a second. Violence tripped over his feet, trying to move away from the bars. Natalie saw the first hint of fear in his eyes.

"You forget who owns this house. Who this book belongs to. You forget this is *my* house," she said with a thundering emphasis on every word. "I did not lie. I have stayed true to our arrangement. Your terms were to be released. You did not specify for how long."

"You know I meant forever!" he shouted, snarling at her.

"Then, you should have said what you meant. I released you for a measurement of time as per our deal. Now, remain still," the goddess said.

In a flash, she reached through the bars and plucked a dirty hair from Violence's head. The creature shrieked and clawed at her, but the goddess was too fast. She retracted her hand before Violence could fight back.

"Come now," the goddess said as she held a hand out to beckon Natalie. "We know your next location. Hopefully, it will be your last, and you will find your goddess."

Natalie followed without hesitation. Violence continued to yell and curse them, but she tuned it all out. She enjoyed the smug satisfaction of knowing Violence lost once again. There was no need to give him any more of her time.

The goddess led her to a small pond inside an oasis of palm trees. For such a small bit of water, Natalie thought it sure looked bluer than it ought. When she peered down to see how deep it was, she could not spot the bottom.

They both gazed into the pool, their faces reflecting up to them. Natalie had not seen her face since the women's tent in Africa. Back then, she appeared much changed. Now, the anchor child stared at a near stranger. Who was this girl, she thought. Natalie knew it was impossible, but she could have sworn she had aged.

Anchor children did not grow up, nor did they change. That was the luxury of the goddess. They could turn themselves into anything but not the anchors. They were forever children, forever immovable.

Yet, here she was. An anchor who moved. One who adventured. One who changed. Someone who fought pirates, traversed deserts, faced sphinxes, battled storms, and survived a Mayan sacrifice. The girl in the pond appeared braver and more capable than Natalie. At least, the way Natalie had been before all of this.

When the goddess dropped the hair into the water, their reflections skewed. Ripples erased their features, and a scene took its place. It was a farm. No, not a farm, Natalie realized. It was a plantation.

There was a dirt road cutting through acres and acres of cotton plants, all in neat rows. The sky was cloudless, with a blistering sun beating down on the backs of the slaves bent over in the fields. A lavish manor house stood tall in the distance, painted all white with red bricks. A fine horse and carriage trotted its way up the road toward the manor house.

"That's where Nan is?" Natalie asked.

"It is."

"And that is where Nat is?"

"It is a possibility," the goddess said. "I am sure you would have found your way here, eventually. Violence just provided the door."

"What do you mean?"

"Grief. It brought you to me. Nan would logically be the next."

"But… you are the original goddess. You reigned the longest."

"In every life, there is grief. Everyone has loss. Some tolerate it better than others. I did for the first few centuries. When you bury your great-great-grandchild, it is too much to bear. To be the goddess is to invite grief. Nan was the smartest of us all. She passed on the power before her burden left her twice."

"What does that mean?"

"You will see," she said cryptically. She pointed to Natalie and gestured to the pool of water. "Jump inside, and it will take you there."

"Wait. I hafta ask you somethin' first."

"Go ahead," the goddess said patiently.

"How did you overcome it? The grief, I mean. If I find Nat, I hafta convince him to come home with me. Home to where Polly's grave is. I don't know if he can stand it. How can he move forward?"

"This is a good question. The best I have heard in a millennium. And one that has no good answer. My way was to focus on my children. When I decided to die, I gave the power to my son. I taught him the ways of the goddess magic, and I was happy when I passed on. Peace is the answer to grief."

"How can anyone find peace with so much loss?"

"The key is to bear it with him. No person can do it alone."

"I see what you are sayin'. I'm gonna try real hard to find Nat's peace."

"Now go. There is not much time. In your world, the storm is raging, and Camille will not be able to hold it for much longer."

Natalie squeezed the goddess's hand. It felt warm and solid beneath her small, fleshy one. Something about the sturdiness of it gave Natalie a touch more courage. The courage Mansa Musa seemed sure she owned. She did not want to let them down.

Natalie released the goddess and leaped feet first into the pond.

CHAPTER FORTY ONE

Her rump hit the dusty road first. The shock went up to her sit bones, into her spine, and through her limbs. She raised her hand to shield her eyes from the oppressive sun. It seemed she had been cursed with a harsh sun this entire journey.

As she stood, she noted the plantation in the far distance. It was the same one from the vision in the pond. Opulent and frightening at the same time. Natalie read her history books. She knew what it was, and she knew the horrors underneath the beauty.

The rattling of wheels and hooves sounded behind her. She turned around to see a distinguished-looking carriage pulled by a single horse. The beast was a quarter horse, large and white. It reared slightly as the driver pulled on its reins to stop.

She took a moment to imagine what a sight she must be—a tousled white girl wearing a paint-splattered Roman dress standing in the middle of a Southern plantation road. There were probably still some Mayan feathers stuck to her back. Natalie rotated the snake bracelet anxiously as she waited for whatever was to come next.

The driver was relatively small, barely larger than herself. Of course, it was hard to tell from where she stood. She was so much lower to the ground. Looking at something in the sun made it hard to distinguish features. One thing was for sure. He was clothed in all black, with very little skin showing to the world.

The carriage was black, like the driver's uniform, with gigantic wheels. Its cabin opened to the elements save for a cover on top for shade. Inside, a distinguished-looking man beckoned to her.

He wore tan trousers and a jacket. His waistcoat was ivory with a hat to match. As Natalie approached, she noticed an expensive watch on a chain in his front pocket.

"Come in. Join me. There is no need for you to walk the rest of the way."

He spoke jovially, but with an odd accent. Certainly not from the South. Perhaps not even from America. Yet, there was something familiar about it. Something in him that eased her distrust.

Natalie stepped into the carriage and sat on the opposite seat facing the man. The upholstery felt hot under her rump, and she was thankful for the long dress Aurelia had given her. Had her legs not been covered, she would have surely left some skin wherever the seat touched her body.

"You have traveled far since last I saw you," he said with a smile.

The gentleman knocked three times on the roof of the carriage. The driver cracked the whip, and the horse began its journey again.

Natalie stared at him. He was familiar, though she could not place his face. He was white with grey eyes and white hair cut short beneath his hat. His features revealed nothing in the way of identity.

She struggled to remember if perhaps he was someone she knew from the real world. A visitor to Tanglewood, perhaps. No, she thought. That made no sense. Nineteen forty was far away from the here and now. Perhaps even a hundred years or more.

"You know me?"

"Of course! My dear, little friend. I truly hoped we would find one another again. I just did not realize it would take so long. You have not aged a day. I suppose that is to be expected."

Natalie gaped at the man for a hard minute before the pieces fell into place. His smile was the key. She just knew it. Or maybe it was the freckles. She had met only one other person with freckles like that. Except on this white skin, the freckles were dark.

Natalie gasped and clasped both hands over her mouth.

"Yes, it is me," Claude said with a slight bow.

"But how?" Natalie said, struggling to find her breath.

"Perhaps this will help."

Claude snapped his fingers and turned back into the man she remembered. His dark face was covered in beige freckles. His hair was knotted and braided with colorful beads. That was how she remembered him. She could almost smell the sea air in that moment. He snapped his fingers one more time, and again, he looked like the affluent white man in the carriage.

"I have discovered living as a black man in America is not the best choice if I want to live as a free person. Even pirates have their rules about such things. This is just barbarism."

"But… how? How are you the goddess?"

"Ching Shih transferred it to me when she had had enough. I took it willingly because I wanted to travel to this new world to seek my fortune. I did not know… I mean, she did not tell me…."

"Tell you what?"

"How incredibly *hard* it is. I had no idea what this would entail. I saw Ching Shih use her gifts and thought what a blessing it was, but it is not. Oh Natalie, how wrong I was. I wanted affluence and power, and I thought that would be easier than the battles and the bloodshed."

"Was it easier?"

"No. I miss the old days where things were simple. Attack that vessel. Kill those men. Loot that cargo. Ching Shih made it look so easy."

"She was in pain," Natalie offered.

"I should have stayed a pirate and retired on an island. I should have turned down her offer. Living forever with the burden of immortality is so difficult. Words cannot describe it. And the loss. Oh, the terrible loss."

"I got that feelin' from some of the others," Natalie said as she thought about Eighteen Rabbit and his anchor child.

"It is horrible. I cannot take it. It has only been a few decades, but I cannot take this anymore."

"Wait. This is when you give the power to someone else? You are the one who gives it to Nan?"

"I have to be rid of it, you see. You understand that, dear Natalie. You know first hand what this does to a person. I thought that if I give it to a brother…."

Claude looked past her, just over her head. Natalie turned to follow his gaze. There, on the side of the road, stood a young man in ratty clothes. The shirt just barely hung on his shoulders where one sleeve had been torn away. He was a slave who looked about eighteen, maybe twenty, at the oldest. He hefted a long burlap sack of cotton over one shoulder.

A nervousness wriggled in Natalie's stomach when she spotted the scars on his back. Several long strips of puckered, discolored skin poked out from the holes in his shirt. Surely this was not Nan, she thought. This was not the right person.

Another rap rap rap of Claude's cane signaled the driver to stop. The carriage creaked to a halt, but the slave did not turn around. He continued on his path without so much as an upward glance. It was almost as if he had been conditioned to do just that. Ignore all and do your work.

"You there!" Claude shouted as he leaped from the carriage. "Stop, please. I must speak with you."

The slave dropped his burden and turned to face Claude. Natalie searched his face but could not recognize him. Not in the least. Was this Nan? Could this possibly be her? The boy before the goddess powers.

Natalie hopped out of the carriage and chased after Claude. The slave turned his attention to the white girl in the strange dress and then back to Claude. He appeared entirely confused.

"I would like to shake your hand," Claude said.

"My hand?" the slave said.

Natalie watched Claude remove one ivory glove. She could see the painted brush strokes underneath the sleeves. The immortal paint needed to transfer the power of the goddess.

"Claude! What are you doin'? He's not Nan. Stop!" she yelled.

Natalie ran toward them as fast as she could. She could not let him do this. It was the wrong person. If he never created Nan, then she would not exist. Nat would never be the goddess. This was all wrong.

It was her fault. She went inside the book and changed everything. Now, Claude was creating the wrong goddess. What would she do if that happened?

The man held out his hand, and Claude took it. As soon as he did, a shock wave erupted from between them. Claude smiled and collapsed to the ground. He fell into some nearby grass and let the Earth take him in. Within seconds, there was only a mound of soil with wildflowers where a goddess once laid.

She was too late. It was done—no way to take it back.

CHAPTER FORTY TWO

Much to Natalie's surprise, the anchor child who appeared next to the slave was familiar. It was true they never met in person, but she knew Jacob from Nat's memories. Jacob was Nan's anchor child, but now he stood next to someone she did not know.

The slave backed away with a face full of terror. He looked down at his hands to see them covered in Claude's immortal paint. Colors started radiating up and down his arms, lighting up his bones from within.

He gaped at her, pleading for help with his eyes, but she had none to give him. No words escaped her mouth. What did she know about this?

The colors finally settled. His bare arms looked like they were painted all over, but in his skin tones now. Browns, umbers, purples. He took in his hands and balled them into fists. Fear turned into calm, which shifted into stiff determination.

Natalie reached out one hand, wanting to get a better look. If this were Nan, surely she could tell from looking into his eyes. However, he shot her a stranger's glare and turned away.

He set his focus down the road. The plantation manor house was in his sights.

"Wait," Jacob tried to say.

His voice came out in a harsh whisper. Natalie remembered what that was like in the real world. It took her forever just to figure out how to talk to Nat. Everyone else was out of the question.

"You can tell me," she said to Jacob. "I'm an anchor child too."

"What?"

Jacob reached for his goddess as he receded down the road. As he did, he jerked at his feet. They were already rooted to the ground and refused to budge. The poor boy gaped at her with a wild expression as he tugged on his pants legs.

"Why can't I move?" he whispered in a panic.

"It's okay. That's just how it is now. You get used to it. I promise."

"No! No, you have to stop him!" he said louder.

"What do you mean?"

"Stop him! Stop him! Hurry before he does it!"

"Does what?"

"He's gonna kill them all!"

Natalie swung her body around. She spotted him down the road. His pace was faster than should be possible, but he was the goddess now. Just about anything was possible. Natalie judged how far away she was from him versus how far away he was to the house. She would have to run hard to catch him before he got there.

She took off after the new goddess. Her bony legs pumped hard, kicking her skirt up this way and that. She really, *really* wished she was wearing pants at that moment. He had such a wide lead on her already.

Natalie passed a carriage listing slowly to the right in front of her. She had to dodge it as the horse moseyed to the side of the road to nibble some clover. It did not occur to her until she passed it that it was Claude's carriage. Now that his anchor child was gone, there was no longer a driver.

As the new goddess stomped toward the house, a storm grew above him. He reached his considerable arms to each side of his body, building the thunderhead as though he were sculpting it from clay. Natalie had to will herself to keep moving. It reminded her of the storm that had been chasing her. Running toward such a thing went against everything her body wanted.

The air crackled electric, and the sun disappeared behind a curtain of dark clouds. Shades of green swirled beneath the lowest layer of the storm. Flashes of lightning sparked inside the thunderhead, causing it to glow like a hideous firefly. When the rain fell, it was hard and steady.

"No! Stop!" Natalie screamed.

The storm swallowed her voice whole so no one would hear it. In fact, no one heard anything at all over the howl of the wind and the rolling explosion of thunder. Men and women ran from the fields, grabbed each other, and ducked into ramshackle houses.

"Please don't!"

He was nearly to the manor house, but there was no need for him to get any closer. The goddess reached his arms into the air like he was reaching into the thunderhead itself. He wrenched them apart, breaking the storm as he did so. A wide hole formed in the center, right over the house.

With a feral scream of pain and torment, the slave unleashed Hell straight down. A blast of wind and lightning and rain shot straight through the house. It sounded like someone fired the largest cannon in the world.

The force of the blast knocked Natalie off her feet. She skidded onto her right side and rolled into a tall patch of monkey grass. When the hail fell, the only thing she could do was curl into a ball to protect the most vulnerable parts of her body.

Natalie laid there, shivering under the sudden blast of freezing wind. Of all the terrifying places she had been to in this book, she would have never thought Nan's story would be the most dangerous.

Just as quickly as the storm came, it dissipated. The hail and rain stopped falling, the wind calmed, and the sun evaporated what remained of the dispersing clouds.

Natalie unraveled from her self-made ball to see the world, much as it had been before. There were two significant differences. Chunks of ice littered across the ground, and there was no longer a manor house.

She scrambled to her feet and made her way past the disoriented people to where the mansion had stood mere minutes ago. It was now a mass of rubble. Splinters of wood jabbed into the air, stone and brick crumbled into piles of dust, and shattered glass sparkled in the newly found sunshine.

The slave was there too. He stood heaving at the edge of the site, taking in his handiwork. His breaths drew in and out, ragged and deep. When Natalie sidled up next to him, she got a better view of the center of where the house stood. There was just a black hole, like someone burned straight through the house with all the power of the sun.

"It's done," he said out loud between gasps. Natalie was not sure if he was talking to her or himself. "It's finally over."

Chapter Forty Three

They stood in the silence together, taking in the carnage of his blast of raw energy. The entire plantation seemed to take a collective breath. It was the second before a fall. That moment when you just feel your stomach drop. It only lasted a second because eventually, as it always does, the screaming began.

People ran this way and that, calling out for their loved ones. They were mostly the plantation's slaves, but a few white people stumbled out of an oversized barn in a dazed trance. Women bundled their children together, pressing them to their bosoms. Men gathered workers from the outskirts of the fields, counting their numbers.

The new goddess stood on the edge of the wreckage, seemingly unable to see or hear any of them. He stared as vacant as a ghost. Natalie reached a hand out, desperately wanting to help him. She did not know how.

"Jacob! Jacob!"

He perked up at the sound of his name in time to see a middle-aged woman making her way through the ice toward them. She had longs skirts gathered in each hand as she ran. At long last, he released his fists, and his face softened.

"Mama?"

"Jacob, my baby. What happened?"

"It's over, Mama. It's done. I made them all go away. They ain't gonna hurt us no more."

His mother stared right past Natalie and into the chaos that used to be the plantation manor house. Her mouth dropped, and the tiniest of shrieks emanated from inside her throat. It was a terrible, building, choking sound. When it got too loud for her to bear, she balled up her apron and covered her face with it.

"Mama, why are you cryin'? I did it. Can't you see that? We are free. They ain't never gonna beat us or nothin' ever again," he said.

He tried to put his hands on her shoulders, but they began shaking uncontrollably with her sobs. His mother threw his hands off her and tried to go out into the rubble. She struggled to move a heavy beam of wood in the way, and he lifted it with ease.

"What are you doin'? Mama, stop this. You'll get hurt."

"She was in here! She's *still* in here!"

"Who?"

"Camille!" she screamed, and began sobbing anew.

The look of horror stretched across his face as though it were made of putty. His mother collapsed to the ground, grabbing fistfuls of dirt in her hands and wailing. All Natalie could do was hold her hands over her mouth and stand out of the way. She was afraid to make a sound.

"No. No, that can't be right. Camille said she felt poorly this mornin'," he said numbly.

"When you ever heard the master let any of us stay sick and bed?" she snapped back at him. "How did this happen? How did you make this happen?"

"I don't rightly know. This stranger came and gave me his power."

"The devil!" she cried as she pushed her body away from him. "The devil came and gave it to you, and now, you're one yourself. A demon sent to take away my only baby girl!"

"No, Mama. I ain't a devil. I just... just wanted us to be free. We ain't never gonna have that if they're alive. They deserved it," he said.

"But Camille didn't!" she wailed.

He reached down to take her in his arms and comfort her, but she threw his hands off. She gathered her skirts and backed away from Jacob like he was a feral beast. Like perhaps he would destroy her next, the way he had the house.

"Mama, what you doin'?"

"Stay back, devil!" she screamed as she fished a rosary from beneath her dress.

"Mama, no. Please, don't do this. I'm not a devil. I... I made a mistake."

Natalie could hear the raw heartache in his voice. The broken way his words came out sounded just as jagged and sharp as the glass all around them. She wished she could help him, but she did not know what to say.

"Ma'am," Natalie started. The woman startled as she took in her presence. It was as though she had not seen the anchor child until that moment. "He's not a devil. I can tell you that. He's a goddess now. He was just tryin' to set you free."

"Another… another one! You both are here to destroy us all," she said as she faced the mass of slaves gathering around them. "Run! All of you! Run for your lives. My son will kill us all the way he murdered his sister!"

The screaming erupted from within the crowd. The women began the call for fear. Next were the wails of children, followed by the shouting of men. The mob did what mobs always did. They panicked.

Families grabbed for one another, racing to their homes and away from Natalie and Jacob. Single men commandeered horses and high-tailed it away from the plantation as fast they were able. Children wept as their parents loaded them into wagons.

The new goddess watched it all with an O of shock on his face. When his mother quickened her speed to get away from him, he raised his hands to stop her. She flinched as though expecting a blow.

"I ain't gonna hurt you, Mama. Please don't go. Don't leave me," he pleaded.

"You stay away, demon. Stay away!"

She turned and ran as fast as she could under all those skirts of hers. Jacob dropped his hands to his side in defeat. His shoulders slumped. Natalie reached out to take his hand, but he fell to his knees before she could. He took in a heaving breath and let out a wail that felt like it could crack the universe in two.

Natalie threw arms over her ears and shut her eyes. It was all pain and fire and tears. So much despair it sounded animalistic. The few slaves that were nearby raced to take cover lest another storm accompany his wails.

His scream petered out as his breath gave up. The potent magic behind it dissipated into the atmosphere. Natalie opened her eyes to see a new person on the ground next to her. Not the strapping young man who was there earlier.

An old woman crouched there on her hands and knees. Her body heaved up and down with the waning intensity of her magic. Her hands and arms had sagging skin, and there were wrinkles on the side of her face. Grey and white hair twisted around what little black hair was left of her head. All of it cascaded over her shoulders in a frizzy mass.

This person was no longer the slave, Jacob. He was a woman, one who resembled a much aged version of his mother. Natalie recognized the poor, weeping woman in front of her. She was Nan.

CHAPTER FORTY FOUR

The old goddess reached into the debris in front of her. She swept away some brick and glass with one arthritic hand. With the other, she pulled out a picture. The gilded frame was still intact, even if the glass had shattered. She pulled the photograph from the frame and sat back on her knees.

"I never meant to do this," she said in a soft voice.

Natalie closed the gap between them and sat next to Nan. She gazed over her wrist and focused on the picture.

It was a portrait of a family. Most of them were white, so Natalie reckoned they were the slave owners who lived in the mansion. There were two parents who were elegantly dressed. An elderly gentleman and lady stood to the right of them. To the left were five children, running from ages five to seventeen.

It was not until Natalie honed in on the other person in the photo that she realized why Nan was gazing at it with such intensity. There was a slave dressed in an all-white servant's uniform. She stood at the end of the line of children and was the only one who smiled even slightly. It was because of the baby she held on her hip, which was tugging on her hair. She gazed down at the child with all the love of a mother.

This woman was the spitting image of Camille. No, not just that. It *was* Camille.

"I don't understand," Natalie said.

"I never meant to hurt her. Not her. I wanted to hurt the family, especially the master. The whippin's and the humiliation. I wanted all of us to be free. I knew killin' him would make that happen."

"But she was inside," Natalie added.

Nan nodded. Tears dropped from her eyes and splattered on the picture.

"I didn't think it through. I didn't want to hurt the kids. They never done anything bad to me. The eldest girl taught some of us to read. And I didn't think about Camille working in the house. I didn't think about the cook or cleaners neither. If only I stopped to think. But I was so angry. All I could see was my revenge."

Natalie dared to reach across the great divide between them. She took Nan's wrinkled hand in hers and squeezed. The goddess pressed Natalie's tiny hand against her face. She could feel the heat radiating from Nan's skin, hotter than the setting sun.

"How is it possible? How'd Camille come back? You told Nat she came on the wind."

"And she did. When that baby arrived, I was so happy. She floated into my life from the sky itself. I named her after my sister but had no idea it was her. You see, my Camille was older than me. I never knew what she looked like as a baby. It weren't until she was nearly ten that I started seein' the resemblance."

"But how can that be? I thought goddesses couldn't bring people back from the dead."

"As far as I know, we can't. The best I can figure has to do with the storm. This storm, to be exact. I called upon the force of God to smite these people. When it was over, my longing and remorse for my sister knit her soul into the very clouds above me. Over time, she was reborn. The Hindus call it reincarnation. I don't rightly know if this counts as that, but it's the only thing that makes sense."

"So you did bring her back from the dead?"

"Not exactly. The Camille you know, is a different person. She remembers nothin' about this life. Part of her spirit is made from the clouds."

Natalie gazed down at the picture of the woman smiling at the baby. It was eerie. That face was Camille's. The woman who hugged her and took care of her. The matriarch of the school back home. Thinking her soul had lived such a different life before was quite the mind twister.

"Tell me, please, is she happy? My Camille. Is she content with her life and her school? She always adored children," Nan said.

Reality snapped Natalie back from this little side adventure she found herself on. She was here for a reason. She had a mission. The fate of the world was in her hands.

"She's not alright. Not right now. Nan, I need to know if'n you've seen Nat. Did he come here?"

"Nat? Well, yes, he did. A bit ago."

"Is he still here?" Natalie asked.

"No. He moved on to his timeline."

"Damn!"

"Why? What's happenin', child?" Nan asked.

Her face turned from sorrow to apprehension. When she saw the urgency in Natalie's eyes, it turned to great concern.

"He left to find Polly. We think he's in his timeline tryin' to bring her home."

"What happened to Polly?"

"She... died of a fever. Nat can't bring her back, so he came here to find her. Ever since he left, this terrible storm's been comin' after us. Not even Camille can stop it."

Nan's lips formed into a tight line. She gazed down at their intertwined hands lovingly for a few long breaths.

"We ain't got much time," Natalie said in earnest.

"No, I 'spose you don't."

"Nan, do you know where he is?"

"He ain't here," she said as she met Natalie's eyes again. "But I know where he is. At least, I can take you where he was."

"How do you know he'll be there?"

"Because it's where I left him."

CHAPTER FORTY FIVE

There was no telling where the goddesses got the whole snapping fingers thing. With all the power in their body, they would not have to make any movement at all. Yet, most of them insisted on snapping their fingers to make the world bend to their will.

When Nan snapped her fingers, they were transported to the dusty streets of downtown Tanglewood. The plantation and the wreckage of the manor house disappeared from view, even if it stayed glued in their memories.

Natalie whipped her head around, taking everything in. She had never physically been to Tanglewood. Being an anchor child made any sort of travel difficult, but she recognized it from Nat's memories. The buildings stood as they always did. The streets were made of packed dirt and gravel laid out before them in a grid. The Texas sun sat high in the sky.

It was eerily quiet. At first, Natalie could not put her finger on why, but then, it came to her. There were no people. Not one soul milled about in the General Store or walked across the thoroughfare. No horses, no dogs, no children. A ghost town.

"What are we doing here?" Natalie asked.

"This is where I left him," Nan whispered. "He was having a hard time finding his history. Since our timelines overlapped, I was able to bring him here. I thought I was helpin' him."

"But where is he?"

Nan pointed a gloved finger down the street. She was not sure when the old goddess had found a set of gloves, but there they were. Natalie followed her, pointing until she saw a person in the distance. It was hard to make out details in the sun's glare, but it was definitely a man. He sat on the ground, slumped against a post.

"That's him?"

"Yes. I'm afraid so," Nan said.

"Why is he here? And where is everybody?"

"I wish I has answers for you, child. I thought bringin' him here was a good thing. Now, I'm not so sure."

"Well, we better go get him. Hopefully, the farm ain't gone by now."

Natalie took Nan's hand and marched over to where Nat sat in the street. Her gloves were made of green satin, smooth and elegant for a dusty town in Texas. The material felt hot wrapped around her hand.

Natalie jerked backward when Nan did not move. It was like when a dog runs to the end of its leash. Nan stared at Nat in the distance with eyes that were filling with water. Her lower lip trembled. Natalie released her hand.

"What's wrong? Ain't you comin'?"

"I think this is a better job for you, child," Nan said.

"What? Why?"

"He won't want to see me."

"What are you talkin' about? You are Nan. Other than Camille, there's nobody in the world he respects more than you," Natalie said in an exacerbated tone.

"He… saw. He saw what I done. Just like you did. I don't reckon he wants to talk to me. Not right now, in any case. I'm worried that if I try to talk to him, he won't listen. I'm afraid I'd just make it worse."

"That's ridiculous."

"You didn't see his face."

"Maybe, but…"

"He will listen to you," Nan said, cutting her off. She knelt down to Natalie's height so she could look her straight in the face. "There is only one person on Earth who can reach that boy now, and that's you."

"But I don't know what to do. What do I say?"

"You'll figure that out. I have complete confidence in you," Nan said with a pat and a smile.

"But Nan… he will forgive you."

"I do hope so, and knowing our Nat, I think you're right. But I'm not the person he should see right now. He needs a rock. He needs an anchor. He needs you."

Natalie stood a tad straighter as she gazed over her shoulder at the pitiful figure in the street. She sincerely wished she had Nan's certainty, but if there was anything Natalie learned through all of this, it was that she was far more capable than she gave herself credit.

"Is this farewell?" Natalie asked.

"It's farewell… for now."

"It just feels like a regular farewell."

"If this adventure's taught you anythin', I reckon it showed you that there is no farewell forever. It just doesn't exist. Now, go. Galahad needs you."

Natalie nodded as Nan stood at her full height. Her billowy skirts and shawls started flapping in a newfound breeze. She held one green hand up. The satin was so smooth it made Nan look like she had dipped her arms in vinyl paint. When she snapped her fingers, the air sparked. A single flash and the great goddess was gone.

CHAPTER FORTY SIX

There was nothing left to do and nowhere left to go. Of all the goddesses and friends she had encountered on this crazy crusade, no one was left to help her. Not one. She was all alone, and she had to be enough. Oh God, she thought. What if she would not be enough?

Natalie crossed the dusty street and approached Nat. Everything here seemed to sit still and listen for what was next. She felt a breeze but heard no rustling in the trees. It was summer in Texas, yet no insects buzzed around her ears. She wondered if every living thing was gone from this timeline—all but the two of them.

Nat barely registered her presence. He hung his head loosely downward, sun-streaked hair hanging around his face. As Natalie got closer, she noticed a large chain wrapped around his waist, tying him to the wooden post. Above him was a sign that read "Thou Shalt Not Suffer a Witch."

Natalie knew that location from Nat's memories. She recognized that sign. It was the place where Nat first met Polly. The place where her zealot father left her, thinking she was a witch. Coincidentally, Polly ended up becoming a witch because he abandoned her. Camille took her in when she found the two of them here.

He heaved a deep sigh when her shadow blocked out the sun. With one hand over his eyes, he raised his face to meet hers. His eyes were bloodshot, lost in their own puddles of sorrow. The hair on his chin and jawline came in scraggly and rough.

A deep, unsettled part of her soul felt relief when she recognized her Nat. He was ragged and tired, but it was him. Not Violence. Not a corruption. Just Nat.

It was strange to see him that way, but not as strange as the look he gave her. She assumed he would be shocked or concerned, but he did not seem the least bit surprised to see her. His weary eyes drooped under her gaze.

"I figured it was you," he said in a strained voice.

"I came to bring you home. You can't stay here," she said gently.

"Here is where I found her. Did you know that? Well, of course, you knew because I knew it, but it ain't the same. I met Polly right here. This spot. I just happened upon this poor girl who was chained to a post all because her small-minded father willed it so. She was braver than... than I ever was."

Natalie stepped around him and sat down by his side. She leaned against the adjacent post, much like he had done when he first met Polly. This way, he could talk to her without the sun in his eyes. This way, they could be equals in memories.

"Why ain't she here?"

"I don't know," he said, with the beginnings of a sob in his throat. "I've looked everywhere. There's no Polly. No Camille. No Crow. The only person was Nan, and I only saw her because she brought me from her timeline. She remembered this place."

Nan's name fell between them like a lead pipe. After what Natalie had seen, it was best to leave that topic on the ground where it landed. Things were too complicated to hash that one out, and they had little time.

"If there's one thing I worked out on this journey of mine, it's that our bein' here changes things. Hatshepsut showed me all the branches on the timeline from where I landed. All the bits of history that wiggled around just by talkin' to people or bein' where I never was."

She thought about her journey and the changes. Not just branching lines. There were also circles, loops in time she created. Natalie fingered the snake bracelet around her wrist.

Nat took her in fully for the first time and noticed her strange dress. He examined her face and inspected her feet. When he poked one finger under her shoe, she lifted it obligingly.

"No roots in here," she said, answering his unspoken question.

"You seem so different."

"I've been on quite a ride lookin' for you. I don't reckon I'm the same."

"But... you saw people. There were the other goddesses. All had people in their histories?"

"Yes. All of them."

"Then why don't I?"

"I don't rightly know. Maybe somethin' about you bein' here as the goddess when you never was before," she offered. "I don't rightly know. In fact, no one I met seems to know for sure. But listen, you hafta come home. Everybody needs you there. You've been away too long."

"What are you talking about? It's only been a few days."

"No, Nat. It's been weeks."

"Weeks? No. That's impossible," he said.

"At least, it was weeks when I jumped inside. Who knows how long I've been in here."

"You don't understand. I can't come back. Not until I find my wife. She's not here, but she has to be somewhere. Somewhere in the pages. I won't go home until I find Polly and bring her back home."

"But Nat, if'n this is your timeline, Polly ought to be here. If she ain't, then maybe that's your answer. She's not meant to come home with you. There is no bringin' her back."

"Well, if that's the case, I'm not goin' home at all. I can't face the farmhouse. I can't sleep mere yards away from her grave. I can't look at…"

His eyes welled with tears, and his face screwed into a pinched expression as he tried to hold back the sob. His efforts did nothing. It came in a blast of emotion that made his shoulders jerk. He covered his face with his hands and let the tears flow. Natalie put a hand on his back and gave him the silence he needed to compose himself.

If there is one thing that can be said about Texas landscapes, it is this. You can see the horizon for miles and miles in every direction. It makes for the most beautiful sunsets.

At that moment, the sun was lowering itself and preparing for dusk, but Natalie stared at something else in the distance. Something she knew. Something ominous. Something that had been following her.

It was back. That tremendous and powerful building of clouds and power. Not any old storm. Not Nan's storm, either. No, this was the one that chased her through history. She only shook it when she followed the path of grief, but here it was again, threatening in the distance.

Natalie's gut told her what that meant. Somewhere deep inside, she knew. This was the same storm that raged against the universe, and it was almost upon them. They had little time left.

"That's new," Nat said as he followed her gaze to the storm on the horizon.

"It's comin' for us, Nat. It's comin' for the farmhouse. For Tanglewood. For all of the world. You hafta come back home."

"I don't understand. Can't Camille handle it? Just until I figure this out."

"It's too much for her. The goddesses here told me about the way it works. The universe has always had the goddess's power in it. If there is no goddess, a terrible catastrophe will happen. I saw it with Eighteen Rabbit. His people had an apocalypse for years."

"You're sayin' that's a storm headin' straight for the farmhouse, all because I'm not there?" he said, pointing to the thunderhead in the distance. "It can't be. I've only been gone a few days."

It was growing in intensity and size. Flashes of lightning lit up the inside of the anvil-shaped cloud formation. A deep tremor vibrated the ground when the first roll of thunder sounded.

Natalie was running out of time.

"Yes. You hafta go back with me!"

"I… can't. Camille can handle it, or Mother Alice or any of the other witches. You don't need me. What can I do?"

"Nat, please!"

"Me bein' there can't be nearly as important as you say."

"The original goddess told me herself. Nat, there's not much time!"

"I can't go back there!" he screamed.

The sound split the air around them, causing a deafening silence. For a brief second, the world went quiet. Even the storm stopped swirling for a long pause. It reminded Natalie of being on Ching Shih's ship when she snapped her fingers, making the sound disappear and freezing everyone. Yet again, Natalie feared she could not breathe if she tried.

It came back in a whoosh. The storm redoubled its efforts, filling the space between them with a chest-thudding *boom boom boom*! The ground shook as a funnel cloud descended from the sky and kissed the awaiting ground.

Natalie put her hand on Nat's hand. She loosened his clenched fist and interlaced her fingers with his. She grabbed at his face, trying to get him to look at her. He refused, hanging his head in defeat.

She remembered what the original goddess said. Nat could not bear this alone. He needed her to grieve with him.

"Why can't you come home?" she asked.

Natalie used all the calm she could muster. The storm frazzled her nerves, and she fidgeted internally. She wanted to jump up and scream in his face. He had to get up. He had to save them, but her gut told her yelling would not help.

"I can't live without her, Natalie. Every time I think about goin' back, it's like I'm givin' up on her. It's like I've decided that I'm fine with her bein' dead. How can I live like that?"

"We all lose people. I lost her too."

"I know, but I just can't bear it. I don't know how to move forward."

"You have us. Me, Camille, Vivian. We can help you bear it."

"But I can't… I can't possibly…"

"Nat, your daughter needs you. Faith needs you. You can't stay here and leave her all alone. Polly wouldn't want that."

He lowered his head and wept again. Natalie was torn. She wanted to give Nat all the time he needed to find his way home, but the clock was ticking. He seemed unphased by the tornado building power on the horizon.

This was not her Nat. Not the one she knew. Her Nat was brave and loving. There was no way he would sit here and do nothing. The creature before her looked broken, much like Eighteen Rabbit and Ching Shih. Like Nan and Claude. Grief had replaced pieces of him and twisted it into misery—some of the most essential pieces.

"That's why I can't go home. She looks… so much like Polly. How can I raise her up knowin' I'm the reason her mother is dead. She will hate me forever. How can I face my little girl knowing I failed her so completely?"

"You didn't kill Polly. The fever did."

"But I couldn't stop it. I couldn't find her here to bring her back. I'm the all-powerful goddess, and I couldn't keep my wife alive."

Another *boom boom boom* of thunder rolled across the prairie. This one shook Natalie down to her guts. She leaped in the air out of shock and yelped in pain. Nat appeared unphased, looking up at her as though none of this was concerning at all.

Then it hit her. Nat wanted to die. He welcomed the storm the way Eighteen Rabbit welcomed the release of the sacrifice. Nat wanted to join Polly. With a swift decision change, Natalie hauled back her hand and slapped him across the face. He grabbed his cheek and stared up at her in shock.

"Snap out of it! You are leavin' with me right now. If the storm is this close here, our family ain't got much time!"

"Natalie!"

She got in his face and stared him down.

"I'm sorry Polly died, but we have to go now! Nat, look into my eyes. Hear me," she called over the building wind as she took his face in her hands. "We are goin' to die if you don't snap out of it—all of us. Your *daughter* is goin' to die! Faith won't just lose her mother and father. She will lose her life if'n you don't stand up and save her!"

A fog seemed to lift from Nat's vision. His eyes had been cloaked in a dark haze, but now that curtain drew back. With the thought of Faith dying, the world righted itself.

He took Natalie's hands and peered up at her with the first clear expression she had seen since Polly's funeral. She wondered if he had fully understood her before or if it was just snippets of words that filtered in through the cloud of this trance of his.

She pictured Eighteen Rabbit hauling his screaming anchor child to the top of a pyramid. His face was equally clouded with sadness. So was Ching Shih. The great Pirate Queen who hid her grief beneath violence and conquest. How many people allowed horrible atrocities in the servitude of sorrow?

Nat broke the chain around his waist with both hands and dropped it on the ground. The metal clanged in a heap around his feet. The tornado was so much closer now, and he stared it down with the intensity of the purposeful. When he cast his gaze back to her, it was Nat again. Her Nat. The brave one. Galahad.

"We have to get back," he said as he took her hand. "Hold on tight."

Natalie shut her eyes. She braced herself for whatever was next, and when nothing came, she looked back up at him. Nat was casting his glance around as if scanning for one last glimpse of his wife.

"She ain't here, Nat. You did everythin' you could. Don't worry. We won't ever leave you to do this alone."

He squeezed her hand and smiled. Then they were gone. No snapping of the fingers. No transition into a blinding light. There was no need for that when you were the goddess. It was all for show, and they did not have any time left for theatrics.

CHAPTER FORTY SEVEN

When the real world appeared around them, it nearly knocked them off their feet. A gale swept across the farmland, blowing trees down and throwing wagons like baseballs into the sky. The earth trembled, and ice fell. Rain poured downward and sideways, stinging their skin and soaking their clothes.

The only reason Natalie did not immediately blow away was because of her roots. She had been without them for so long, but now that they were back in the real world, they grew back twice as fast.

A gust of wind sent her skidding across the Earth as she held fast to the goddess book. Natalie shoved one forearm into the ground. She dug in her knees and the toes of her shoes. Tiny white root sprouted from her skin, tethering her in place.

They saved her, but she was not sure for how long. Somehow, the wind picked up speed, blasting rain and dirt in her face. Natalie crouched as low as possible, clutching the book to her chest. She tried to open her eyes, but the rain stung her every time.

Suddenly, a powerful arm scooped beneath her waist and hauled her up into the air. Her roots snapped instantly. Natalie flailed wildly, trying to find something to hold on to. What she found was Nat. He held her to his chest, and she wrapped her arm around him.

"Hold on!" he yelled over the din of the storm.

"They're all gone!"

Her heart pounded in her chest. With the wild storm coming ever closer, how could their family still be alive? Not in this. Natalie figured it must have blown them away.

"No. They're here," Nat said.

Natalie squinted against the rain to see what he was talking about. She was instantly sorry she did. A massive tornado raged toward them. Colossal amounts of Earth swirled upwards into a funnel connected to the sky. It picked up trees and fences, throwing them miles away like someone flinging chicken bones. The noise rose louder and louder, sounding like a freight train roaring along the tracks.

At the top, it cradled something large and familiar. Natalie squinted to focus on what the storm was holding. It did not throw it. It held the thing as if inspecting what it was just before tossing it away. When Natalie recognized the farmhouse, she gasped. Their home. The storm had their home.

It was so close; she feared it would suck her up at any moment. At least, she thought, they would all be together. She did not want to die, but it would be better than living alone with the knowledge she and Nat caused it all. If only she found him sooner.

Just then, something miraculous came into view. A giant bubble appeared about twenty yards away from them. It was big enough to encapsulate several people and what appeared to be a mule and a horse.

Nat made a beeline for it, and Natalie got a better look.

Camille braced herself against the power of the tornado. She had created a protective barrier against the storm, much like the umbrella she had made by the gravesite. Dirt, hail, and rain battered the invisible bubble. So much debris sprayed around her that Natalie could barely make out everyone inside.

The weather had never been a problem for her in the past. Now Camille gritted her teeth to hold on to her spell, sweat pouring down her forehead. Her feet dug into the Earth as though something was pushing her downward.

Vivian, Calliope, and Delphia huddled together as they clutched Jack Jr. and baby Faith inside the bubble. The infant cried, but no one could hear her over the roaring freight train. Just behind them, David held fast to Johnny Sanders and Calliope's horse. He whispered bespelled words in their ears so the beasts would not buck and gallop away.

"Camille!" Nat screamed as loud as he could.

Camille met his eyes, and she instantly looked relieved. She still struggled against the force of the storm, but now there was hope. Nat got close enough to toss Natalie inside.

"Let her in! Catch Natalie!"

It appeared to be quite the struggle, but Camille jutted one hand out of the bubble while keeping its integrity intact. Her feet skidded backward a few inches, but she did not flinch. Nat wrapped two arms around Natalie.

"Don't let go of the book! Grab her hand!" he yelled.

Nat positioned his hands on her waist and tossed Natalie toward the bubble. In that second, Natalie spun in the air, and she thought she would die. She swore this was it. The tornado would surely blow her away. All of her work, and they would be too late.

The dirt and rain pounded against every inch of her body. Her feet begged to touch the ground again. Everything in her being wanted to be rooted once more.

It was only when she felt Camille's hand grabbed her arm that she thought she might be alright. One beautifully solid thing in a world of chaos. Natalie clung to Camille, her lifeline. She tried not to dig her nails into the witch's skin.

With one hard yank, Natalie fell into the bubble. The relief felt supernatural. No longer was she thrown around like a rag doll. The Earth was so beautifully still. She sat on her knees and took it in as she clutched the book to her chest.

Camille was back to bracing the spell against the tornado. The hail and dirt swirled around them, beating against the bubble. Natalie locked eyes with Vivian, who held young Jack against her bosom.

"Natalie! What's happening?" Vivian asked.

Natalie opened her mouth to answer, but found she had no words. Of course, she thought. She was back in the real world. Here the anchor child had roots, and she could not speak. There was no way to answer her.

Then, a thought came to her mind. Vivian was a psychic. Perhaps if she sent her words as a form of focused attention to Vivian, she would be able to interpret her message. There was no precedent for it, but she had to try.

Natalie concentrated all of her energy on her message. She shot her words to Vivian with all the psychic energy she could muster.

"I found Nat and brought him home."

Vivian's eyes glazed over for a moment. She seemed to both stare at Natalie and beyond her at the same time. She squeezed the book with all of her nervous energy. Natalie did not know if her experiment worked until Vivian spoke again.

"If you found him, why has the storm not stopped?" Vivian asked.

The returning fear quickly overshadowed the exhilaration of knowing it worked. She shot her another message, and this one was a horror.

"I don't know. We might be too late."

They all trained their eyes on Nat, who stood in between their bubble and the massive tornado. It still held their farmhouse high in the air, as if taunting them with it. It appeared to be threatening to drop their home at any second. Possibly on their heads.

This was no ordinary tornado. Any regular twister would have already torn the building apart, throwing pieces away as it had already done with the barn. Natalie could not see it anywhere. No windmill or wagons either.

No. This twister acted as though it were alive. It toyed with them like a cat with a mouse. If it dropped their house, no amount of magic would save them. Everyone would be crushed.

The only thing standing in between them and death was Nat, and he marched toward the beast like a man possessed. He did not seem afraid at all. Not an ounce of hesitation. Natalie hoped against hope that he could do this. She prayed Galahad would be enough.

CHAPTER FORTY EIGHT

The tornado shot a bolt of lightning straight for the bubble. Everyone screamed in unison and braced for the worst. Natalie refused to turn away. After all she had gone through, she was determined not to cower. Never again. If she died today, it would be with her head held high.

Nat raised one hand and caught the lightning in mid-air, mere feet away from Camille, who was still straining to keep their protective barrier in place. His arm lit up from the impact, showing his bones glowing red hot beneath his skin.

The electricity did not come and go as a lightning strike normally would. A burst of energy that dissipated once it found a host. This pulsed from the cloud into Nat's hand as though the storm meant to do it. Like it was trying to blast Nat away.

Everyone gasped as they watched Nat play a reverse tug of war with the lightning. For every step he took forward, the electricity shone that much brighter. She knew storms did not have personalities. They were not creatures unto themselves. But at that moment, it appeared to all the world like the tornado was fighting the goddess for control.

When the storm shot another bolt of lightning, Nat caught it in the other hand. He dug his heels in as the force of the electricity shoved him backward a few feet. There were skid marks on the ground from his boots scraping.

"How do we help him?" Calliope yelled over the gale.

"What if he can't stop it?" Delphia asked.

She looked at Vivian, who was clutching Jack Jr. and the bundle between the women. Natalie shot her a questioning glance and a new set of words. Ones that asked for her psychic help.

"Can you see our future?"

Vivian merely shook her head. She did not know what would happen, either.

"He's got this!" Camille yelled over the din.

Sweat poured down her face, making her words sound empty and small. Natalie tried to think that way. She poured all of her energy and thoughts into supporting Nat.

As if buoyed by their love, Nat found surer footing. He moved forward easier, pushing the electricity back into the tornado. The bolts snapped back like rubber bands, filling the anvil-like storm with light. The tornado faltered, teetering this way and that.

Everyone gasped as the farmhouse fell from its perch and smashed into the ground a mere thirty yards away from their bubble. It shattered into a pile of splinters and glass.

Nat balled his fists, cupping the excess energy in his hands. He molded it into a glowing ball. When the tornado righted itself, Nat hurled it directly into the heart of the beast. No baseball pitcher had ever been so accurate. Then again, it was hard to miss the heart of a gigantic storm.

As it reeled from the blow, Nat strode toward it with all the power and anger of an enraged goddess. His arms sparked with blue magic as he got closer. He reached into the sky with both hands and made a violent pulling motion. The tornado shook and ripped in half under his command. Two lesser funnels staggered away from each other.

They tried to shoot lightning at him, but the bolts were small, and he batted them away with little effort. Nat grabbed the smaller twister and snapped it in the air like chicken farmers do when breaking a hen's neck. It dissipated with a faint scream.

He took the larger one by the tail and drew it toward him. Had Natalie not known any better, she could have sworn the twister was trying to flee. Nat gripped the storm with both hands and ripped it into quarters, stomping each one into the ground.

The sky cleared as the storm clouds evaporated. A bright orange sun poked its head out to inspect Nat's handiwork. He stood in the middle of the torn Earth with a smile on his face.

It was done. It was over.

Nat was every inch of his best self at that moment. The goddess they called Galahad. Natalie had never been prouder of him.

CHAPTER FORTY NINE

Camille collapsed to her knees after she released the barrier of the bubble. The sheer will alone to keep it solid took every inch of her strength. Nat ran to her and helped her up. She took his arm before wiping the sweat from her forehead.

"It's about time, Galahad," she said.

"I'm sorry. I didn't know... well... that's not an excuse. I should've known."

"You made it here. That's all that matters."

"I wouldn't have if it weren't for Natalie," he said, gesturing to her.

Natalie pulled her hands from the ground, snapping at the roots that had grown there. She stood up straight and brushed the dirt from her Roman dress. Camille took her in with a curious grin.

"You look very different, child," she said. "Went on a proper adventure, did you?"

Natalie nodded to her with a bit of a salute. Camille laughed, and Nat patted her on the back. The three of them set their eyes on what remained of the farmhouse.

Pieces of the old building littered the area. The parts of the house that stayed together slumped over and downward as if someone deflated a balloon. It was like looking at an injured animal, one they had loved for a century.

The scene reminded her of the plantation's manor house. A massive home destroyed and turned into rubble. While their farmhouse was not lavish, it was theirs—their sanctuary from the brutal world around them.

No one said a word for a minute. They just took in the carnage. Their home, their precious home, was gone and broken beyond repair.

"Faith!" Nat exclaimed. A light flashed behind his eyes as a realization hit him. He turned to Camille with terror written all over his face. "Camille, where's Faith. She wasn't in there, was she?"

"Don't worry. She's here," Camille said.

She pointed to the group huddled together behind Natalie. Vivian and Delphia were unraveling themselves from their embrace and standing up. Delphia held Buck, the taxidermy deer bust, in her arms. Jack Jr. still clung to his mother as she righted herself. He whimpered into her dress.

"It's alright, baby. It's over. Uncle Nat took care of it," Vivian cooed at her son.

"Well, it is about time, if I do say so myself," said Buck in his formal voice. "We were nearly killed. Not to mention, the whole ordeal scuffed my perfect nose!"

"I'll fix it. I promise," Delphia said, petting his ears.

"Faith. Where's Faith?" Nat asked frantically.

He raced to them, looking from one woman to the other. It was not until they stepped aside that Calliope was in full view. The nun stood up carefully and removed a quilt she had wrapped around her body. Beneath it, she held a bundle close to her chest. It wiggled and coughed. As soon as the fresh air hit the baby, she cried.

Nat closed the gap between them and took the baby from Calliope. He flashed her a grateful smile as he gathered the infant into his arms. Tiny baby Faith fussed as he shifted her, but she calmed as soon as he brought her close. When she focused on her daddy, she smiled and grabbed for his chin.

Tears welled in Nat's eyes. He ran a finger across one of her golden, wispy locks. When he leaned in to kiss his daughter, she used the opportunity to put her mouth over his nose. He laughed and hugged her close to his chest.

"Thank you all. I can't… I'm just so sorry." Nat said.

"You came back when it mattered," Camille said.

"I knew you would be back in time," Vivian said.

David led Johnny Sanders and the Clydesdale back over to the rest of them. The mule still had the wild eyes of the recently scared, and David had to keep his reins tight. With his free hand, he wiped the dirt and sweat from his forehead.

"Did you find Polly?" he asked.

Nat swallowed hard. Fresh tears were forming again, but he held them back with a brief sniff. No words came out. It was almost like he was an anchor child, unable to speak to anyone.

Now that she was back in her own world, Natalie could feel things again. She always had a rough idea about the short-term future, and she usually could sense Nat's deeper emotions. When he locked eyes with her, she knew why he could not speak.

If he said it, it was over. Saying the words meant she was really gone. To tell them his failure admitted the worst thing in his life. Polly was truly gone, never to return. He failed.

Everyone turned their attention to Natalie. Even though they knew she could not talk, they still looked to her for the answer. She held back her own tears and shook her head.

"I'm sorry, Galahad," Camille said, sidling up to him as he hugged his daughter again. "We're here for you. All of us."

Vivian, Calliope, and Delphia gathered around him. Calliope placed a gentle hand on his shoulder. Natalie wished she could join, but her roots kept her in place. Luckily, David led Johnny Sanders in her direction, so she did not have to be alone. He nodded down to her in an approving way and tussled her hair.

"What are you wearing?" he asked with a smirk.

Natalie elbowed him playfully.

"Golly, Camille. Your house," Delphia said, pointing to the wreckage. "What are you gonna do? Where will the kids go now if there's no *Camille's Home for Wayward Children?*"

Everyone looked at what was left of the farmhouse together. As if sensing it was being discussed, the heap of wood and glass collapsed in on itself. It appeared to all the world like a noble beast who took its terminal breath and passed right in front of them.

Jack began crying all over again as Vivian pulled him closer. Delphia hugged Buck closer when he started blubbering incoherent things about his one and only home. Natalie felt a deep sinking sensation as she marked the passing of a house that felt more like a family member than anything else.

"We can rebuild," Nat said, breaking the moment of silence. "It was our house, but we can make a new one. Until then, we can stay with Percy."

"But… it was more than that. It was our home," Camille said, wiping a tear from her cheek. "The only home I've ever had. It was our sanctuary. *Your* sanctuary, Nat."

Natalie looked at Camille and wondered if they should tell her the truth. This was not her only home. She had a life with a different home before all this. One that Nan destroyed. Nat locked eyes with her and shook his head. Maybe later, Natalie thought.

"It was my sanctuary—all of ours. But we can make a new one. It wasn't home. Home is right here, with all of us," he said as he held Faith closer to his chest. "The building is just where we hang our hats. As long as we are together, we are home.

Camille wrapped her arm around Nat and laid her head on his shoulder. He leaned back into her hug and let out a long breath. There was no telling how long he had held in it, but that one exhale took all the tension out of his body.

"Well said. We will rebuild better than ever," his mentor said.

"Camille," Nat said as he gazed down at his daughter.

"Yes, Nat?"

He paused and held his breath.

"Her eyes."

"What about her eyes?" she asked.

"They are just like Polly's eyes," he said.

Nat's voice broke with the most heart-wrenching crack. He slumped down to the ground, and Camille went with him. He held onto his daughter and leaned into his surrogate mother's arms. She wrapped him in a warm embrace as the all-powerful goddess broke into a round of sobs.

Camille held him in the breaking. She petted his messy hair and brushed some of the grit from his forehead. Everyone around him stood still in reverence for his pain. They did not turn away. They did not hide from it. They acted like the family they were and sat vigil for his mourning.

"I know she does, kid. I know. It's the worst and best part of it all."

CHAPTER FIFTY

Someone already hung the decorations when Nat stepped off the front porch of the farmhouse. He was not surprised. It was quite possible that Camille and Vivian were more excited about Faith's birthday than she was, if that was possible. He smiled and let the dusky sun kiss his face as he stepped off the porch steps.

Pink and yellow streamers radiated out from the roof like rays of crepe sunshine. They dipped in and out of tree branches leading to the barn. The weeping willow trees were Nat's idea. He planted them all around the property, hoping they might do all the weeping for him. It turned out to be a great idea since they provided endless shade, even in the hottest of summers.

Delphia bespelled groups of lightning bugs to fly inside small circular jars that hung alongside the streamers. They resembled tiny, electric lights flashing beautifully against the impending twilight.

"I wonder what Delphia promised those fireflies to get them to stay put," Nat marveled to himself.

"I'm pretty sure it had to do with their own koi pond or somethin'," Camille said, joining him.

They took in the scene together—a beautiful day for a party among the willow trees. The intoxicating scent of food wafted from within the house. Nat took it in and relaxed inside this perfect scene of family.

The house may have been new, but the spirit of it felt old. It was built much the way the old house was, looking to all the world like a run-down shack positioned in a patch of dried prairie. Inside, it expanded to fit however many people needed it. There were dozens of marvelous living rooms, bedrooms, and a kitchen that could feed an army. Nat insisted on that since it was where Natalie spent much of her time when here. They also enlarged the library to three times its previous size.

They needed the space. *Miss Camille's Home for Wayward Children* had grown in size over the years. In the past, she had only taken in a handful of children at a time. Now, her school was bursting at the seams with over two dozen students.

A group of younger children blasted through the back door and raced past Nat and Camille. They chased one another, playing some unknown game of tag. One boy had grown a set of ram horns on his head, and he charged at a smaller boy who was pinned against one of the willow trees.

A tall, older girl reached through the tree and pulled the smaller boy through just as the other boy rammed into the trunk. The branches shivered from the impact. He looked around, confused what happened. When he saw the boy, he frowned.

"Hey! Teleportation is against the rules!" he shouted.

"I didn't," the boy said.

"Then how did you move through the tree?"

"I moved him," the girl said as she stepped into view. The boy's face fell when he took her in. She just smiled and patted the little boy's head. "I can use teleportation any time I want. And you are not supposed to be so rough."

"I... I... I'm sorry, Miss Faith. I got carried away," the older boy said.

He ran his hands over his horns, turning them back into a messy mop of hair. Faith tussled it under her fingers as she turned them both toward the farmhouse.

"Go on. Get cleaned up. I can't abide smelly children at my birthday party," she said with a loving pat on their backs.

The boys ran toward the house, giggling and tugging at one another. Camille pretended to grab at them as they passed, and they squealed with excitement. Faith walked up to her father and hugged Nat with all the affection of a loving daughter. He hugged her back and smelled the scent of sunshine in her hair.

He knew he had to take in every nuance, every detail, before it was all done. He had a finite amount of time left, and he had to make these moments count.

Faith grew up beautifully. Nat knew she would, being Polly's daughter. With her wide hazel eyes and sandy blond hair, she resembled her mother so much it hurt Nat to look at her. She was taller than Polly, one of the few traits she got from Nat, and could stand eye to eye with Camille.

"Are you excited for your big day?" Camille asked Faith.

"I'm so excited," Faith said. She met Nat's eyes, and a faint shadow passed over her face. "Well, I'm excited for most of it. Are you sure this is what you want, Daddy?"

"I am ready, honey. Are you?"

"As ready as anybody could be," she whispered.

"You don't have to, you know," Nat said, taking her hand in his. "It can be someone else."

He folded her elegant hand inside his gloved ones. They were the gloves Polly made him so long ago. She had embroidered little compasses on each hand with bespelled thread. No matter where he went, the stitched compasses always pointed him in the right direction. At that moment, both arrows pointed to his daughter.

"No, Daddy. I'm not afraid of that. We've been trainin'. It should be me. I'm ready for that. It's the other part…"

"Don't worry, honey. That part is inevitable, but then again, it always was."

CHAPTER FIFTY ONE

The twilight came in a sweeping curtain of soft purple. A veil that dimmed the sun but allowed the world to swim in fuzzy enchantment before night enveloped them all. Nat took in the scene, breathing in the heady scent of lilacs and sugar.

Children of all ages buzzed around the picnic tables and decorations with smears of food on their faces. Delphia whispered to a box full of bunnies and pointed to a group of girls. The rabbits leaped from their box and ran at the giggling brood. They all turned with a round of squeals and dashed away from the pursuing cottontails.

David sidled up next to Nat with an easy smile and shook his hand. He smelled like hot dogs and smoke. He had volunteered to handle the cook fire for the party.

"Some party," David said.

"Yes, it is. Thank you again for bringing Delphia and Calliope up here for the celebration."

"No problem. We wouldn't miss it for the world."

"How's that family of yours at the cathedral?"

"Mary and I are good. We just welcomed our second child. A boy this time."

"I had no idea. Congratulations, David. What about Delphia? Has she got designs on anyone?"

"No. She seems to be content with being Auntie Delphia. I don't know what we would do without her," David said, looking lovingly at his sister as she scooped one of the more petite girls into her arms. "We've been talking about possibly opening up a school of our own somewhere."

"That's a wonderful idea. If there's anythin' I've learned from my time here, it's that there is always need for sanctuaries."

Vivian appeared from the house carrying a giant, two-tiered strawberry cake. Twenty candles covered it with colorful bursts of sparks. It was a spell provided by Jack Jr. to make the cake look like fireworks. Faith's eyes lit up as everyone started singing the birthday song. Her cheeks turned into two pink rosebuds.

Nat marveled at his little girl as she blew out her candles. Jack Jr. appeared at her elbow, swiping a dollop of frosting from the cake and dotting her nose with it. She giggled and play-slapped his hand away. He smeared frosting on his own nose and kissed her on the cheek.

Luckily, the only thing Jack shared with his terrible father was his height and brown mess of hair. He had grown into a handsome, capable man, and Nat was grateful he would be there for Faith after tonight. Anyone would be hard-pressed to find a kinder son-in-law.

After David joined the hoard waiting for slices of cake, Nat ducked out of the way before anyone saw him leave. There was a much more important place to go.

***

The graves had not moved, even after the great storm. They rebuilt the farm and planted the trees around the stones. Nan's grave still sat as a rectangular mound of colorful wildflowers. They never withered, even in the winter. Next to her grave marker stood Polly's tombstone.

Nat ran his fingers over her carved name the way he always did. Down the P and around the O several times. The path was so known to him that the edge had worn smoother than the other letters. It was soothing somehow—a sort of prayer.

The only sound around him was the muted party raging behind the house. He felt utterly peaceful by himself. So when the sudden flapping of a gigantic bird's wings flew next to his head, he startled to his feet. A huge, black crow perched on the gravestone, looking at Nat as though he knew him.

"Hello, brother?" Nat asked.

Crow squawked at him.

"I figured that was you. You are welcomed here. You know that, don't you?"

Crow shifted along the stone and pecked next to one talon. At any moment, Nat expected Crow to turn into his human form, but it did not happen. There was no denying who he was. This was Crow. Yet, he did not change. Something was wrong.

Nat looked deeply into his obsidian eyes. The story was in there, even if it was hard to understand. He could see into Crow's memories and thoughts, but so many were like a bird, the complete picture jumbled in shattered fragments. One constant was the memory of Polly. She came up in both of his memories as a human and as a bird.

A well of guilt opened up in Nat's belly. Crow indeed loved Polly, and she chose Nat over him. Crow had never quite been the same after that, staying away more and more until they rarely saw him at all. It had been ages since anyone had seen him.

When he stared deep into the bird's thoughts, Nat saw no hint of anger in his mind. Just frustration. Suddenly, the answer took shape. It was buried deep within the bird's memories. When Nat finally made the connection, it all made sense.

"You can't turn back anymore, can you? We haven't seen you in years, and now I see why. You've been a bird so long you don't know how to be anythin' else."

The bird squawked and flapped its wings.

"Let me help you with that," Nat said.

Crow held still as Nat removed his gloves. He gingerly tapped one finger to the bird's beak. In a flash of feathers and dust, the bird crow turned into the man Crow. He stumbled and placed one hand on the tombstone to steady himself. His legs wobbled, and Nat took his other arm. He wondered how long it had been since Crow had stood in a human body.

"Thank you, Nat," Crow said in a scratchy voice.

It sounded like he had not used his human vocal cords in ages. The words fell clumsily from his mouth.

"Are you alright?" Nat asked.

"Yes. I... just heard what today is. I wanted to try to turn back."

"I'm glad you came."

"Ummm. Who is this?" said a feminine voice behind them.

The men turned to see Calliope walking in their direction from the barn. She was just as beautiful as she had always been. The past years had been kind. Only the finest of laugh lines spidered away from her eyes. A few grey strands glittered among her dark mane, almost making it look like she sparkled. Her skin was just as golden, and her almond eyes just as fine.

In one hand, she held a heavy book. A large blanket was draped over her other arm. She averted her eyes when she noticed Crow was utterly naked. The slightest of blushes flashed on her cheeks.

"I saw you change, and… uh… brought a blanket," she said as she handed the blanket to Crow.

He wrapped it around his waist clumsily. Nat wanted to laugh. Crow was completely unaware of his nudity, and Calliope refused to look back down until his nethers were covered.

"This is Crow. Crow, meet Calliope."

"Pleasure to meet you," Calliope said.

She stuck her hand out, but Crow just looked at it questioningly. The long moment of confusion drew out, so Nat broke the silence.

"Crow is not used to being a human," Nat said. He gestured to the book in her arms. "Is that for me?"

"Yes, of course," she said.

Calliope handed *The Goddess Stories* to Nat. He took it and ran his hand over the embossed title with the little lock on the cover.

"And the key?"

She brought out a thin gold chain from around her neck with a key dangling on it. Calliope undid the clasp and handed the key over to Nat. He took it with reverence.

"How long has she been in there?" he asked.

"She has not come out since you left."

"That was six months ago. I think that's her longest one yet."

"She wanted to have one last great adventure," Calliope said.

"Well, she deserved it," Nat said.

"Who are you talking about?" Crow asked.

They ignored him for the time being. Nat unlocked the book and handed the key back to Calliope, who refastened the chain around her neck. He reached one hand into the book and paused.

"How will you find her?" Calliope asked.

"She knows where to go and when. We discussed it," Nat said. Suddenly, his arm jerked a touch like a fishing pole that just got a bite. Nat smiled. "And there she is. Right on time."

With one long yank, Nat pulled a small girl from within the book. Natalie landed on the ground with ease. She was clad in all white and maroon silk with multiple gold chains around her neck. Her hair was pulled into an elaborate hairstyle. An Egyptian headdress covered in blue and gold stripes with a golden cobra perched on the top.

Natalie stood straight and proud, meeting everyone's eyes with a wide grin. Nat patted her shoulder like a proud older brother. Even though he had allowed himself to age with the passage of time, she stayed forever a little girl. Well, in physical appearance anyway. Her mind and maturity blossomed beyond her years. It doubled every time she went into the goddess book and visited her friends.

"Did you have a good farewell adventure?" he asked her.

She nodded enthusiastically.

"And how's the Wise King and Pharoah Queen? I see they dressed you before you came back. Were they sad to say goodbye?"

Natalie's smile faded a touch. She took Nat's hand and squeezed.

"Yeah, I know. Farewells are hard. Are you sure you're ready for the next one?"

She pulled Nat down to her level so the other two people could not hear her. He leaned in close to hear her whisper.

"No farewell is forever," she said in a tiny voice.

"You're right," he said with a sad smile. "All we have left to do is wait for the birthday girl."

CHAPTER FIFTY TWO

It was hard to tell what drew them to the small cemetery. No one said when it was time or where they were supposed to go. One by one, the partygoers filtered away from the happiness of the birthday party. They made their way to join their friends in front of the two graves. Nat, Calliope, Natalie, and Crow waited patiently.

When Camille saw Crow, she ran to him with the excited energy of a child. She threw her arms around his neck and squeezed. He leaned into it awkwardly and only winced a little when she kissed his cheek.

"You're home! I've missed you so much. Are you gonna stay awhile? I'll make whatever food you want. Just please don't go away," she said.

"You have more lines on your face than last time," Crow said without a hint of emotion. He gave the same amount of weight to the words as one might give to the description of a tree. Crow turned his gaze to her hair, which was pulled up into one of her elaborate wraps. Tendrils of grey peeked in between the vibrant patterns. "And your hair is changing."

She smacked his arm playfully.

"Ouch," he said.

"That'll teach you to point out an aging woman," she said.

The indignation did not last long. Within seconds, Camille was hugging on him again. Despite his stoic manner, Crow shut his eyes and leaned into her. She smiled as he wrapped one arm around her waist. The other held up the blanket.

"Now, what do you want me to make you for dinner?" she asked, trying to hide the tears in her eyes.

"I would like tomato pulp and grasshoppers," he said plainly.

Camille laughed and squeezed him again.

"Anything for you."

When Faith appeared holding Jack's hand, everyone quietened. The group held their breaths collectively as the duo walked toward Nat and Natalie, who stood next to Polly's grave. Her father smiled at her, and she smiled weakly back.

The scene was reminiscent of a wedding. A group of people stood on either side, forming a path through the middle. A family watching on as something momentous happened. The beautiful woman in white walked up the aisle hand in hand with her beau.

Nat awaited them at the end as he removed his other glove, showing the swaths of paint on his arms and hands. Faith stood in front of her father and fidgeted nervously. She bit at her lips and tried to swallow back her emotions. None of it looked natural on such a lovely creature.

The world was silent as Jack released her hand. He stepped back a few paces. This moment was, after all, not about him. It was about Faith and her father.

"I'm right here if you need me," Jack whispered to the back of her hair.

Faith nodded and faced Nat. He smiled at her, trying to take in every last nuance of her face. Every freckle and every pore.

"Are you ready?" he asked.

"Y…yes. I think I'm ready."

"Don't worry. It doesn't hurt," Nat said.

"But will it hurt you?" Faith asked.

"No, baby. Nothing hurts me anymore."

"What happens to you? Will you see Mama?"

"I am not sure. I do hope so," Nat said.

"If you do, could you tell her… I don't know rightly what to tell her. Somethin' though. I mean, shouldn't I have a message to give her? I don't remember her, but I want to. That seems like the proper thing, right. To have a perfect thing to tell her from me. Wouldn't that make a good ending here?"

"Baby girl, this is not an ending. Far from it," he said as he brought forth the two compass gloves. He handed them to Faith, and she took them with a sigh. "Your mother made these for me when I was lost. They were meant to point me in the right direction."

"Yes, Daddy. I remember the story. It was my favorite at bedtime for years."

"What I didn't tell you was the rest," he said.

"What rest?"

"See that there," Nat said as he pointed to a brown stain next to the thumb. "That's a speck of blood from where your mother pricked her hand mending these things. And that little pink smudge on the pinky is where she accidentally dotted her lipstick on one of our dates."

Faith's eyes went wide. She suddenly looked at the glove with renewed interest. These tiny imperfections, it was like she was seeing them for the first time.

"This pinched part is where Johnny Sanders crushed my finger after our wagon broke down. I was supposed to be takin' her to the picture show. Didn't live that one down for weeks."

His daughter giggled despite herself. The laughter quickly turned into barely concealed tears.

"Why are you tellin' me this now, Daddy?"

"Because I want you to have the gloves. Not to hide behind, but to use. Your mother put so much of herself into making them, and I put so much of ourselves into using them. You will never be alone or lost if you have these with you."

"See," Faith said, choking back a sob. "You did it. You went and found the words. The perfect good ending words."

She threw herself into Nat's arms, and he clung to her. He shut his eyes tightly and held his daughter, completely taking in the moment. When he lifted his gaze, he saw Jack fidgeting just behind her. The poor man was teetering on the edge of proper etiquette. To run to his love or to leave her alone with her father.

Nat nodded to the young man, and he rushed to Faith, collecting her against his chest. Jack appeared relieved to be helping. Faith took his handkerchief, dried her eyes, and faced her father once more.

"Are you ready?" Nat asked.

Faith handed the compass gloves to Jack and nodded.

Nat turned to Natalie and took her hand.

"Are you ready?" he asked the anchor child.

Natalie grinned at Faith and nodded.

"Alright then. It's time."

Tears streamed down Faith's cheeks, finding fresh paths over the dried roads of her previous weeping. Somewhere in the crowd, Vivian cried openly, and Camille sniffed back an impending sob. Calliope stood perfectly still next to David as he held his sister to his chest. Delphia held her sobs back with a wad of handkerchiefs.

"Goodbye, Daddy," Faith said as she held out her hand.

Her arm trembled as it extended. Nat took his daughter's hand in his. He made sure his hands were warm and firm. Everything she needed them to be right then. Cold felt like death, and he would spare her that.

"Don't worry, dear heart. I love you. That's never gone. Nothing can take that away."

He squeezed his Faith's hand and transferred all of his paint to her. In his last moment, he saw it smear across her fingers. Nat breathed a sigh of relief as he fell backward, landing softly on the ground next to Polly's grave.

In that moment, the world held its breath as the goddess known as Nat faded into the Earth. No one exhaled until every scrap of Galahad vanished from sight. A plot of sunflowers bloomed in his place.

Epilogue

I was not sure exactly what to expect. To be fair, I'd never died before, so there was nothing to compare it to. Those who were religious touted the virtues of heaven, but how did that work for goddesses? The bible always seemed a jumbled mess when I tried to read it, but I was pretty sure it held no passages explaining what happened when I died.

The world of Tanglewood faded away, and the passing felt peaceful. I was relieved, knowing my friends and family were safe. Faith was the goddess now. I knew she would be a better goddess than I could ever be, and she had all the support anyone could ask for.

I woke up lying on my back on the ground. When I peered around me, I realized I was not at the farm anymore. Buildings replaced the trees, and the Earth beneath me was hard-packed dirt instead of the spongy garden outside our home.

Sitting up was a tad disconcerting, so I took in my surroundings. There was no Natalie anywhere to be seen. No Faith. No Camille. The streets formed a grid the way most small Texas towns did. I spotted the General Store to my right and realized I was in the town of Tanglewood. At the end of the road stood the post. The place where I'd first laid eyes on Polly. The place where everything changed.

Someone was there, standing next to where the chain laid in the dirt. It was hard to make out who they were in the midday sun, but my heart soared at the sight. I stood up quickly and walked over to them. She came into perfect view when I got close enough.

Polly. My Polly.

She wore the simple white lace dress she'd worn on our wedding day. Her hair pulled back into a loose braid with baby's breath flowers in the folds. When I looked down at myself, I wore the suit from the same occasion. A modest grey one Vivian picked out for me.

"You're here," I said through sticky lips.

It was a stupid thing to say. Of course, she was here. She stood right in front of me, but it was all I could muster in my shock.

"I've been waitin' for you," she said.

"But… how? How is this possible?"

"Natalie found me."

"She *found* you?"

"Yes. She told me you would be here. It was only a matter of time. So, I waited for you. That reminds me. Where is Natalie?"

I looked around as though she might appear at any moment, but she did not. There was a warm sensation inside my stomach—a comforting wiggle nudging my heart.

"I think she's back inside me. I can feel her. I reckon I don't need an anchor anymore."

Polly smiled, and the world seemed to right itself. All of this time without her, I felt the constant ache of her absence. Every birthday celebrated without her hand in mine. Every holiday without her laugh. Even the happiest moments dimmed without her in them.

We ran to each other, and I took her in my arms. I breathed in the flowers and sunshine in her hair, and I held her against my chest. My bones shook with the relief of her, and I struggled not to weep from joy. When she pulled away, silent tears were rolling down her cheeks.

"I'm so happy you're here," she said.

"Me too. I've missed you more than you can imagine."

"I knew, you know. I just knew this was going to be the place," Polly said.

"What place? What are you talkin' about?"

"Natalie said to go to the place where we fell in love. I guessed it!"

She looked so much like Faith right then. Her eyes sparkled with joy but also accomplishment. The bright-eyed wonderment of someone who figured out a riddle. No one illuminated from within like my girls.

"Wait. Natalie told you to go to the place where I fell in love with you, or where you fell in love with me?"

"Both, I think."

I could not help but stare at her incredulously. This place was an obvious choice for me. I was head-over-heels for Polly the second I met her. Even though she was in a sack of a dress and dirty as an urchin, she had my heart immediately. But Polly? This spot marked the most challenging moment of her life.

"You loved me from the start?" I asked.

She leaned in and kissed my nose lightly. I felt the warmth of it even after she pulled away.

"Did I fall in love with the boy who risked everything to protect me? Yes, dummy, I did."

"But…"

Polly grabbed the back of my neck and pulled me down to kiss her. All other thoughts ran from my mind, and I didn't bother chasing them. There was no need. She loved me from the beginning, and she loved me now. We were home.

"Wait, does that mean we are… in the book?"

"Yes. This is our heaven. It's where the goddesses go, thanks to you. They can visit all histories as much as they like in the book."

"But when I tried to find you before, you weren't here. I looked everywhere."

"You weren't supposed to be here. Not yet. You bein' here pushed us out. Goddesses can't live in this place until they die."

"Then how did Natalie find you? How did you get the message?"

"She found me in Nan's timeline and told me to come here when *it* happened."

Polly blushed and looked down at her feet when she mentioned "it." We both knew what she meant, and I was not afraid to call the beast by its name.

"My death, you mean."

"Yes, your death," she said as she brushed a light hand across my forehead.

"Now that I'm dead, everything's how it should be," I said.

Saying dead out loud felt strange. I was dead. That was a fact, but it sounded hollow and surreal at the same time. The word "death" was like a period in a sentence. The halting of that particular story. The end of something important. Was this a death? How could it be when I lingered?

Perhaps that was why people called it a passing. I used to think that word was a kind of cheat—something nice to soften the visceral blow of the end of a life. Now, I was not so sure. It felt more accurate, like a comma instead of a period.

My story lived on. Not just because of the book, but because I lived. One would find it hard to live a life without making some sort of mark. The image of my life in Tanglewood flashed before my eyes. My friends and family. The witches under my protection.

Their memories of me would continue. There was no death in shared history. Not to mention the legacy I left behind. My pride and joy. My daughter. The story of her mother and father was written into her blood and etched into her very bones.

I took a moment of silence. In it, I bore witness to the passing—not death—of my truly original story. If nothing else, I lived as a unique creature surrounded by people I loved. In the end, goddess or no, that was all anyone could hope for.

"We can go relive our happiest memories," she said with a wide grin. "Our wedding, our lives at the farm, when our daughter was born."

Polly halted at the mention of Faith. Her hand flew to her chest as though something suddenly choked her. It all hit me at once, staring into those perfect hazel eyes of hers. Her last memory of our daughter was when she was a baby. It was right before the fever took her.

"Nat, how is she? How is our Faith?"

"She's… perfect. So much like you, it hurts. She's the goddess now. I gave my powers to her."

Polly's eyes flew wider.

"She's the goddess. Oh Nat, are you sure that was a good idea?"

"I've trained her for years. It's what she wanted. Natalie showed me the past histories of the goddess. The happiest ones are when it's passed down to family."

"I don't know. It's such a hard burden," Polly said.

"But such a blessing at the same time. Nothin' that powerful comes without pain. It just doesn't. But the best part is when she passes, she'll come here. She can be with us. We can visit her timeline and see all the amazin' things she did."

Polly's grimace faded, and she took Nat's hands in hers.

"I want so desperately to meet her," she said.

"Well, you can," I said.

"How?"

"If I'm dead, and this is my timeline, you can meet her. All of my life's memories are here. That means she's here too."

"You mean I can watch her grow up?" Polly said with a ray of hope in her voice.

"Yes, my love. You can come to every birthday, every party, every first our baby had. You can watch her skip for the first time. Or the time when she trapped Jack Jr. in the wall for burying her teddy bear in the snow. Did you know Camille made her green pancakes with chocolate chip faces every Sunday and called them 'Daddy Cakes'?"

She smiled up at me and wrapped her arms around my waist. I heard her sniffle against my chest. When she pulled away, there was a light of excitement on her face. That gorgeous beam from within her that never dulled. Not even when she was sick. Not even when she passed in my arms all those years ago.

"What would you like to see first?" I asked.

"How about... I don't know. Gosh, how do I pick? There's so much I missed."

"Anythin' you want. We've got all the time in the world."

"What about her first birthday? Can we see that one?" she asked with all the innocence of a hopeful child.

"That's one of my favorites."

I took her hand, and we walked away from the post, away from the town of Tanglewood. We had much to see and all the time to see it in. If heaven existed, it was here with her. This perfect place where nothing was dead. Everything was but another chapter. In here, like in life, farewell was not forever.

About the Author

Michelle Rene is a creative advocate and the winner of multiple indie book awards.

Her YA historical fantasy, *Manufactured Witches*, won the OZMA award and was honored by the Indie Author Project as Texas' Best YA Novel in 2019.

Its sequel, *The Canyon Cathedral*, won first in category for the Dante Rosetti Award and was a finalist for the Next Generation Indie Book Awards for LGBTQ+ Fiction.

When not writing, she is a professional artist, belly dancer, and autism mom. She lives with her husband, son, and ungrateful cat in Dallas, Texas.

Note from the Author

Word-of-mouth is crucial for any author to succeed. If you enjoyed *Goddess Stories*, please leave a review online—anywhere you are able. Even if it's just a sentence or two. It would make all the difference and would be very much appreciated.

Thanks!
Michelle Rene

We hope you enjoyed reading this title from:

BLACK ROSE
writing™

www.blackrosewriting.com

Subscribe to our mailing list—*The Rosevine*—and receive **FREE** books, daily deals, and stay current with news about upcoming releases and our hottest authors.

Scan the QR code below to sign up.

Already a subscriber? Please accept a sincere thank you for being a fan of Black Rose Writing authors.

View other Black Rose Writing titles at
www.blackrosewriting.com/books and use promo code
PRINT to receive a **20% discount** when purchasing.

Made in the USA
Las Vegas, NV
07 December 2024

13446276R00132